# A
# HEART
# OF
# STONE

HARPER A. BURGE

This book is dedicated to:

+GMG+
My family
My friends
My dog
Readers
Nappers
And
Those
Searching
For
A
Portal
To
A
Fantasy
World

# PROLOGUE

It snowed the day Ma died.

Ma baked a fresh loaf of bread that morning. The fluffy insides steamed when we tore it apart in our cramped cottage in the woods. It was a good day when we ate fresh bread. That meant Pa caught something in his trap that sold. That meant we had enough money to eat.

Ma was the teacher in town. Her hair was tied back in a scarf to cover her red curls, the red curls that marked her a foreigner. A ringlet fell that day, showing itself to the class. That's what started her foul mood, the laughter.

But that day she'd had enough of our nonsense. She slapped skinny, little, freckled Jimmy Horner across the head. Jimmy Horner, whose father was Councilman Jim Horner, mayor, and closest thing to nobility in our small town.

Ma hanged the next morning.

I didn't cry when I watched her life escape. I imagined her soul floating away into the clouds, going to a better world. A world with full bellies and warmth. I'd seen my fair share of death. Six of my nine brothers and sisters passed to the next life. It was just how it was. Pa was still alive. He would protect us. Or so I thought.

A snowflake landed on my nose as I watched my mother swaying lifeless. It didn't melt. It clung to me like life. Maybe that little snowflake had come from a somewhere else. Maybe it was a soul falling down to earth like Ma's soul was falling up. I brushed it away. You don't want any part of this life, I thought to the flake.

I trudged back through the snow to our cabin in the woods. Pa was there banging around, making an earful of noise. He didn't come to watch Ma hang. Too much for his tired eyes, he'd said. I think maybe his soul broke a little too. There is only so much heartache a man can take.

"Where're you going, Ceceil?" I asked my oldest brother.

"Collecting the body. We'll bury her out back with the rest."

Ceceil didn't look at me. He trudged forward. He was getting tall and lanky, stuck somewhere between a man and a boy. His dark hair was matted against his brow, so thick and black like molasses. His nose outgrew his face, but soon it would catch up. His eyes were sunken like the rest of us, tired and hungry.

Ma said I was an anomaly. I didn't know what an 'anomaly' was, but I figured it just meant different. My hair was red as fire, same as Ma's, though it fell like a waterfall not in ringlets. I was the only one born with the foreigner's traits. Like Ma, I had to keep it covered. Foreigners were not welcomed here. Times were tough enough without outsiders coming in taking the hunt and the crop land from the locals. I understood it some, but still, we needed to live too.

When I was little, I didn't know much about surviving. But since moving here I'd learned to trap and gather. I recognized plants and animals, knew how to track, to forage, to live off the land. Before we'd settled in this village, we'd lived in the Old Country, back where Ma wasn't foreign, and neither was I. The snow didn't fall so heavy there. Back then I knew comfort, or so I'd been told.

I didn't remember.

We left the Old Country quickly and quietly. Pa came for us in the middle of the night, said we needed to leave with haste. We trudged across mountains and valleys to the lands where Pa was born.

Pa wasn't from our village, Innesbrown. He said his home was nearby, though. And the people here tolerated us well enough on account they'd heard of Pa's hometown. I guess a mighty fire burned his town to the ground. So, there hadn't been anywhere else for us to go but here.

I never asked why we had to flee. I was young, and then time slipped away. I never asked my brothers and sisters either. Those first years had been marked with death. Death holds the curious at bay.

My breath puffed in clouds of steam, and I felt like one of those creatures that lived in the northern passes. My brother, Ceceil, and sister, Yesimia, both older, stood on either side of me. Their breaths puffed as well.

No one cried except Timtim, who was still sensitive to death, maybe too sensitive for this world. He stood apart, by the old oak tree, where little stones protruded from the ground at jagged angles, marking my other six siblings' bodies.

Timtim and Ceceil dug the hole. Their gloves were dirty and torn from plowing the frozen ground. My Pa took off his hat and recited an ancient prayer.

Weeks later my birthday arrived. I was eighteen and an adult. It had been ten years since we left the Old Country. Ten years, four sisters, two brothers, and one Ma dead

# PART ONE:

# THE NORTH

# CHAPTER 1

Yesimia took a deep breath next to me. Though we looked alike, my sister didn't share my rough features. She was taller, more beautiful, and soon to be married to a local boy. I didn't envy her.

"Finish your needlework," she demanded. Yesimia had been quick to take over Ma's role. But I already poked myself several times in the hand, and even the warmth of the crackling fire wasn't enough incentive to keep me here injuring myself.

"I'm off!" I jumped up and scrambled to the door, dawning my furs, boots, and lastly my large raccoon hat that fell over my ears and covered my hair. I grabbed a machete off the wall and strapped it on my belt.

"Don't you dare, Meeka." Yesimia glared but made no move to come after me. I shrugged and opened the door to the cold. "Be back before dark at least!" Yesimia shouted as I took off in the wild.

Since Ma died, school shut down. They hadn't found a replacement that could both read and write, so in the interim, the kids all were helping around at home. I didn't feel too helpful though. I was bored.

As I trudged through the snow, I counted my steps. I liked to do that when I was bored, it passed the time. Scanning my surroundings, I looked for any predators, but during this coldest time of year I didn't expect to see many. Still, I kept my hand on the hilt of my machete in case a snow worgel hid nearby.

I paused. A twig creaking, a breath intake. I turned around but was too slow. A hand clamped over my mouth.

I elbowed my attacker in the stomach. He peeled off with a groan.

"Who are you?" I demanded, pulling my machete out of my belt.

"Shh-" he whispered. I looked him up and down. He was covered head to toe in furs. He pointed up at a tree a few paces away. Turning to where he pointed, I spotted a snow worgel perched on an upper branch, eyes glaring in my direction.

"Careful now," I drawled, backing slowly away, and gesturing to the man, who was now suddenly on my same team.

We stood together, moving carefully as the snow worgel readied to pounce. The beautiful creature was perched on all fours, a cross between a wolverine and a bear, with razor sharp teeth and a spotted coat to blend in with the snow.

They rarely came close to town, but at this time of year there would be slim hunting up in the mountains. The worgel would be looking for food.

The man slowly pulled a dagger from his scabbard as we continued to back away.

"If we move quietly, it should leave us alone," he whispered.

"Fat chance," I snorted next to him, "that beast's as hungry as an orphan. He's not leaving without food. We're probably looking like a juicy turkey leg to him about now." I had to be practical. The man just glared at me sideways and shook his head.

We continued to back away, but in the deep snow we didn't get very far, and the worgel seemed to get hungrier staring at his slowly retreating meal. I took a deep breath, knowing what was coming.

"Be ready," I commanded the man.

I wasn't sure if he was a fighter. I thought I knew everyone in these parts but didn't recognize him.

Occasionally, we'd have a stray come looking for work, or a hermit come down from the mountain, but they weren't usually dressed all in furs like this fellow. It was unnerving to meet a stranger.

As I sized up the man next to me, the worgel took advantage and pounced. It leapt gracefully yet aggressively from the tree, barreling right into my distracted self. I tried to roll out of its grip, kicking my legs to throw the beast off. It was clumsy but it worked, though not without a scratch to the face. My racoon hat went flying, but so did the worgel.

The man's eyes went wide eyed. He looked between me and the beast, momentarily stunned before lifting his dagger and rushing forward. He leapt at the worgel the same time as the worgel leaped for me.

Fortunately, the man reached his target first, tackling the creature, and after a bit of wrestling, slit its throat.

So, yes, a fighter then.

"Thank you," I stammered as I stood dizzily, wiping blood off my cheek.

"Your hair," he replied then seemed to think better of it, shaking his head. "Are you alright?" He asked instead.

"I'm fine," I replied, lunging toward my hat, and quickly putting it back on my head, tucking my hair in uncomfortably. "It's just a scratch."

"Let me see." He came to me, his large strides reaching quicker than I could respond. He pulled off each glove, raising my chin and moving it around, assessing me for any more injury besides the scratch on my cheek. His hands were warm against my cold skin, and the touch sent a jolt down my middle. I shivered.

Seeing him up close, he was younger than I thought, closer to my own age. He had light green eyes, the color of summer emeralds. They sparkled as if amused, even though he spoke with gravity. I couldn't see his hair, wrapped in furs as it was. But those eyes were penetrating.

Noticing the intensity with which I was staring back, he quickly dropped my face and stepped back. He took a deep breath as he glanced away.

"You should take that worgel with you. It'll give you lots of meat, and that fur will keep you mighty warm-" I paused looking him up and down, "though you seem to have an awful lot of fur already," I trailed off.

"You have it. I'll help you take it back to town," he responded. I looked at him with suspicion.

"You don't want it?" I narrowed my eyes. "Snow worgel is worth a whole lot."

He only shrugged, which made my apprehension grow.

Suddenly, I realized I was alone in the woods with a stranger. My machete was still lying on the ground, having been ripped from me during the worgel's attack. I glanced at it now, then at the young man.

I jumped quickly, grabbing my weapon, and rounding on him.

"Who are you?" I growled.

He slowly put his dagger to the ground and raised his hands. But there wasn't fear in his eyes. No, he was amused. I clenched my jaw in annoyance. "Despite the fact that worgel pounced on me, I promise you I'm a quick blade."

"I don't doubt that," he grunted but couldn't keep the chuckle from his voice.

"I will hurt you if you don't tell me who you are and why you're here."

He must have sensed my threat was serious, as he raised both eyebrows at me, again piercing me with those glassy green eyes.

"I'm the new stable boy in the village. My name's Johnny Pullver." He stuck out his hand to shake mine. I looked at it, suspicion sharp.

"And what are you doing following me in the woods, Johnny Pullver?" The name didn't sit right on my tongue. It was a name from these parts, but those eyes were not dark and haunted like most northerners.

"I wasn't following you at all. I'm looking for a horse." He nodded to the ground beyond us, where hoof marks sunk in the snow.

"You lost your horse?" I snorted skeptically. "And you're supposed to be a stableboy? A stableboy who lost his horse and doesn't want to take a prize worgel home for warmth, a full belly, or the wealth it could bring? Forgive me, Johnny Pullver, but your tale unfolds." I kept my machete raised.

"When you say it that way, I agree," he shook his head, looking amused, "but you've got it all backwards. I didn't lose my horse. And I would've found it sooner if you hadn't gotten in my way. Also, the worgel doesn't interest me. As you can see, I'm already warm, I don't much like the taste of vermin, and I have no desire for money."

I looked at him, mouth ajar.

"An odd stableboy indeed," I whispered under my breath.

I lowered my machete, not entirely sure I should trust his word. But his eyes shone with the sparkles of a hidden lake, and I couldn't find much fault in that.

"Seeing as I am incredibly bored and have nothing else to do unless I go home to my pestering sister and poke myself with an embroidery needle, I will help you find your horse and drag this beast to the stables. Despite your ridiculous statement, Johnny Pullver, no one in their right mind doesn't like the taste of worgel."

# CHAPTER 2

We trudged through the snow in silence. Occasionally, I glanced warily in Johnny's direction, but he didn't seem to notice or care. He was intent on tracking this horse, which he seemed to be doing purely based on instinct. Despite the few tracks he had shown me, we had discovered no more. The snow began to fall, covering any helpful hints where the steed may have gone.

Meanwhile, Johnny tied a rope around the legs of the snow worgel and slung it over his shoulder. He carried it with ease, making me wonder at the muscles that lay hidden underneath all those furs.

Focus on the horse, Meeka, I shook off the thought.

"So, Johnny Pullver, where are you from?" I asked, stealing another glance in his direction.

"A few days ride from here. My family sent me." He continued forward unfazed.

"To be a stableboy in Innesbrown?" A little town in the middle of nowhere. I wasn't sure Innesbrown was even on a map.

"To look for...work. Now you know all about me. And I don't even know your name." He didn't look at me, but I saw the corner of his mouth twitching upward.

"I'd hardly say I know anything about you," I grumbled, "besides, what've you done to earn my name?"

"Well, I do recall saving your life only moments ago," those sparkly eyes met mine, "but if that's not enough to earn a name, what then?"

I pondered the question. I wanted to come up with something clever, but he was right, he had saved me from the worgel.

"What can you do?" I asked instead.

"What can I do?" He repeated with a grunt. "What's that supposed to mean?"

"It means what I asked. Tell me, Johnny Pullver, if that is your real name, can you sing? Can you dance? Can you fly?" I turned to him, fisting my hands on my hips.

He stopped, turning as well, depositing the carcass at his feet between us.

"What kind of silly question is that?" He asked, looking at me with renewed interest.

"You want my name? Entertain me and it will be yours." I bit my upper lip trying to remain serious. He narrowed his eyes, and I could tell he was weighing me.

"Ok, then, Nameless. In fact, I know many ways to entertain a lady. Are you sure you'd like me to preform them here?" He gave me a wicked smile.

My knees wobbled and I turned away. I felt my face growing hot.

"You're no gentleman."

Johnny laughed, a sweet sound that made my stomach flutter.

"No, just a stableboy, bent on entertaining you, at your wish." He lifted the worgel throwing it back over his shoulders as though it weighed nothing.

"Where is that bloody horse?" I muttered under my breath, quickening my pace. The space between us suddenly felt too small.

"Ah look," Johnny drawled, pointing ahead where the trees gave way to a meadow and small stream. A large black stallion stood at the water's edge, drinking. The fast-flowing spring had not yet iced over.

"Perfect timing," I huffed under my breath.

"Are you often in the habit of mumbling?" Johnny asked, as he came up beside me. I didn't answer but instead turned up my nose and continued toward the horse.

"Not so fast, Nameless. You wait here with the worgel. I'll retrieve the horse." He tossed the worgel down, pushing past me. I made a disgruntled sound but didn't argue. As skilled as I was with nature, horses never seemed to like me.

I watched Johnny slowly approach the massive steed. The horse whinnied and backed away, but Johnny held out a gentle hand and spoke quietly, calming the beast. He stroked the horse's waxy black coat, an almost intimate gesture. I was mesmerized by his ability to tenderly appease the creature, and when he looked back at me smiling, he winked. I turned away.

Johnny pulled another rope from somewhere buried in his layers of fur and tied it gently around the horse, leading it over to where I stood watching.

"Shall we head back to the village, Nameless, and I can prove to you I am in fact the new stableboy?" He asked with those sparkling eyes.

"You want the two of us to ride the horse together?" I asked with only a tinge of panic at the thought of being so close to this stranger.

"Nope." He grabbed me around the waist before I could protest. His large hands fit almost all around my middle, and he lifted me easily on top of the horse. I sucked in a breath, staring at him wide-eyed. He didn't seem to notice as he seized the worgel and thew it on the horse behind me. He took the rope off from around the horse's neck and used it to tie the creature around the stallion's rump.

Then he jumped on the horse right between me and the worgel, straddling the steed with his strong thighs. Strong thighs that now pushed up against my backside as he wrapped an arm around my waist.

"I mean for all three of us to ride together. The worgel can be our chaperone," he spoke softly in my ear as he tightened his grip.

He leaned forward grabbing the stallion's mane with his other arm, folding his body over mine. "If you don't mind, there is no saddle, so this is the only way to ride."

"If it's the only way," I managed to squeak out. I heard him chuckle in my ear.

"Careful, Nameless. As you said, I am no gentleman. Yaw." He kicked the horse, and we set off galloping through the woods.

# CHAPTER 3

We made quick time getting back to the village. Johnny rode with expertise, the possibility he really was a stableboy becoming more likely. We didn't speak on the ride. The wind whipped against our faces, making it impossible. I knew I should be wary in the presence of a stranger but instead all I felt was pure thrill.

I jumped off the horse a little before the village came into view. I couldn't imagine the scandal if anyone saw me on the stallion, rosy cheeked and bright eyed, with a young man wrapped behind me. Especially if Pa got word.

"Thanks again but I should be getting home now," I told Johnny as he swung off. I straightened out my jacket and hat, making sure it was covering my fiery hair.

"You don't want to walk me to the stables? Check my story?" He smirked.

I narrowed my eyes at him. "Well, I suppose I can take the long way home through the village. Just to make sure, that is." He laughed but looked at me with more intensity than was right for a stranger. It was hard to look away.

I closed my eyes and turned. We made it out of the forest where the edge of the village opened to muddy, hay-lined streets. The town was only a few avenues long, dotted with rotting wooden buildings with makeshift signs reading various titles. We passed the druggist and the market, the cobbler, and the millinery.

Turning left at the end of the road, we passed the inn and the tavern, where my Pa had spent too much time since Ma died.

I ducked below the tavern window as we passed, crawling on my hands and knees, not caring about the mud that would soil my furs. Johnny looked at me curiously.

"And to think, Nameless, I thought you were a person. But indeed, you may be a dog." He looked down at me then glanced around. "What in the world are you doing down there?"

"Shh. My Pa's in there." I crept past the tavern window then stood, brushing off what mud I could from my knees and hands. Johnny didn't say anything but looked through the window, a darkness crossing his brow.

We continued the rest of the way to the stables in silence. Johnny seemed to be brooding the closer we got, whether from my actions or having to return to work, I was unsure.

"Took you long enough." Old Roy, the stable master came out to meet us. "And you picked up some extra weight while about it seems." He gave me a dark look. Old Roy hadn't been too fond of me ever since I'd experimented with some ale and threw up in his stables a couple years past.

"Good day, Old Roy." I gave him a sheepish grin. He scowled and took the horse from Johnny, noticing the worgel.

"I suppose this snow worg will make up for you keeping questionable company." Old Roy glared at me. Johnny gazed at me curiously, and I shrugged. "Careful with that one," he told Johnny. I smiled at him innocently.

"So, this Johnny here really does work for you?" I asked Old Roy.

"Where else do you think he works, girl? Have you gone daft?" Old Roy shook his head but didn't wait for a reply. Instead, he brought the stallion and the snow worgel into the stables. Johnny hung back. He looked at me expectantly.

"I should go," I said. I turned but Johnny gently grabbed my wrist, pulling me back. Twisting, I met him face to chest. I sucked in a deep breath as I looked up. His crisp green eyes met mine.

"You really won't tell me your name?" He let go of my wrist and stepped away.

When I didn't answer, he moved toward the stables, removing his large fur hat. Dark locks spilled across his brow, and he pushed a hand through them in a gesture I found too alluring. Without his hat, I saw that he was indeed closer to my age than I first expected. His jaw was sharp and refined, and the muscles in his neck alluded to a strong figure.

"I find you rather mysterious, Johnny Pullver," I responded after some time, angling my head.

"You as well, Nameless," he winked at me, "I'll be seeing you around. Hopefully with less danger next time."

"I don't mind a little danger. See you around...maybe," I narrowed my eyes.

He chuckled.

I looked down the street to see Pa stumbling out of the tavern. "Time to go."

I ran from the stables, not waiting to see Johnny's reaction. Pa would not be happy to see me here, but the way he was stumbling, I knew I had to help him home. I got to him just before he pitched to the mud.

"Pa, I'm here." I grabbed onto him before he fell, using all my strength to hold him up.

"Meeka? Is that you?" Pa slurred looking up at me, "What in the hells are you doing here? You should be home with your sister." Pa's voice tinged with anger as he batted me away.

"Was just out for a quick walk. Needed some fresh air," I lied.

Turning his gaze on me, he glared with one eye closed.

"You stupid woman." He batted at me again but missed. I slung his arm around my shoulder, holding him up and leading him away from the tavern toward our cabin in the woods. Jeers came from the open window, but I turned glaring at them all. It didn't stop the laughter. Pa had become a fool.

I dared to sneak a peek down the road toward the stables. Johnny still stood, facing us, though I couldn't clearly make out his expression. I shook my head, annoyed with myself for caring what he thought. I didn't even know him.

"Let's go, Pa."

I dragged Pa down the road toward the woods. It took a long while to stumble home to the cabin, and my arms were mighty sore by the end.

Ceceil was chopping wood as we approached and quickly threw down his ax to help. He glanced at me and sighed, shaking his head. He was awfully quiet since Ma died.

"Meeka, get inside now." Yesimia stood in the doorway to the cabin, anger mixed with concern across her brow. I nodded, giving Pa to Ceceil as I marched up the steps to the cabin.

It was no secret to any of us how Pa would take out his anger. He only had one child who looked like Ma. Only one child whose fiery red hair reminded Pa of his loss.

Yesimia quickly ushered me into the bedroom and told me to lock the door until morning.

# CHAPTER 4

The first time Pa beat me was after Ma died. He was well behaved before that, if not a bit aloof, but the pain of Ma dying had been too much. I hardly even blamed him. Ceceil and Yesimia did their best to protect me. Yesimia knew how to make a sleeping brew and it worked most nights to keep the demons at bay. But soon Yesimia would be married. She wouldn't always be here to help.

Timtim often would hide with me, though I don't think he was in any real danger. It was the red hair that made Pa go mad. It was the red hair that reminded him I was an outsider. I had made their lives more difficult. And now I reminded him too much of the woman he had lost.

I woke the next morning in a foul mood. It had been early when I arrived home with Pa the previous day and locking myself in that room the remainder of the day and night had been enough to boil my blood.

"Where's Pa?" I asked Yesimia as I entered the living room, which doubled as the kitchen and dining area. She sat on the worn leather sofa, a thick embroidered blanket hung across her lap. The fire roared, but no bread baked, no smell of porridge or meat came wafting from the kitchen.

"He went out early again." Yesimia looked up at me, sorrow in her eyes. "I can't believe the wedding is in a week's time."

"Don't worry about me, Yesimia. I'm mighty happy for you," I attempted a smile, but it wouldn't meet my eyes.

My foul mood and rumbling stomach had the final say. "Is there any food to eat?"

"Pa took most of the money and trading furs with him." Yesimia looked downcast. "I hid a bit in the top drawer – go get something for you and Timtim to eat in town."

"What about you?" I asked, my grouchiness fading at Yesimia's look of false hope.

"I don't need anything. I've got to fit in my wedding dress after all." She smiled but I knew she was lying. There just wasn't enough for all of us.

"Where's Ceceil?" I asked.

"He's out hunting, trying to get some more pelts to trade and meat to eat," she sighed.

At least someone was trying to work for this family. I needed to find something to do. I felt idle and worthless.

I went to Yesimia's dresser and pulled out a few coins from the top drawer.

"I'll go get something to eat," I told Yesimia as I donned my clothes.

"Come right back home, Meeka. I mean it. Don't give Pa any more reason to be upset." She gave me a pointed look. I glared at her resentfully. I knew she was trying to help, but her implication that I was part of the problem irked me.

"It's not my fault he gets drunk, Yesimia. It's not my fault I was born with this cursed red hair. Just go get married and leave me alone!" I shouted at her, anger getting the better of me as I slammed the door on the way out. I know I shouldn't take out my anger on her, but I was starting to feel something bubbling under my skin. I needed a release, and I wasn't even sure from what.

I trudged through the snow picking up rocks and sticks and throwing them at nearby trees. After a while I fell to my knees and buried my face in my hands, screaming into my gloves to muffle the sound. I hated this feeling. This loss of control.

I wanted to throw off my hat. I wanted to let down my hair and let the world see me as I truly was. But I knew I couldn't. Not here.

I took a deep breath, closed my eyes, and shook my head. I needed food. I was hungry, that was all. As soon as I got something in my belly, I would feel better. Resigning myself to that thought, I continued toward the village. I would apologize to Yesimia once I returned home.

The door to the market screeched on its hinges as the bell at the top simultaneously rang. The portly woman behind the counter, Mrs. Potsrow, stretched her neck to see who had entered.

"Morning, Meeka," Mrs. Potsrow sighed.

"Good day, Mrs. Potsrow," I replied with a small smile.

The townsfolk had been wary of our family since Ma was hanged. No one liked a scandal. They had overlooked the peculiar red hair on account of her always covering it, as they did mine, but when she stepped out of line showing her anger like that toward little Jimmy Horner, the folk said it was on account of her being foreign - and they didn't like foreigners. Though we'd been living in the village for ten years, we were on the outskirts not only physically, but in their hearts.

"What do you need, child?" Mrs. Potsrow asked with waning patience.

"Just came for a bit of broth, some dried beans, and canned potatoes if you have any." I unwrapped my gloves and shoved them in the satchel I brought from home.

"We got canned potatoes but no fresh broth." Mrs. Potsrow busied herself with the beans and potatoes while I looked around to see what else my measly number of coins could buy. There was fresh meat behind the counter which made me salivate, but I knew I didn't have enough for that.

"Any dried bones?" I asked hopeful.

"Not today," she shook her head. I continued looking around.

"I think just the beans and potatoes then," I stated with a hint of disappointment. The bell to the door rang again as another customer entered.

"That will be twenty-three centiar." Mrs. Potsrow put the potatoes and beans in a brown bag and held out her hand for the change.

"Twenty-three?" I counted out my change. I only had nineteen. "When did the prices go up?" I felt a bit of panic as I wouldn't be able to pay for all this. I was also slightly embarrassed knowing whoever had entered was now standing behind me pressuring me to hurry.

"It's winter now, girl. Harder to come by food and trade. Less product, more money." Mrs. Potsrow was growing irritated. "Do you have it or not?"

"I only have nineteen." I looked at her hoping she was in a bargaining mood.

"You can have the beans or potatoes but not both. Now hurry and pick, I've got customers waiting," Mrs. Potsrow snapped in my face. I clenched my jaw.

"The bean -" I was about to finish when a hand reached across my shoulder depositing a handful of centiar on the counter.

"This should be enough and throw in one of those cuts of meat. The big one on the bone." A familiar voice rang behind me. I turned to find myself staring up at Johnny Pullver.

"That's not necessary, Mrs. Potsrow," I stammered while staring up at Johnny. "I don't need your charity, Johnny Pullver," I growled.

"It's not charity, I'm coming over for supper tonight," he winked. I stood there dumbfounded.

"You what?" I asked confused.

"I am coming for supper tonight. I'd like a nice meal. It's purely selfish motives, I assure you," Johnny smiled.

"This has become a tiresome affair," Mrs. Potsrow continued her sighing as she bagged up a piece of meat, took the change, and held out the bag. "Take it or leave it."

I grabbed the bag before I could think better, my growling stomach ultimately winning the battle over conscience.

"Thanks," I managed to mumble out, though I'm not sure exactly which person I was thanking. I left as quickly as I could.

A little way down the road, I heard a whistle behind me. I turned to see Johnny jogging and waving in my direction. I clutched the bag of food tighter, ignoring him. However, it wasn't long before he caught up to me anyway.

"Not only are you an ungrateful one – especially when it comes to chivalric matters like saving your life and buying you dinner – but you seem to be a poor listener," the corners of his lips twitched upward as he looked at me with those sparkling green eyes.

"The snow worgel wouldn't have killed me, I was just distracted. And I told you before I didn't want your charity, but you insisted." I turned up my nose refusing to look his way.

"So, I distract you, Nameless?" He tilted his head, leaning down toward me, hands in his pockets.

When I didn't answer and only glared, he continued, "it wasn't charity. I do plan to come tonight for supper." At this statement I rounded on him.

"What nonsense are you talking about? Thank you for the food. I left my purse at home and only had a few centiar. I will pay you back, I promise. There, does that please you?" I asked him, mighty frustrated.

"Your hospitality tonight is payment enough." This time he smiled in full, not hiding his amusement.

I wanted to punch him.

"Since you look like you want to murder me, I'll explain. I met Ceceil last night. He was with your Pa, so, I assume this Ceceil is your brother. We had a fine night, and after some good conversation he invited me to supper. Tonight."

"You met Ceceil? And my Pa?" I couldn't help the flush that crept up my cheeks. Embarrassment and dread boiled beneath my skin, as well as anger at Pa for going back out to town.

"Don't worry. He mentioned he had two sisters, but he didn't tell me their names. Your secret is safe. At this point, Nameless, I think it would be a disappointment not to hear it first from your own lips." He raised his eyebrows in question.

I didn't reply. I was dumbstruck. This young man in front of me had charmed quiet Ceceil into inviting him to supper? And Pa had agreed? I narrowed my eyes, new suspicions rising.

"How did you get them to invite you for supper?" I glared.

"Don't you think I merit an invitation on my own friendliness?" He questioned.

"No." I continued to glare.

"You're a funny one, Nameless. Anyway, I think they took pity on me being new in town. They said your family had been new once," he shrugged.

"Ceceil is not sympathetic. And neither is Pa," I bit my lip.

"Regardless they invited me, and I am attending. So, whether you like it or not, I'll be eating supper with you tonight." He patted me on the shoulder, tipped his hat, and walked away, leaving me there on the road, speechless.

# CHAPTER 5

Pa came home that afternoon a bit drunk but not angry. He was excited, with a slight pep in his step none of us had seen since Ma died. He was energized to have a guest, someone from outside the village who could tell him news of the world that had forgotten us, and us it in return.

Yesimia and I eyed each other nervously as we prepared the potatoes, beans, and meat. Pa didn't ask how we afforded the meat. I wasn't sure he remembered he'd spent all our money on drink.

It wasn't a lavish feast, but rarely did we eat meat we hadn't killed ourselves, and the juicy piece of steak felt luxurious on its own. I wasn't the best cook, but Yesimia coaxed me along, helping me prepare the potatoes with a splash of cream from a neighbor's farm. The beans were rinsed and baked with onion from the cellar even though we only had a few remaining for the winter.

Timtim and I sacrificed yet another meal to keep the food available for our guest tonight. Therefore, my mood barely improved, though having a guest seemed to put us all in higher spirits. It was not often we had company.

"He should be arriving soon," Ceceil announced, "Yesimia and Meeka, if you're done go make yourselves presentable. And for gods' sake, Meeka, wear a dress."

I rolled my eyes but took off my apron and went to my room to change.

A short while later, a knock at the door indicated our guest had arrived. Yesimia and I sat at the fire, embroidering, as commanded by Pa. Really, I was just pretending to embroider, I had no desire to war with the needles this evening. My dress had grown tight and uncomfortable. I had grown into a woman's body since the last time it had been worn. My hair was pulled up and covered with a scarf, no locks showing. I wish I could let it down and put on something more comfortable.

Johnny Pullver entered and handed his large coat to Ceceil who hung it on the hook by the door. It was the first time I'd seen Johnny not bundled in layers of fur. He wore rough grey trousers, and a collared shirt rolled up at the sleeves revealing his muscular forearms. He had one button too many undone in the front, which I found mighty excessive and distracting. He shook the snow out of his unruly dark hair, then used his fingers to run it back.

I sat gawking, my fingers frozen, needle in hand. Yesimia kicked me and I snapped to attention, closing my mouth, and glaring at her with wild eyes. She bit her lip, laughter shining in her eyes. I shut my jaw as my attention was pulled back toward Johnny. He was staring at me with eyebrows raised, amusement on his face.

"Daughters, this is Johnny Pullver, our guest." Pa gestured to us. Yesimia and I both stood and curtsied. Johnny's eyes never left mine.

"Nice to meet you, ladies." Johnny nodded in our direction, green eyes hovering as he took me in, dress and all.

"Johnny Pullver, these are my daughters, Yesimia, the elder, and Meeka, the younger." Pa stumbled toward the kitchen table pulling out a seat. "Come and sit. Ceceil, whiskey."

Johnny lingered, his gaze roaming my face as he mouthed "Meeka," one side of his mouth turning upward. He put his hands in his pockets, nodding at us once more before turning to sit with Pa.

"My sons, Ceceil, whom you've met, and Timtim over there." He gestured to where Timtim sat playing on the floor. "Ceceil, I said the whiskey," Pa shouted.

Ceceil quickly found a bottle of whisky, which only contained an inch of the brown liquid. It should have been full. He poured a small drink for both Pa and Johnny, as the rest of us sat watching.

"Your children have unusual names," Johnny mused as he stirred his whiskey. Pa sat with his back to Yesimia and I, but Johnny had a perfect view of my face. His eyes met mine again. I looked away.

"My wife wasn't from here," Pa admitted with a touch of embarrassment in his voice.

"And your children were born in your wife's country?" Johnny asked rather intrusively, I thought.

"All but Timtim, hence he's got a Northern name like me. I hail from these parts you see, which is why folk have tolerated us here well enough." Pa looked down at his empty cup, which he had already consumed in a single swallow. "I said whiskey, Ceceil!" Pa stomped his fist on the table.

"Should we eat, Pa?" I asked standing up and trying to distract from the growing tension in the room as Pa's belligerency grew. Yesimia stood up behind me, and we both made our way to the kitchen, grabbing supper and placing it on the already set kitchen table. Ceceil poured what was left of the whiskey into Pa's cup.

Yesimia sat and gestured for me to serve the food with a waggle of her eyebrows. I picked each dish up in turn, going around the table and portioning the food with a wooden spoon. When I arrived at Johnny's side, I bent down as he turned his face toward mine. He was so close I could feel his breath against my skin.

"Thank you," he breathed. It sent a shiver down my spine.

As I straightened, a lock of hair came loose falling down my shoulder. Johnny's gaze fixed on my scarf then slowly followed the fiery tress in a line, stopping where it rested low on my chest. I heard his sharp intake of breath before Pa banged his fist on the table again, scattering his plate.

"Hells, Meeka, put that away," Pa shouted. I almost dropped the potatoes I'd been serving, but Johnny steadied my hand. I tightened my fist around the wooden spoon, daring Pa to come at me now, in front of a guest. Pa looked around, noticing everyone at the table, as if he had forgotten where he was. "Eat everyone," he gestured, ignoring me as though nothing had happened.

I walked to the kitchen sink, turning my back on the table, and tucking the lock of hair back under the scarf. I gathered my composure before taking my seat. The only open spot was across the table from Johnny, thanks to Yesimia's meddling.

He peered at me with slight concern, but I shook my head. I felt vulnerable under his gaze.

"Any news of the outside world? I heard a rumor the Old King died. Is it true?" Pa asked Johnny. I heard no such rumor. We had no king in the North, which meant he must be asking about the Old Country.

"I believe so," Johnny took a mouthful of potatoes.

"I knew that old bastard had to die eventually," Pa smirked, downing his whiskey. Johnny choked on his potatoes, sitting up straight and pounding himself on the chest. After a minute, he composed himself.

"Yesimia is to be married in a few days' time," I spoke, looking down at my plate, trying to make friendly conversation while changing the subject.

"Is that so?" Johnny asked, now recovered, looking to Yesimia who nodded. "Who is the lucky man?" Johnny smiled, but it was merely friendly, none of the intensity he reserved for me in his eyes.

"Carson Front. He's the son of the cobbler," Yesimia smiled happily.

I liked Carson. He was a nice fellow. But their marriage would be dull, Yesimia cooking and cleaning, having lots of village children, while Carson continued his apprenticeship in his father's shop. There was nothing wrong with that; Yesimia seemed content with her lot. But there would be no grand romance, no adventure, they would continue in the cycle of living and dying in this small village, generation after generation. I wanted more.

"Ah yes, I met him only two days ago. A nice fellow," Johnny mimicked my thoughts, and I wondered if he had the same dreams of adventure, of a greater love. I studied him, my head tilting. As if he knew I was watching him, he looked up meeting my eyes. I suddenly found my food very interesting.

"You must come," Yesimia sat up and clapped her hands, "it will be such a joyous feast, there will be dancing and cake, you must be there." She looked between Johnny and I, smiling. I wanted to wring her neck. She was so obvious. Johnny seemed to think so too as he looked at me, raising his brows again.

"Then I must," he agreed not taking his eyes off me.

The rest of the evening passed uneventfully. Pa had grown tired of us girls, sending Yesi and I to bed, but soon the liquor had him snoring on the couch.

Ceceil and Johnny retired to the porch to have a pipe, and I tiptoed out of my room, hoping to join them.

"Meeka, where are you going?" Yesimia stopped me in my tracks.

"Why are you still awake?" I asked her, annoyed.

"Why are you? And where do you think you are sneaking off in your nightgown? And your hair uncovered?" Yesimia looked scandalized.

"I was going to put on my hat and coat..." I said, though now I realized that she was probably right. "Ugh, never mind. I'll go back to bed."

"Yes, you very well shall, Meeka," Yesimia gave me a pointed look.

I rolled my eyes.

As I crept back to the bedroom, the door creaked open.

Johnny and Ceceil walked in.

Yesimia yelped and grabbed a blanket covering herself and her nightgown. I looked around panicked but had nothing to cover myself.

My hair cascaded around my shoulders. My bare arms hung at my sides. My nightgown was only a thin layer of fabric, which did little to conceal my body.

Johnny's gaze trailed up and down my body.

"For gods' sake, Meeka, get back in bed. Pa's sleeping right there," Ceceil whispered loudly, gesturing to Pa snoring on the couch.

Johnny quickly turned around.

"I apologize," Johnny stammered, "I better be off. Thank you, Ceceil, for a fine night. Ladies, a delicious dinner." He waved, still turned toward the door. He was already wearing his coat, but he grabbed his hat off the hook and left with haste.

"Meeka, you imbecile," Ceceil shook his head once Johnny had left.

"I didn't know you were about to walk inside," I raised my hands in surrender.

"Just go to bed," Ceceil seemed tired. I looked at him closely. I often overlooked Ceceil. He'd been trying to take care of us all, I realized. Him and Yesimia. But soon Yesimia would be gone, and it would all fall on Ceceil's shoulders. I suddenly felt like a burden.

"I'm sorry, Ceceil. I know it's been hard on you since Ma died. I'll try to be more helpful," I gave him a sad smile. He ruffled my hair.

"Go to bed, Meeka," he patted me on the shoulder and went off to his room.

# CHAPTER 6

The next morning, I woke extra early, determined to go trapping. I hadn't contributed much lately, and I felt the need deep in my bones.

It was particularly cold, but the air was clear, and the sky was blue. It was a beautiful day, and the joy of it was encompassing.

I hummed to myself as I lay traps in a large perimeter. I was hopeful of catching a muskrat or two, maybe even a fox. The pelts wouldn't sell for much, but if I caught anything at all, it would be enough to buy us food for a week, at least.

It took a considerable amount of time concealing the traps under the snow, making sure they were close to a water or food source, spreading them out to ensure diversity of catch. By the time I was done, the sun was well overhead, and I needed a break.

I sat with my back against a tree, taking deep breaths, enjoying the fresh air. Before long, my eyes grew heavy, and I dozed off.

I awoke to voices.

In a clearing beyond the bushes, two men were talking in whispers. Obscured by the brush, I remained unseen. One of the men was Johnny Pullver.

What are you up to, Johnny? I asked myself. And who was he meeting? It was not a man I had ever seen before. He had long grey slicked back hair tied at the nape of his neck with a ribbon. He was strong and gentrified, even beyond Jim Horner, the most gentrified man I knew in these parts.

"I need more time. It's been less than a week since I arrived, I hope you know." Johnny wasn't wearing his hat, but ran his gloved hand through his hair, looking annoyed.

"We don't have that much time. The council is restless," The man spoke aggressively. I wondered if it was Johnny's father, but he was dressed too fine to be a stableboy's sire.

I scooted through the snow to get a closer look but as I crawled toward the clearing, a stick cracked beneath my weight. The noise reverberated through the trees. Both men turned their heads in my direction. I ducked behind a shrub.

"I need to get back to work," Johnny said after some time. I didn't dare look, but I heard the whinnying of a horse as the man galloped away. I waited some time before I was confident that Johnny had left.

I knew he had been keeping something. Had he really come here looking for work? Had his family fallen on hard times? Or had he fled in the middle of the night like my family? Maybe he also escaped some unknown threat that lurked in the Old Country. I had no answers. His affairs should not concern me, even though something nagged at the back of my mind.

It had been a few hours since laying my first traps, so instead of mulling about Johnny, I dragged myself through the snow checking the traps. I was right – it was a good day. I caught two foxes. I'd go to the trading post right away to sell them.

Though the air was crisp and my breath was blowing mighty smoke plumes, I was getting hot in my furs trudging through the snow. I pulled off my thick hat, hair tumbling into my face, as I shook it out. The icy wind blew across my brow and chilled the sweat beaded on my forehead. It felt good. I felt alive. I was far enough out of town no one would see me here.

"Meeka."

Well, maybe I wasn't so far out after all.

I startled, turning toward the source. He was resting against a birch tree, arms crossed, head tilted, staring at me.

"Johnny," I nodded in his direction but continued barreling through the snow.

"So, that's your name. Meeka," he stated, and I could feel him watching me, though I didn't turn to look. "It's a good name, though I wish I heard it first from you."

"Now that you have my name what will you do with it?" I sunk a little too deep in the snow and had to pry out my foot. Johnny ignored my question.

"Why do you hide your hair, Meeka?" He asked, not moving from his spot against the tree.

"It's a foreigner's hair. People here are wary of foreigners." I still didn't look at him. The way he continued to purr my name made me more unsettled than I wanted to admit.

"I think it's beautiful," he spoke softly. I looked at him then. I couldn't help it. There was no amusement on his face now.

"Careful, Johnny. That sounded like a compliment," I stopped in my tracks, the foxes swaying at my belt.

"And why shouldn't I compliment you, Meeka?" He asked, pushing off the tree and stalking toward me.

"Stop saying my name like that," I groaned, not answering his question.

"Were you following me earlier?" He stopped right in front of me. Our bodies stood perilously close. If I reached out, I could touch him. I tensed at his question.

So, he knew I had been there in the woods. He knew I heard his conversation with the strange man.

"No, I'm out trapping, see?" I unbuckled the two foxes and held them in front of his face. He gave me a wicked smile full of danger and secrets. I had to remind myself that I didn't know this man at all.

"Then what were you doing spying on me?" He asked, assessing.

"I wasn't spying on you. I fell asleep and you happened to have your little secret meeting right next to me. Maybe next time you should be more discreet, Johnny Pullver, if that is your name," I glared at him.

"So, you didn't hear what we said?" His eyes narrowed suspiciously.

"Only a little," I shrugged. "Who was that man anyway?"

Johnny peered deeply in my eyes. There was a calculating coolness to his look, and something more I couldn't place. He shook his head.

"Just a messenger from my village, checking in on me," he smirked, amusement back intact.

"He was dressed mighty nice for just a messenger." I tied the foxes back on my belt. When I looked up, Johnny was staring at my hair. The wind whipped it across my face. Johnny bent down, taking his gloved hand and pushed a lock behind my ear.

I tensed at his touch but didn't shy away. I looked into his green eyes, which moved down my face, finally meeting mine. I licked my lips. He watched, a pained expression briefly crossing his face before he turned away.

"You should really be more careful out here. I've snuck up on you twice now. Plus, the snow worgel did too," he shook his head, eyes back to smiling.

"I can take care of myself just fine. What did you do with the worgel anyway?" I asked, genuinely curious.

"I sent it home." He turned away.

So maybe his family had fallen on hard times. A worgel would definitely help with that. Maybe that messenger was here to gather the worgel.

"Do you plan to stay here long?" I asked, remembering the conversation I overheard, that he needed more time.

"Just until I finish my task. Here, let me walk you back to town." He paused and waited for me to join him.

I grabbed my hat and worked at stuffing my hair underneath.

"I wish you wouldn't hide your hair like that," Johnny stated as he started marching toward the village.

"Me too, but it's necessary," I huffed as I caught up to him.

"Necessary for what?" He sounded annoyed.

"To hide from the townsfolk," I stated simply. I had kept my hair hidden since I could remember. Most of them had seen it at one point or another but they didn't like being reminded someone was so different.

"Hm. Curious," he snorted.

"What do you mean, 'curious'?" I glanced at him from the corner of my eye. He was running his glove through his hair again. Ugh, I wished he wouldn't do that.

"Are you sure it's the townsfolk you're hiding that hair from?" He met my sideways glance.

"Who else would I be hiding it from?" I asked confused.

"Now that's a good question, isn't it?" He smirked.

# CHAPTER 7

We made it quickly to the village where we parted ways. Johnny went back to the stablemaster for work, and I headed to the trading post to sell my pelts.

The post was crowded, as it usually was when the weather was pleasant. Lots of folk had come to trade before the snow started falling heavier and the roads closed.

I bargained with Mr. Happen, the clerk, for a while, but finally was able to get close to the price I wanted. My good mood continued, that is until I bumped into Jim Horner.

"Watch it, girl," he sneered down his nose. I gave him a dark look but bit my tongue against the words I really wanted to say. Murderer. If it hadn't been for him, Ma would still be alive.

He was a weasel of a man, both by looks and by virtue. He stood tall and lanky, balding but for the greasy side-slicked hair trying and failing to cover his head. For all that, he was still the richest man in town. He wore a three-piece suit with a gold chained pocket watch looping across his middle. He walked with a slight limp, on account of a hunting accident several years back, but other than that he was all pompous and pride.

I hated him fiercely.

I clenched my fists, pushing past him and out the door.

"Jim Horner, I hope you rot," I growled under my breath. I kicked at the dirt, angry by the sight of that wretched man but there was nothing I could do. He was the mayor and therefore also the judge of the court. Jim Horner was the law.

I spit on the ground.

"Meeka!" I looked up to see Yesimia staring with wide eyes.

"Yesi, what are you doing here?" I asked, startled to see her in town. She rarely came into the village.

"I'm headed to meet Mrs. Front. I'm trying on my wedding dress, remember? You're supposed to meet me. That is why you're here?" Yesimia put her hands on her hips, giving me a very maternal frown.

"Of course," I stammered, having completely forgotten about the appointment with Yesimia's future mother-in-law.

Yesimia huffed as though she could smell my lie.

Shrugging, I followed her down the road to the cobbler's shop. We took the stairs up the back to the small living quarters above the storefront. This would be Yesimia's home in only a few days' time.

"Ah, girls, come in, come in," Mrs. Front waited for us in the doorway. She was short and fat, but she was friendly, and her rosy cheeks and kind eyes did more for her beauty than her girth did against.

"Mrs. Front," Yesimia kissed her on both cheeks, "so good of you to have us."

"Thank you, ma'am," I agreed stepping into the warm room. It smelled like cinnamon, and I hoped to the gods we were going to have pie.

Mrs. Front ushered us to sit on the sofa. She placed a small hand mirror on the table in front of us, and I picked it up, curious to see my reflection. We didn't own a mirror.

I still pictured myself as the scrawny little girl with sunken eyes but was surprised to see a young woman staring back. I had most defiantly matured in the last year.

"Quit staring at yourself," Yesimia scolded under her breath, snatching the mirror away. She placed it back on the table. "Don't you know if you stare in a mirror too long it will steal your soul?"

I snorted, but before I could respond, Mrs. Front returned with both tea and some sort of delicious smelling pastry. Thank the gods.

"I've laid the dress out in my bedroom, dear girl. Don't worry, I've sent the men away for the day. They won't bother us. Now hurry and go change." Mrs. Front looked giddy with delight.

"Are you excited your only son is off and getting married? He'll be stuck with the same woman, same village, same job, for eternity," I asked with a mouthful of whatever the delicious cinnamon concoction was.

"Off and married! Eternity! Who speaks like that!" She looked at me aghast.

"I just mean he's your only son, that's all. I'm just saying there are other things than marriage." I grabbed another pastry.

"And it's no wonder it isn't you getting married, girl, stuffing your face with pastries and speaking nonsense. You should learn to behave more like your sister," Mrs. Front chided.

Yesimia entered the room before Mrs. Front could further reprimand my stomach or my tongue. She was swimming in a rough, off-white fabric, that could have fit the two of us together. I spit out my tea.

"Meeka!" Yesimia clenched her jaw wide eyed.

"Sorry. I mean, I apologize, you just look so...beautiful. What a voluminous dress, Mrs. Front." I had to bite my lip from laughing.

"Oh hush. It needs a few alterations, but...Oh, Yesimia, you will be a beautiful bride!" Mrs. Front laughed with joy, then was standing, hugging Yesimia, wiping tears from her cheeks. Yesimia beamed, looking truly joyful, regardless of the hideous dress.

I schooled my features and hugged my sister. Gods forbid I would be married off to a village boy. I shuddered at the thought.

# CHAPTER 8

The next few days went quickly, wedding preparations taking precedent to other chores. I was grateful for the money the fox pelts brought in, as it meant we had enough to eat.

Mr. Front had insisted on paying for the wedding, which was a testament to Carson's love for Yesimia if you ask me. Pa would never have been able to afford it.

Before long the wedding day arrived.

The ceremony was set to take place in the small chapel in town, followed by dancing and cake in the city hall.

"Do you think I need more ribbons, Meeka?" Yesimia asked as we sat in our room in the cabin getting ready.

"No, Yesi, you'll look like a present," I finished pinning her hair, putting the last ribbon in place, "I take that back, you already look like a present."

Yesimia smacked my arm. I laughed.

"At least the dress looks better with the alterations," I noted. Yesimia rolled her eyes.

"You look awfully pretty too, Meeka," Yesimia looked at me with tenderness in her eyes. I saw the love but also the sadness.

"Don't worry about us, Yesimia. We will all be fine. Besides, you will still be close by," I reassured her.

"You know how Pa is. Promise me -" she started but couldn't finish. She just shook her head.

"I'll stay out of his way and lock the door at night if he comes home with too much drink in him. I promise," I patted her shoulder. She smiled, slightly reassured, but the haunted look still lay beneath.

"Sometimes I dream that you have magic and could run away," she looked at me softly, "Ma always said there was magic in our blood."

"Ma is dead. Her blood turned cold. No magic saved her," I spoke harsher than I intended. Yesimia clenched her jaw and yanked free of my touch.

I ruined the moment. I shouldn't have said it, but it was true, and Yesimia and her fairy tales were getting on my nerves. But this was her day, I reminded myself. It wouldn't do to be selfish.

"I'm sorry, Yesi, I shouldn't have said that." I tried to smile.

"None of that, now. It's time to go." She busied herself moving about the room, but we already dropped her belongings at the Front's, and she had nothing left to do.

"Yesimia, I'm sorry," I tried again. She stopped moving around and looked at me. She sighed but came and gave me a big hug.

"I meant what I said, you look beautiful, Meeka." Yesimia held me at arm's length taking in my dress. It had been one of Yesimia's now that I had outgrown my own.

I looked down at my outfit. The dress was a crimson fabric that shimmered when I twirled. The tight bodice dipped low, accentuating my figure. The dress sinched at my waist, then flowed gracefully down below my ankles. It was worn and faded in areas, but it did fit me well. I wore a matching headscarf, covering my hair, though with the color, I pretended it was my real hair tied up elegantly.

I smiled at Yesimia.

"Let's go," she said, all giddiness back.

Pa, Ceceil, Timtim, Yesimia, and I trekked through the snow to the small chapel. When we arrived, most of the villagers had already taken their places inside.

The chapel resembled a stone cave. It was covered floor-to-ceiling in paintings of the gods at war, blood, gore, and glory, all. It was a rather daunting place for a joyous celebration, but marriage was daunting, I supposed.

There were no seats inside, everyone stood around the room in circles, the happy couple now standing in the center.

Something dripped on my shoulder. I looked up to see a fresco of a woman crying. How odd. Though it was only a painting, she stared directly into my eyes. Her arm stretched out across the ceiling, reaching desperately for a muscular man. The man returned her desperate stretch, lunging for the woman before the god above her wielded his heavy axe. I wiped the tear off my shoulder and licked my finger. It tasted salty. I shuddered but looked back to the ceremony.

The cleric begun his chanting, and I zoned out. I took deep breaths and swayed from leg to leg, not used to being so confined. I searched the faces of those in the room. Most I recognized but there were a few strangers among the crowd. I assumed they must be relatives from out of town.

My eyes met Johnny Pullver, who was looking at me with concern.

What? I mouthed, crinkling my nose. He just shook his head. I narrowed my eyes in his direction as Ceceil elbowed me.

"Ouch," I said under my breath to Ceceil, "what was that for?"

"Quit moving around so much. And quit flirting with the stableboy," Ceceil glanced at me sideways.

"I am not!" I glared at him. He shrugged.

The ceremony lasted longer than I'd hoped, but soon they were married, and it was time for cake. That was the part I looked forward to the most.

"Meeka." A shiver traveled down my spine.

"Do you have to say my name like that?" I asked Johnny Pullver who caught up to me as we made our way down the street to the village hall.

"Like what, Meeka?" He purred.

"You know what you are doing," I murmured.

"Now that I know your name, I can't help myself. Can I escort you?" He held out his elbow. I rolled my eyes and sighed but took his elbow all the same.

"Did you ever wonder why we don't hibernate?" I asked, my mind wandering.

"No. But it sounds like you have." He gave me a curious look.

"It's just mighty interesting to me how some creatures do, and some creatures don't," I shrugged.

"And do you wish you could hibernate?" He smiled playfully.

"No, not really. I rather like the snow," I sighed wistfully as we arrived at the hall.

"It would be a shame if you slept all winter. Who'd provide the much-needed entertainment?" He bumped my shoulder. I bumped him back. He laughed that sweet sound again, making my heart flutter.

"You better stop laughing, Johnny Pullver, that sound could turn a heart of stone to fire." I meant it playfully, but it sounded grave. He gave me another one of his curious looks.

"Come on, let's go dance," I took his hand and pulled him toward the dance floor. He didn't budge, but instead tugged back, flipping me around until our bodies were facing.

"And you better be careful, Meeka," he grinned down at me, "I like to play with fire."

# CHAPTER 9

I lost myself in the whirling music and rhythm of the dance floor. Johnny joined me reluctantly, but when it was clear he didn't know the steps, he excused himself. I didn't mind; I twirled and stomped and clapped my hands following the country steps I had spent the last ten years dancing. I loved to dance. It was freedom and movement and tempo flowing through my veins. I laughed as I twirled with my arms out and looked up to the open ceiling of the village hall. The stars shone down on us like the tiny eyes of the gods peeking in the darkness.

"Meeka, may I?" Dilly, one of the village boys from my class, stood before me with his palm out. I smiled sweetly and took his hand. We laughed as we spun and swooped around the other couples, the fiddler jumping off the stage to play amongst the dancing.

"Dilly, you right stepped on my foot," I chided Dilly as my toe throbbed, but I didn't stop moving and neither did he. Instead, we both laughed and continued to relish in the thrill of the dance.

I snuck a glance across the room where the cake was being served. Johnny stood in the corner, starting right at me. I frowned at him.

I continued to glance around the room, until my gaze settled on Pa and Ceceil sitting at a round table. Pa already looked taken with drink. I took a deep breath then looked back to Dilly. I wouldn't worry about that now.

The music slowed and I excused myself, wiping my sweaty brow, and heading for the refreshments. I was thirsty and it was time for cake. I wandered to the corner for food and drink; not to see Johnny Pullver - or so I told myself.

Sipping a sweet punch, I grabbed a large slice of berry cake and settled in a corner where I could enjoy the rich dessert.

"Gods, to find a girl who'd look at me like you look at that cake," Johnny Pullver drawled, joining my side. After all, he had only been standing a few steps from where I settled.

"You want a wife who would eat you?" I raised my brows at him. He chuckled.

"Who said I wanted a wife?" He stared at me with those green eyes, and I couldn't help but blush.

"Nevermind," I mumbled.

"So, is that your beau?" Johnny asked, leaning back against the wall. He nodded to where Dilly stood staring in our direction. Dilly waved as I found his gaze, but I ignored him.

"Dilly Putnum?" I snorted, "what a thing to say." I tried to contain my amusement. Dilly was a nice boy and all but, no. Never.

"You two look good dancing together," Johnny glanced at me from the corner of his eye.

"Anyone would look good compared to your dancing." I peeked up at Johnny, unable to control my laughter. "I suppose they didn't teach you country dancing in your village?"

"Not quite," Johnny looked away. He didn't seem to share my amusement.

"Oh, quit being a sour lemon. You just didn't know the steps, that's all. I could teach you?" I asked taking a big sip of my punch and not looking him in the eye.

"Maybe another time." Johnny pulled his hands from his pocket, slicking back his hair in that infuriatingly distracting manner.

"Have it your way," I shrugged, trying not to feel rejected.

"Actually," he pushed off the wall and turned toward me, grabbing my punch and cake and depositing them on the nearest table, "where I come from, we dance like this."

Johnny grabbed my hand with his, our fingers gently sliding together. My skin tingled from the contact. He placed his other hand gently on the small of my back. His fingers curled against the fabric of my dress, sending butterflies up my chest. He pulled me in until our bodies were touching. I was exceedingly aware of every inch where his met mine. My breath hitched.

The music was quick, but he swayed back and forth slowly, bringing my body along with his in a soft and intimate rhythm. I breathed out slowly and looked up into his bright green eyes. He pierced me with those eyes, an unspoken question lingering that neither of us was willing to answer.

"This is how you dance back home?" I barely managed to whisper out.

We held each other's gaze, but he pushed me away, forcing me into a twirl. He caught me on the other side, pulling me in closer still, the warmth of his body filling me in a way that made my heart hammer.

"Yes." He stared down at me lips parting.

"Meeka," Yesimia interrupted. I jumped backward, cheeks flaming as I turned toward my newly married sister.

"Yesi! Johnny was just showing me how they danced back in his village." I gave her an innocent smile, trying to hide my embarrassment. She looked at me and then at Johnny, holding back a smile, though her eyes twinkled. I was too self-conscience to look at Johnny.

"Ceceil is taking Pa and Timtim home," Yesimia glanced over her shoulder nodding to where Pa was trying unsuccessfully to rise from his seat. Ceceil pulled him up and lifted Pa's arm over his shoulder.

I peered up at Johnny, but he looked away, occupied by something at the other end of the hall.

"Do you want me to go help them?" I asked Yesimia.

"No," she said a bit too forcefully, then looked up alarmed at Johnny, who still appeared to be paying no attention. "You stay put for a while. Go home when its safe."

The last part she whispered. I didn't think Johnny could hear, yet I thought I felt his body tense slightly next to mine. He turned and excused himself, giving Yesimia and I a chance to talk.

"Yes, of course, Yesi. I promise." I gave her a reassuring pat on the hand and then kissed her on the cheek. "Enjoy your night, Yesimia. It should be a night to remember." I waggled my eyebrows, and she smacked my arm.

"You too, Meeka," she raised one brow at me then looked questioningly at Johnny, who walked toward a group of men at the opposite side of the hall. I shook my head but couldn't help the smile that broke through.

"Go away, you are married now. I am young and free and can't be associated with old married hags," I shooed her away, laughing.

"Meeka, you are awful," Yesimia shook her head but laughed as well.

"Go, Yesimia, for real this time. May the gods shine down on you. A piece of my heart is with you always." I meant it.

"You say that like a goodbye," Yesimia gave me a sad smile.

"Never a goodbye, Yesi, only until next time," I squeezed her shoulders and then we hugged.

We were two sisters who had been through so much death, so much hardship, so much loss. But in this moment, we held each other, thankful that we hadn't been alone through all our trials. For once, we allowed ourselves to hope for a better future.

# CHAPTER 10

Yesimia and Carson left shortly after their goodbyes to enjoy their wedding night. I was happy for them, but it felt like a small hole had been carved out of my chest. I supposed that was the consequence of giving away a piece of your heart to someone.

I sighed taking another sip of sweet punch. Pa should be asleep by now and there would be nothing to worry about. Timtim had left with Ceceil and Pa, and it was only a matter of time before I'd follow. I'd be the only woman in the house now. I hope they didn't expect me to embroider.

Johnny Pullver had disappeared shortly after I said my goodbye to Yesimia. All the better. There was a line drawn between the two of us that felt too fragile. It would be better to keep our distance, especially as he wasn't planning on staying long. Just a little more time, he had said - or something like that. It wasn't really my business and getting involved would only make that line between us blur further.

The party was beginning to die down, which I took as my signal to leave. The remaining guests were mostly drunk, and those sober few were ushering their belligerent loved ones home.  I suddenly felt trapped.

I was stuck in so many ways. Stuck in this village where I didn't really belong. Stuck home with a Pa who couldn't look at me, a brother who shouldn't have to take care of me, and another too young to know better. I wanted to get out of this village, away from all this. But that would be impossible. I had nowhere to go. I was already a foreigner in this land, but I had been reluctantly accepted. No one would welcome me in a village where I was completely unknown. My cursed hair would always betray me.

The Old Country. My thoughts whispered of the homeland I tried so hard to keep from my mind. No, I couldn't go back there. I didn't even know where it was. I didn't even know it's real name.

A man stumbled in the hall as my thoughts wandered.

"Fire!" He shouted to those who remained. "At the tavern. All hands needed!"

I shot to my feet with the others except for the few who had fallen into a deep sleep, who wouldn't awaken from their inebriated slumber until morning.

We ran out of the room and down the road, turning the corner to the tavern, where the wooden shack was indeed on fire. Several others had already made their way, grabbing buckets, barrels, or anything they could get their hands on, making a long assembly line from the town well.

I joined the formation and helped usher bucket from hand to hand, until those nearest the flames threw the water on the licking flames. I noticed Johnny Pullver near the front, grabbing the heavy buckets and heaving them with a strength that was both mesmerizing and impressive.

It took a while, but soon the fire was contained. The villagers all but fell to the ground, wiping sweat off their brows even in the frigid night air. It wasn't unusual for a fire to break out in the village. The whole town was practically a dilapidated wooden tinder box.

Mr. Willard, the tavern owner, sat crying on the stoop of his burned down establishment. It was mighty unsettling watching a grown man cry. Instead of offering comfort, I thought it best I made my way home.

"Meeka, wait up," Johnny Pullver jogged to my side while I was retreating, "what are you still doing here, shouldn't you be home by now? It's well past midnight."

"I know, I was just heading there," I closed my eyes against the distracting way his strong muscles glistened with sweat, "you look like you need a shower."

His eyes sparkled with amusement.

"Goodnight, Johnny Pullver," I nodded at him, cheeks reddening, and continued my retreat. I was sore from fighting the fire and dancing all night. I felt tired to the bone.

"I'll walk you home." He fell in line next to me.

"That won't be necessary," I tried sluggishly to shrug him off, but I couldn't lie, I appreciated the company.

"It's my pleasure," he smiled at me and winked. I rolled my eyes.

"Johnny Pullver, I don't know who you were in your past town, but here you seem to be all charm and a bit of stalker. I bet you had a mighty lot of girlfriends," I met him with a challenging smile.

He laughed. That sound again, my heart.

"Are you asking if I have a girl back home, Meeka?" His eyes shone as he met my playful tone.

"No," I shook my head, ignoring the way my cheeks burned.

"I think you are," he teased.

"Johnny Pullver, are you really so arrogant?" I shot back.

"So, if that Willy Dilly," he ignored my question waving his hand in the air, "or whatever his name is, doesn't spark your fancy, is there someone else for you here?"

"Well, well, well. It seems like you're the one interested in me, not the other way around," I smirked. His face grew red.

"Your face is as red as a beet in winter," I laughed, I couldn't help myself. Johnny stopped in his tracks and folded his arms across his broad chest. I had a feeling he wasn't usually easily rattled.

"You really are irritating," he huffed.

"Don't I know it," I brought my hands to my face, cupping my chin, and gave him my cutest smile. He scowled and continued walking toward the cabin.

"So if you don't have a girl, why do you wear that ring around your neck?" I asked.

I'd noticed the chain around his neck a few times since I first met him. It was made of an unusual metal I'd never seen before.

"Oh, this?" He asked, pulling the ring forward. "This is nothing, just a reminder from home." He tucked the ring back under his tunic. A dark look passed across his brow before he covered it with a smug smile.

We made our way through the forest until the cabin was in sight. A light was still on – someone was awake, and I hoped to the gods it wasn't Pa.

"This is far enough. I suppose I should thank you for walking me but that would be rather atypical of us, so I'll just shake your hand," I held out my hand to Johnny.

A bang came from the cabin, and I flinched. Johnny furrowed his brow, but I tried not to show my fear as I continued to hold out my hand.

"And I am supposed to accept this offering?" He stared down at my outstretched palm. Grabbing it with two hands, he turned it over back and forth, inspecting. "I suppose it is a good hand," he shrugged playing with me, "but I won't accept."

I tried to ignore the way my stomach tumbled at his touch. He dropped my hand, and I fought the need to step closer.

"Fine then, what would you like?" I tilted my head, folding my arms across my chest and raising my eyebrows in question.

"I believe I asked for your name," he stated.

"You know my name," I challenged.

"I want it from your lips," he looked at my lips as he said it. They felt suddenly dry, and I resisted the urge to wet them with my tongue.

"I will give you my name in exchange for a handshake."

I don't know why I said it, but I had the irrational desire to touch his hand one last time. Then I would be done with these games.

"Very well," he agreed, his lips pulling up on either side in amusement.

I held out my hand and ever so slowly he stepped toward me, extending his own palm, his large hand encapsulating mine. The contact sent a jolt of fire up my spine.

"I'm Meeka," I slowly brought my gaze from our hands to his crystal green eyes. I thought his touch was electrifying, but the look he gave me now made my heart pound and the world slow.

"Have you ever been kissed, Meeka?" Johnny stepped closer.

My heart stopped in my chest as my body tingled with nerves.

"There was this one time, but it hardly counts," I stammered, "we skipped out on the school play. He didn't really know what he was doing."

"Let me rephrase. Have you ever been kissed properly?" His eyes twinkled.

"I-" but I couldn't finish.

Another crash came from the cabin. I broke the contact between our hands and our eyes.

"Got to go. See you around, Johnny Pullver," I rushed.

"Meeka-" he started but I didn't wait for his words. I didn't look back at all as I raced toward the cabin. My hand was still warm where he held mine, a smile still tugging at my lips.

# CHAPTER 11

Pa was awake.

Worse, Ceceil was dead asleep.

I crept across the floorboards trying to sneak past where Pa was rummaging through the cupboards in the kitchen. He was mumbling to himself, clearly looking for more to drink but coming up empty handed. He'd already drank the house dry.

I tried to tip-toe, but the room was small and quiet and the floorboards creaked. I winced as I stepped on a particularly loud plank, but Pa didn't flinch, too distracted on his scavenger hunt. I sighed in relief, only steps away from my door.

I turned the knob but it was locked. Timtim you bloody fool. That would complicate things.

I didn't have time to come up with a new plan, however, as I was suddenly jerked backward, Pa grabbing my shoulder and pulling me around to face him.

"It's you, you red devil," he spat at me, pushing me to the ground.

"It's me, Pa, Meeka," I yelled up at him, hoping the commotion would wake Ceceil. It didn't.

"You brought this hell upon our house," he kicked me in the ribs, "be gone, devil!"

I curled up in a ball absorbing his blows and trying to remind myself that he didn't recognize me. He didn't want to hurt me. He thought I was someone else. But my pity for the old man dried up with each blow. Anger stirred inside.

"Pa, stop!" I yelled again, trying to rise. My hair spilled out from under my scarf, loosening from the blows.

"I knew it was you, red devil," he stared at me wide eyed, "it's all your fault."

"What's my fault, Pa?" With effort, I stood facing him. He stopped beating me and looked at me with fear. He backed away slowly.

"You're the reason we're here, it was all 'cause of you, I tell you!" Pa stumbled, falling to the floor as he retreated from me. I looked around in confusion. Pa had beat me and called me a red devil before, but this was the first time he looked at me with true fear in his eyes.

"I don't know what you mean, Pa. It's me, Meeka. Your daughter." I pleaded with him.

"You're no daughter of mine," Pa continued to retreat toward the door, "be gone, red devil!" He shouted and grabbed a machete off the wall.

He meant to kill me.

"Pa, stop," I put my hands up in protest, trying desperately to show him I meant no harm.

He held the machete in both hands swinging it through the air, though I was still several feet out of his reach. He stumbled on his feet, still thick with drink.

"Pa, it's me, Meeka," I tried again. He came at me, swinging the machete wildly. I ducked and he knocked into the table, sending chairs flying and falling to the ground. I had a moment to think but I had no idea what to do. I could run away, but where would I go?

Instead, I did nothing. I panicked, a fox in the path of a hunter. Pa got back to his feet, machete still in his hand. His head was bleeding where he hit it on the side of the table.

"Pa, this isn't right. You are sick," I clenched my jaw, angry now. Even if I made it through the night, what would I do? I couldn't stay here with Pa mighty crazed as he was. Eventually he would kill me.

I jumped over the worn sofa, trying to make my way to the door, but Pa was somehow quicker on his feet. He grabbed my ankle as I leapt, flinging me to the ground. I winced as my elbow hit hard but rolled over to find Pa looking down at me, machete pointing at my face.

"It's about time I got rid of you, red devil," Pa looked triumphant, "you've taken everything from me."

He raised the machete, preparing to cut off my head.

I rolled to the side as he brought it down. I lay there in shock as Pa yanked the machete out of the floorboards, where he just nearly missed my neck. He truly meant to kill me. He had beaten me before, called me names, but I never thought it would go this far.

I stood slowly, the pain in my ribs searing, my elbow throbbing. I took a deep breath and spun toward him, mustering all the courage I could find. I would not let my own Pa be my downfall.

He swung back around to face me with the blade raised. Our eyes met and this time I thought I saw a spark of recognition before his face again hardened. He let out a warrior's cry.

The door swung open at the same time Pa lunged for me.

# CHAPTER 12

"Stop."

A man stood in the doorway. I didn't know him. No, that wasn't quite right – he was the same man I saw in the woods with Johnny Pullver.

Pa backed away mid strike, but not quick enough. The blade came down as Pa retreated, opening a small flesh wound across my eyebrow. The blood dripped down my face. I licked it as it passed the side of my mouth. It tasted like copper.

"You-" Pa shouted looking to the man, then back at me, "and you...I knew you must be in league; how did you find me? It was the red devil, wasn't it? She's working for you?" Dad looked accusingly at me then back at the man.

"Shut up, Sir Tomkin," The man replied with ice in his veins. Sir Tomkin? That was the my Pa's name. This man knew my Pa.

"Who are you?" I demanded.

Before he could reply two more men entered the cabin.

"What's going on?" I looked around between the men, confused. Johnny Pullver stood facing me, his eyes hardened into stone, none of the glimmering amusement that had been there earlier tonight.

"You," Johnny pointed in my direction, "are coming with us."

"I knew it!" Pa shouted, "You've been working with them all along."

I ignored Pa's paranoid outburst.

"Johnny?" I asked, my voice barely a squeak.

"You shall address him as 'Your Royal Highness'," the man behind Johnny spoke, reprimanding.

"What's going on?" Ceceil finally emerged from his room. His timing couldn't have been more horrible. Where were you ten minutes ago, Ceceil, I wanted to demand.

"The red devil's been working against me," Pa pointed at me, "she led them right to us."

"What in the bloody gods are you talking about, Pa?" Ceceil asked looking around alarmed, "Johnny, what's going on?"

The man behind Johnny stepped forward, presumably to rebuke Ceceil as well, but Johnny stuck out his hand, quieting the man.

"My name is Prince Ajax Radjmir Vissarion, heir prince to the throne of Skirsgard, and we will be taking your sister with us." Johnny motioned for the two men to grab hold of me.

I stammered to my feet and kicked one of the men in the shin, but the other grabbed my arms behind my back. I squirmed but couldn't release his grip. Pa didn't come to help and Ceceil stood frozen looking around like it was all a dream.

"I knew your name wasn't Johnny Pullver," I snarled at Johnny – no, not Johnny, Prince Ajax. He raised his eyebrows and smirked, as if I was the least threatening thing he'd ever seen.

"Let's go," he motioned for his men to take me.

"Wait, you can't have her," Ceceil finally stepped forward, grabbing the prince by the arm. The prince looked down where Ceceil's hand squeezed him, then back up to his face.

"She belongs to Skirsgard." Johnny stared Ceceil down with a look that would make most people go running.

"She belongs to us," Ceceil, to his credit, stood his ground.

"Sir Tomkin, permission to take the girl?" The prince asked, still glaring Ceceil in the eyes.

"Yes, yes," Pa said eagerly, "you can have her for a price."

Ceceil dropped his hand from the prince's arm.

A look of disgust passed the prince's face before he collected himself and pulled out a centiar purse. Tossing it on the ground, he motioned for his men to drag me along.

"Take it all," he muttered.

I stood speechless, the fight drained from my body. All I was good for was a few centiar that pa would spend on drink. Pa sold me out to the enemy, and I knew Ceceil wouldn't go against Pa's word.

I looked at Ceceil, pleading, tears threatening to run down my face and mix with the blood from my cut eyebrow. Ceceil looked devasted but shook his head. He would do nothing.

"Ceceil, you coward," I whispered under my breath. And though he may not have heard me, he understood my meaning.

I'm sorry. He mouthed. But it was not enough.

Years of death had hardened Ceceil and made him immune to heartache. He had lost so many family members. In a sense he was probably relieved I was leaving. I would no longer be his burden.

Looking between Pa and Ceceil, I knew I would get no help. I was all alone.

Pa had gone mad, and Ceceil had gone cold.

# PART TWO:

# THE COLD

# CHAPTER 13

I swore under my breath and kicked at the snow. We had been walking for some time now, trekking through the dark forest, heading south. The moon shone overhead like a candle too far out of reach to truly light the way.

I continued to glare at the prince and my other handlers, steering me like sheep dogs as if I were a measly sheep. The prince refused to make eye contact. He didn't have any remorse for the way he treated me. It had all been one big lie. It didn't really matter, though. He kidnapped me. He bought me. He was a traitor.

"Where are you taking me anyway?" I asked for the millionth time. Once again, I got no answer. I kicked the shin of the nearest man. He bent over grabbing his leg, swearing in pain.

"You little-" he cursed at me. I pushed him back down, attempting to make a run for it.

The prince caught up in a matter of steps, grabbing me by the waist and pulling me back in line.

"If you don't quit trying to run, I'm going to have to carry you the whole way," the prince whispered in my ear from behind. I turned and glared at him, willing every ounce of hate to show on my face. He laughed. I wished I had my machete to slice off his smirk.

"You're a mighty rotten person, Johnny Pullver, prince of lies," I spat on the floor at his feet. The other men tensed, waiting to see what this so-called prince would do. He slowly smiled.

"Careful, Meeka. Where we are going, some have been killed for talking to their prince with disrespect." He gave me that mischievous grin again, but this time his eyes were laced with danger.

"You aren't my prince. And you never will be." I hardened my eyes and my jaw. I met his stare, glaring, but he didn't back down. Neither did I. For one brief second, I thought I saw his eyes soften, but it was so quick I couldn't tell if I had imagined it.

"We'll see," the prince spoke low then turned, ignoring my presence as he continued forward in the dark.

I stumbled in the snow but didn't get up. Instead, I turned toward the night sky, watching the stars shine down in beautiful patterns, immune to the problems of my small world.

I assumed one of the men would force me up and make us continue but instead, they all seemed to pause, waiting. The prince looked around and sighed.

"I suppose we'll break here until daylight. Besides I don't think anyone is coming after her."

Did he really think so little of me? But if Pa and Ceceil had given me up, who would come for me? Yesimia? She wouldn't even know I was gone. No, the prince was right, I realized with a twinge of pain. I was truly alone.

"Are you sure, your royal highness?" I asked mockingly, "I thought you'd want to continue to torture us as long as you could."

The prince glared my way again but only shook his head. I sat up suddenly, grabbing a handful of snow and ice and threw it as hard as I could in his direction. It hit him right in the upper thigh. I tried not to smile in triumph when I saw the look of anger on his face.

"That was awfully close to hurting," the prince clenched his jaw.

"His royal highness is so weak to be hurt by a lump of snow?" I leered in his direction. The other men looked around unsure what to do.

"You know, you are going to get yourself into trouble," the prince warned, but there was a sparkle that touched his eyes.

"You better pray to the gods you aren't on the other end of my trouble," I threatened.

"My lady, you may not speak-" one of my guards began before I cut him off.

"Yes, yes, I know. I may not speak of his royal arrogance in such a demeaning manner," I waved my hand at him in dismissal, "and I am not a lady."

"Leacher, leave her alone," the prince told his man. The guard stood at attention and looked down at his feet embarrassed by the reprimand. My eyes narrowed.

"You really think you are so high and mighty, don't you?" I scowled at the prince.

It took two steps for the prince to reach me. He pulled me up by the arm until we were standing face to face, more like face to chest the way he towered over me.

"Now listen up, Meeka," he purred my name again, his face leaning down only inches away from mine, "this can be easy, or this can be hard-"

"I'm not easy," I taunted him. He threw me back down on the snow.

"I can't deal with you." The prince shook his head, turning away from me and walking several paces away. "Guards make camp here. I will set up my own tent further along. Goodnight."

The prince left me alone with the three other men who so far had been silent. I didn't watch him leave, nor did I see him making his camp, as the men around me suddenly sprang to action.

They pulled out tarps from their packs, assembling them into makeshift tents. One of the guards even somehow managed to start a fire among the ice.

"Are you making something to eat?" I asked the guard. Leacher, the prince had called him.

"Yes, my lady. Would you like some?" He asked, opening a tin can with his knife, and placing it atop the fire.

"I'd love some," I replied genuinely starving.

We waited in silence until whatever sludge was in the can began to boil. When it was ready, Leacher retrieved a wooden spoon from his pack and handed me the can. It was so hot, it burned my fingers though my gloves, but the heat was inviting, and I didn't mind the burn.

"This is surprisingly good for how disgusting it looks," I told Leacher, digging in even though I seared the tip of my tongue.

"You are just hungry, my lady," Leacher broke out into an honest smile, "it really is disgusting."

I choked on the boiling sludge, laughing, still not sure at all what was in it, but it was salty, and it was filling.

"I like you, Leacher," I told him, smiling back.

"And I, you, my lady," he reached a hand across the fire, "my name is Finyalreg Leacher, royal guard to prince Ajax."

I took his hand and shook it.

"Meeka," I offered my name.

"Will you two stop playing. Leacher, she is supposed to be your captive not your friend," the other guard scolded Leacher, but didn't look upset, instead he rolled his eyes and smiled, sitting next to me, and holding out his hand.

"Name's Demetri," he shook my hand and grabbed the can and spoon from me, taking a large bite and passing it over to Leacher. I glared at him, amused.

"Meeka," I repeated my name to him.

"I'm the one you've kicked in the shin twice now," he raised his eyebrows looking down at me.

"Well, maybe if you didn't abduct me, I wouldn't have had to," I rebutted.

"Only following orders, my lady," he shrugged unconcerned.

"And who's the one over there?" I whispered leaning in conspiratorially, "the one who knows my Pa?"

"He's a mean fellow, don't mess with that one," Demetri whispered back. I couldn't tell if he was joking.

The mean-looking one stood apart from our group. He sat outside his makeshift tent, smoking a pipe and glaring at me. I wasn't sure if Demetri was telling the truth, but he did look nasty. He narrowed his eyes but continued to glare, taking a long drag of his pipe.

I didn't like the way he stared at me deep in concentration, as though he knew a secret that I didn't. I looked away and shuddered.

"But who is he?" I asked again, this time hoping for a less vague answer.

"He's the late King's brother. Prince Ajax' uncle. Now that the King is dead, it's up to him to ensure a smooth changeover of power," Leacher answered.

"So, the prince will be king. Then what is he doing here?" I asked confused.

Leacher and Demetri looked at each other, but neither answered my question.

"Ugh. You're all infuriating," I got up and went to one of the makeshift tents. "I'm going to bed. Goodnight."

I lay down under the small tarp propped up with branches, barely large enough to fit my whole body. It was freezing in the dark, but whatever material the tarp was made of somehow kept the cold at bay.

I lay there thinking, trying to fit the puzzle pieces together. If the prince was going to become king, then what could he possibly want with me?

I suddenly sat upright and bumped my head on the branch holding the tarp.

I rubbed my head as I realized exactly where we were headed. In the confusion of the night, I hadn't pieced together the obvious.

We were going to the Old Country. My homeland. I was going home.

# CHAPTER 14

Skirsgard. The land of my birth. I pinched myself for never asking more questions about my homeland. It would really come in handy now. I remembered nothing; I hadn't even remembered its name. I was going back to the Old Country as good as blind.

I lay under the tarp, sleep alluding my tired body. I planned to wait for Leacher and Demetri to fall asleep before trying to escape, but now second guessed my decision.

There was no point in going back to Innesbrown. Pa didn't want me. I was a burden to Ceceil. Yesimia was married. And Timtim – I felt a slice of guilt in my gut for leaving Timtim behind. He would be raised by Pa and Ceceil. What would become of him? I could only hope Yesimia would be there for him, a mother figure like she had been for me in the time since Ma's death. The gods knew I couldn't fill that role. No, I would not go back to Innesbrown.

I would go to Skirsgard.

If these men hadn't killed me yet, I was hopeful they needed me alive. I had never really felt at home in Innesbrown. Maybe there would be answers in Skirsgard that I didn't even know I had been looking for. I lay down and finally closed my eyes, but still, sleep would not come.

After another hour of tossing and turning, the sun began to peak over the mountains. No more point in trying to sleep. I got up quietly, hoping to find a moment of peace to take care of my business and maybe find a small stream to wash my face, still caked with blood from last night's fight.

I snuck around the other tents, where I heard Demetri snoring loudly. Making my way further into the woods, I steered clear of where the prince had set up his own tent. My tracks would be easy to follow in the snow, but I would only be gone a short time.

I never tied my hair back after the fight with Pa. It flowed around my face now, the rich color a sparkling contrast against the surrounding white. I put my thick fur hat on but didn't tuck my hair underneath. If we were going to Skirsgard, I hoped I would no longer need to hide. My Ma had said my hair was that of a foreigner. None of these men had fiery hair like mine, but I figured Ma meant it wasn't so uncommon back in the Old Country. The thought made me smile. I knew I was supposed to be a prisoner, but maybe this wouldn't turn out so bad after all.

"Ahem," came a voice from behind. I startled. I was bent down at a small, quick-moving stream.

"Prince," I replied, putting as much disgust in my voice as I could muster.

"And what do you think you are doing?" He asked, looking bored.

"Can you not see what I'm doing?" I crouched, washing my face. "Are you not only fragile, but stupid?"

"Very well, if it is going to be this way," the prince mumbled as he turned around and began walking back toward camp, "but don't even think about running away, you won't get far; that's a promise."

"I wasn't planning on it. I want to go with you. And not because you are forcing me, but because I made up my mind," I countered.

The prince halted in his tracks and turned quickly to face me. He looked me up and down, distrust wrought on his furrowed brow.

"Why?" He asked, narrowing his eyes.

"It's my homeland, isn't it?" I scoffed.

"And what do you remember about it? Of your time there?" He tilted his head, taking me in.

"Nothing," I replied truthfully.

He hesitated then nodded.

"Meeka," he began. His eyes softened and he took a step toward me, "about everything that's happened, I want you to know-"

"There you are, my prince," the prince's uncle, whose name I still did not know, appeared suddenly from behind an oak tree, "I was looking for you. We should get on the road."

The prince kept his gaze on me, mouth open as if weighing whether he should finish his thought. Instead, he clenched his jaw and nodded. He slowly turned toward his uncle and followed him back to camp.

"We will be waiting for you. Don't take too long." He spoke to me with his back turned but I could see the way his shoulders tensed. I smacked the water with my hand, hating him. He was a liar, and I hated lies.

Despite my anger, I made it quickly back to camp where the men were standing in a circle sharing another can of the questionable sludge. The tents had been packed in my absence, and evidence of our camp erased.

I grabbed the can and spoon from Leacher, taking a large bite. The prince sauntered over to my side, eyebrows raised looking impressed.

"Wouldn't have taken you for being fond of tallow worms," his green eyes looked amused.

"Tallow worms?" I choked out, swallowing the thick mucousy substance with difficulty. The prince chuckled.

"Didn't know what you were eating did you?" He bit his lip, trying not to smile.

"I knew exactly what it was," I said stubbornly taking another bite but failing to keep the disgust completely from my face as I swallowed, "you learn not to be picky when you don't know when you'll get your next meal."

I said it defensively but the prince's face hardened.

"My prince, it's true. Last night she even said she liked it," Leacher cut in.

"Leacher, stay out of it," the prince chided him.

"Hey, leave him alone," I shot back, smiling at Leacher then scowling at the prince. The prince looked between Leacher and I, eyes narrowing.

"Don't fall for her charms, Leacher." He looked annoyed as he grabbed the can and spoon. He took out a small cloth from his pocket and wiped the spoon that had been in my mouth only seconds before. Then he took a large bite – rather too large to prove a point – and ate it hungrily, all the while staring me down.

I grated my teeth in anger. He was clearly trying to provoke me. He raised his eyebrows, daring me to say something, so instead I stayed quiet, clenching my fists. Oh, I wanted to smack him.

"Is there something you want to say, Nameless?" The prince asked.

I shook my head in fury, not wanting to give him what he wanted – a peak at my temper. He laughed and then winked at me. That was the final straw. I rushed him, knocking him to the ground before he or anyone else could stop me, the can of worms flying and landing in the snow.

Leacher and Demetri immediately came to the prince's defense, grabbing my arms and pulling me off him.

"My lady, that is the prince," Leacher said in horror. But the prince wasn't upset or hurt. No, he was laughing.

"Leacher, did I not tell you to stay out of it?" The prince said with amusement in his voice.

"You're lucky you have your lackeys, you wouldn't last in a fair fight," I panted out as Leacher and Demetri let go reluctantly.

The prince stood, shaking off snow, and stalked over to me, so close I could feel the rise and fall of his chest. He towered over me. He was stronger in every way possible. I lifted my chin in defiance.

"Are you sure about that?" His voice sounded like gravel. I tried to ignore the way it made my toes curl.

"I guess we'll never know since you have other people do your dirty work for you," I wrinkled my nose.

The prince continued to glare, his eyes catching on my red hair, where it flowed from under my hat. But instead of answering, he bent down, wrapped his arms around my legs, and flung me over his shoulder.

"Alright, men, let's move out." He gestured for his men to lead the way, ignoring my fists beating his back.

"Put me down!" I yelped.

"I warned you I would carry you the whole way if you continued being a pill," he smirked.

"Johnny Pullver – you little-" I beat at his back.

"That's not my name, Meeka," he replied, and I could hear the smile in his voice. It irritated me beyond measure.

"That's right, it's the Prince of Lies!" I tried to lift myself up, but I was too laden down with layers and fur. Instead, I smacked him on the back of the head.

"Ow," he rubbed his head but laughed that low, soft, chuckle I found too enticing.

"Are you seriously going to carry me the whole time?" I asked giving up the fight and lying limp, becoming as heavy as I could. Maybe that would make him put me down if the hitting did not. But he seemed to barely notice, as the strong muscular arms that held me easily handled my weight.

"Do you know what it means to be the prince of Skirsgard?" He asked as we continued along, following his men.

"That you're a mighty prick?" I responded annoyed, yet not all together hating the feel of his arms around me. No, I would not admit that. I was resigned to hate this man.

"It means that from a young age, I have spent my days in the training ring. And when I have not been in the training ring, I have been out fighting."

"You've fought in battle?" I asked intrigued.

"Yes." He sounded less amused as he trudged through the snow.

"What's it like?" I asked, curious.

"Dirty. Smelly. Cold. It's a belly full of hunger. It is humanity striped to its base and exposed like an open wound," he sighed lost in some memory I couldn't understand.

"It sounds exciting," I mused.

"Exciting? No," he spoke in a whisper, "war is not exciting."

"Is there a war in your country now?" I asked. He was quiet for some time. Finally, he stopped walking and set me down. He faced me, looking serious now.

"That," he spoke with an emotion I didn't understand, "remains to be seen."

# CHAPTER 15

We trudged through the cold for most of the day. The prince was deep in thought, and I was too weary to bother him. With only the tallow worms to sustain us, we were all running out of energy.

"How much longer?" I asked Demetri who had fallen in step beside me.

"There's an inn a little way ahead. Maybe an hours' time," he shook his head, spraying snow everywhere from his long brown curls. I wiped snow off my face where it landed.

He was tall and handsome – not quite so tall or handsome as the prince though, my invasive thoughts whispered. His hair fell in ringlets to his shoulders, and his face was full of bright hope and energy. He had big, round, blue eyes, and a sharp nose, with a small pattering of freckles across his cheeks. He was easy to like and to chat with. We had made quick friends throughout the day, much to the annoyance of the prince.

Leacher was also warming quite nicely. He was more reserved than Demetri, and definitely scared of the prince, but he had an innocence to him only found in someone young and loyal. He couldn't be much older than eighteen, if that. He had mousy hair, and a squinty face, but his brown eyes were kind, and his devotion to the prince was unwavering.

The prince's uncle, however, was a mystery. There was something slimy about him, despite his regal look. He rarely spoke, unless to give directions, but I felt his glances throughout the day. He didn't seem to like me, and I felt much the same way in return.

"Will we stay at the inn?" I asked Demetri.

"Up to the prince," he shrugged.

I sighed. A bed sure did sound nice. My hands and feet were starting to go numb, but I was used to spending days and nights in the cold. I glanced around at the others. I could tell they were not as used to the freezing temperatures by the way they fidgeted and pulled at their hats and gloves.

"Hey, Prince," I shouted up to where the prince was walking at the head of the group. He looked back, eyebrows raised in question. "Your men are going to freeze their weak little southern heinies if you make them trudge through the snow much longer."

The prince stared at me as if I'd sprouted horns.

"I beg your pardon?" He choked, the corners of his lips curving upward.

"Your...men," I spoke slowly as if he were dumb, "they...are...going...to...freeze."

"Yes, their 'heinies' was the word I believe you used." He pressed his lips together, suppressing a laugh.

"Oh, you know what I mean," I huffed.

"I know what you mean, just never heard it put quite so cute." This time the prince broke out in a grin. There was laughter in those shiny green eyes. I scowled.

"I am not 'cute'." I made my way to where he was standing. The men parted, not wanting to interfere. Although, Leacher looked ready to tackle me if needed.

"You look put out. Do you need to be carried?" The prince's eyes shone with devilry.

I pushed him, but this time he didn't budge. Gods, he was solid. He chuckled as I continued to pound against his chest. One would have thought I was tickling him. Finally, he grabbed both my hands, stilling me, holding them against his chest.

"If I didn't know any better, I'd say you are looking for excuses to get near me," he grinned wickedly and pulled me close, "is that so, Nameless?"

"Let go of me!" I wrenched my hands away from him, although he gave no resistance.

"We will stay at the inn tonight, men," he spoke loudly to the group but didn't tear his gaze away from mine, "it's just a little further on."

I shook the snow off and huffed past him, nudging his side. He grabbed my wrist and spun me around.

"Meeka," he looked sincere, "you don't need to fight so hard. I'm not going to hurt you, I promise."

"Too late, prince. You already have." I stared deep into his eyes letting him see the hurt and betrayal that lay beneath the surface. He studied me then slowly dropped my arm.

"I see," he replied quietly, then turned and continued through the woods.

With those words I felt my heart harden.

"You know, he isn't just any man, my lady," Leacher fell in step next to me, encouraging me to continue forward, "he is the prince of Skirsgard."

"I don't care. I know nothing about Skirsgard," I said flatly. I was tired and sick of all the lies and secrets.

"You've never been there?" Leacher asked then looked at my hair, stammering, "well of course you have, I mean, it's just, you haven't been there since you were a child. Do you remember anything?"

"I came to Innesbrown when I was a child, I don't remember anything although maybe I should, I wasn't that young after all." I hadn't ever really thought about it before, but I had no memories before coming to the North at all. It was as though my life was written in a book, but if I went back through the pages long enough, they were suddenly blank.

"Ah, that's the magic that will do that," Leacher nodded in understanding.

"What do you mean 'the magic'?" I looked up sharply.

"Ah – I – I – I'm not sure how much I can say," Leacher glanced to his side, where Demetri was approaching.

"What he means is he's too much of a butt-kisser to tell you anything," Demetri interrupted, "anyway, there is no magic in the North, that's what he's talking about."

"What does that have to do with my memory?" I asked perplexed.

"Your memory is tied into your magic, when you came North – no magic, no memory," he swiped his hands together twice as if that explained everything.

"But I don't have any magic," I protested. Both Leacher and Demetri looked up at my hair. Demetri started to laugh, and even Leacher looked like he was suppressing a grin.

"Ok, my lady," Demetri nodded and looked at me like I had gone mad, "whatever you say."

At that, I had no words.

# CHAPTER 16

We walked the rest of the way in silence. I was lost in my thoughts. The way Leacher and Demetri spoke was unsettling.

Shortly before we arrived at the inn, the prince's uncle told me to hide my hair once again. I suppose it was still offensive in these parts.

We rounded a bend and came upon a snow-covered road. After following it for some time, it broke into a small clearing where a stone cottage welcomed us. Moss and snow covered its entirety, smoke wafting from the chimney into the cold air. It was late afternoon now and the sight of the inn gave hope to my weary bones.

"Thank the gods," I mumbled as Demetri held the door open. Warmth spilled out from within, and I relished the feeling.

We entered a small tavern. A bar lay across one end and a few wooden tables with straw benches were scattered throughout. A large hearth with a roaring fire heated the room. It wasn't a big space, but it seemed clean enough, and at this point anything out of the cold was welcome. I followed the men, taking over two tables in the corner.

"Drink, food, or shelter?" The barmaid came round our tables asking.

"All three," the prince replied, stripping himself of his furs.

"The barmaid looked us over with squinting eyes, judging our ability pay. Her gaze roamed over the prince's uncle, dressed in finery as he was, and she nodded, "how many rooms?"

"How many do you have?" The prince asked looking around the establishment. There was a small set of stairs behind the bar, presumably leading to the sleeping quarters.

"We've got two vacancies," she put her hand on her hip. She was a big woman, plump in all the wrong places.

"We will take two then," the prince brought out a centiar purse, "a meal tonight, and one in the morning, and ales all around." He counted out several centiar until the barmaid nodded. He placed them in her outstretched palm.

"For your discretion," he nodded, adding a few extra.

"Very well," she pocketed the coin and turned toward the bar.

When the ale arrived, I moved from the table I was sitting at with the prince and his uncle over to the table where Demetri and Leacher sat chatting.

"You know any good drinking games?" I asked Demetri and Leacher as I sat down.

"You bet we do." Demetri smiled, taking a deep sip of his ale. I followed suit. It tasted sour but filled my body with warmth.

"How about I teach you one and you teach me one?" I slammed my beer down on the table, grinning.

"Ha, deal." Demetri took his ale and clinked glasses with mine. Leacher followed, a shy smile across his face.

"Does anyone have a centiar?" I asked. They both shook their heads. I frowned.

"Hey, prince of lies, can I have a centiar?" I turned around to the prince's table sticking my hand out and wiggling my fingers.

The prince looked me up and down but reached into his pocket and held out a single centiar. I went to grab it, but he pulled his hand away.

"You sure you can keep up with them? You are a wisp compared to my men," the prince's eyebrows rose high across his brow.

"You don't know what I can and can't do, prince," I sneered.

"Easy on the 'prince' around here," he looked around to make sure no one was listening, but there were only a few others in the room, and no one appeared to be paying us much attention.

"Oh, that's right, Johnny Pullver. I forgot in the North you are a liar." I grabbed the centiar out of his hand and turned back to my table. I took a long swig of my ale.

I explained the game to my guards. One person would spin the centiar, while the other two had the amount of time the centiar spun to match gestures on their forehead with their hands. Flat hand for the valleys, fist for the mountains, pointing finger for the skies, wiggling fingers for the plains, four fingers for the four seasons, or a hand over your eyes for the darkness. The number of times the two made the same gestures in the amount of time the centiar spun, was the seconds they had to drink.

The first couple of rounds, the men were still comically confused by the hand gestures, but after the third round everyone seemed to understand, and we were laughing and drinking and thoroughly enjoying ourselves.

"Drink four seconds!" I shouted and pointed at Demetri and Leacher after the centiar I spun dropped. They had matched four gestures in the time it spun. They grabbed their ales, laughing, and chugged as I counted.

"More ale," I shouted across the room to the barmaid. The prince cleared his throat and I turned to look at him. He gave me a glare that seemed to say 'oh really' but I ignored him and turned back toward the bar. The barmaid nodded and soon brought us another round.

"Ok, your turn," I told the men.

"Fine. I'm in." The prince dragged a chair and sat next to me at the table, "I know a good game to play." He gave me that wicked smile.

"Very well," I rolled my eyes. The prince winked. My stomach fluttered but I shook it off. Maybe I was drinking too much.

"The game is a truth and a lie. It's simple, you tell one truth and one lie, if we correctly guess which is which, you drink. If we guess wrong, we drink," the prince explained.

"You ought to be mighty good at this game then. At least the lying part," I narrowed my eyes at him. He kept my gaze, that mischievous look beneath his green eyes melded with irritation.

"Leacher, you start," he turned toward his guard.

"OK, hm," Leacher cleared his throat, "I have a mole on my shoulder. And I love butterflies."

Demetri broke out laughing, "those are the two you picked?"

"Well, I didn't have a lot of time to think," Leacher turned red.

"I think the mole is a lie and you do love butterflies," I said unable to keep the chuckle from my voice.

"Wrong! Drink!" Leacher pointed at me looking victorious.

"You hate butterflies? Who hates butterflies?" I asked incredulous.

"Apparently, the guy with the mole," the prince responded, also unable to contain his mirth.

"Oh, fine," I said taking a long sip, "you go, Demetri,"

"Let's see. I have four brothers. I have a horse named Viktor," he sat back in his chair folding his arms.

"You have four brothers but no Viktor," I narrowed my eyes.

"Drink! I only have one brother," Demetri laughed.

"This seems unfair," I said taking a sip and looking around at the prince and his men, "you already know all this about each other, don't you?" They all started laughing.

"I'm sorry, my lady, you are an easy target," Leacher chuckled but looked slightly apologetic.

"A bunch of cheaters you are. Anyway, now it's my turn and you all know nothing about me," I huffed but tried to think of something that would stump them. "Once, when I was nine years old, I locked myself out of the house on accident. Instead of banging on the door, I went into the woods and made a camp. I stayed there for three days, and no one ever came looking for me. That's the first, here's the second. When I was seventeen, I had to make up a test at school. There was another kid, a boy named Tom, who had to make it up at the same time. He cheated off my paper, but when it was discovered, they thought I was the one who cheated, and they beat me."

The men all sat up, glaring at me.

"Those are awfully detailed," Leacher said rubbing his head. The prince crossed his arms and tilted his head assessing me. Demetri looked up at the ceiling in thought.

"I think the camping is a lie and the cheating is the truth," the prince said but didn't look happy about it.

"Nope, drink! All of you this time – you're in this together, you cheaters," I grinned at them.

"So, you weren't beat when this boy cheated?" The prince asked while lifting his ale to his lips. I tried not to stare at those full lips.

"No, I was beat. Mighty bad in fact. But Tom didn't cheat off me, I cheated off him," I broke out in a grin. Demetri slapped his knee and threw back his head laughing.

"You are a sly fox," Dimitri grabbed his ale and threw it back. Leacher chuckled and shook his head, taking a long drink as well. The prince only narrowed his eyes, his gaze boring into mine, but the corner of his mouth turned up.

"Looks like we aren't the only cheaters here. My turn," the prince said.

"Sorry, prince, but game's over. Time for me to rest. Besides, I've had enough lies from you," I gave him a false sweet smile and downed the remainder of ale.

"She's right, my prince," his uncle turned toward us. I almost forgot he was there. "Go settle in the rooms, I'll have the food sent up. We leave early, it is time to rest." He stood and we followed suit.

It was the first time I'd stood since starting the drinking games, and I had to admit I was a bit wobbly on my feet. Drinking all that ale on an empty stomach didn't help, and the rush to my head was suddenly intoxicating.

"Ok, you. You're coming with me. Men, see you at first light," the prince grabbed my elbow, steadying me and steered me toward the stairs.

"Take me to my rooms, prince," I commanded in a haughty way trying to imitate him.

The barmaid eyed us at my use of 'prince' as we passed her, but the prince just shook his head.

"Don't mind her, she's drunk," he told the barmaid.

"Am not!" I swatted his hand on my elbow.

"Bring our food to our room," he fished another centiar out of his pocket and threw it to the barmaid. She caught it and nodded.

"What do you mean 'our room'?" I turned to look at the prince but lost balance and fell right into his chest. He grabbed me with his arms and held me at length.

"You will be staying with me in my room. The other men will have the second room," he explained as though it were no big deal.

"I'm not staying with you alone," I said horrified.

"What? Are you afraid of me?" He leaned in close and whispered in my ear, "I'll only bite if you ask me to."

I told myself it was the ale that was making my head spin and my cheeks hot.

"I'm not afraid," I stood tall and raised my chin.

"Prove it," he gleamed down, those green eyes sparkling, "or will I have to carry you to bed?"

"No, that won't be necessary," my heart beat too fast but I turned toward the stairs attempting to climb on my own. The prince had to nudge me along a few times, but we made it to the top without incident. I clenched my fists, my heart continuing to beat nervously, as the prince led me down the hall to our room.

"Here it is." He stopped at a small door with number two branded in the wood.

He turned the knob and opened the door to a very tiny room with one very tiny window and one very singular bed.

"There is only one bed," my jaw dropped. I looked up at the prince, he grinned at me with that wicked smile.

# CHAPTER 17

"Even if I wanted to, I couldn't share that bed with you," I said adamantly.

"Are you saying you would want to?" The prince chuckled.

"Absolutely not!" I stammered, "I just mean it's mighty small."

I rubbed my forehead and looked around. The room was so tiny, if this was how all the quarters were, I could not possibly imagine how three men were going to fit in the other room. It suddenly made me laugh.

"Do you think Leacher and Demetri will share the bed with your uncle on the floor?" I couldn't help but giggle at the thought. The prince, it seemed, couldn't help himself either. That laugh – it made my heart skip a beat.

"Stop laughing," I clenched my jaw and sat on the bed.

"Oh, that's right, it could 'turn a heart of stone to fire' I believe you said?" He raised his eyebrows at me and leaned against the now closed door, arms crossed.

"Of course, you remember that," I mumbled feeling slightly embarrassed.

"I remember everything, Meeka," he said softly.

I looked up at him. The expression on his face was earnest, like it had been when he was Johnny and not the prince. He sauntered slowly to where I was sitting on the bed and sat down next to me. He turned to face me and stuck out his hand.

"Should we try this again, Nameless?" His hand extended toward mine.

I looked at it unsure what to do. If I grabbed his hand now, would that mean I forgave him? I didn't even know who he really was or what he wanted with me. It irritated me that despite all that, it felt like I did know him; it felt like we were connected. But he had lied to me, kidnapped me. And I still was in the dark about the reason for it all. No, I couldn't shake his hand. Not yet.

"Why did you take me? Was that the reason you were in Innesbrown, just to steal me away? Or would any girl have done?" I asked him the pain clear in my voice.

"You are not just any girl," he said, dropping his hand and looking miserable.

"Ugh, won't you give me any answers," I grunted, frustrated.

"Yes, you were the reason I was Innesbrown, and you were the only one I was looking for. There." His face looked so raw that I believed him.

"But why?" I whispered.

"You'll find out soon, I promise," He ran his hands through his hair.

"And what will you do with me when we get there? Throw me in your dungeon? Beat me?" Anger began to bubble inside me.

"I told you I wouldn't hurt you," he sighed, looking as frustrated as I felt.

"That's about all you've told me," I lay back on the bed and turned toward the wall, "I'm sleeping here, you can sleep on the floor."

"Don't you want to eat?" He asked.

"I lost my appetite," I responded stubbornly.

Just then there was a knock on the door. I sat up quickly. The bar maid entered with a tray, placing it on the small nightstand. My stomach grumbled and I couldn't deny the alluring waft coming from the two steaming hot bowls of stew. There was a loaf of bread and some fresh butter as well. It looked delicious. My appetite came back with a vengeance as my stomach audibly growled.

I grabbed a bowl and ripped off a hunk of bread, immediately feasting. The prince snorted but grabbed his own bowl and followed suit.

"This is pretty good," I said between bites, forgetting my anger as my belly filled. The prince just shook his head and continued to eat. But I saw the corners of his mouth tug upward in amusement.

We ate in silence, enjoying the warmth, the food soaking up some of the ale from before. The prince stole glances at me throughout, as if there was something he wanted to say, but I ignored him. I was suddenly so tired I could barely keep my eyes open.

"Sleep, Meeka," the prince stood, grabbing the tray of empty bowls.

"Where are you going?" I asked, my eyelids growing heavy.

"Don't worry about me, I'll be back soon," he strode to the door, opened it, and left.

The room felt colder with him gone, but I tried not to dwell on that as I lay down, shut my eyes, and quickly fell into a deep sleep.

I awoke sometime later. The sky outside was still dark with night. I turned toward the floor, but the prince was not there. How long had I been sleeping?

I rubbed my eyes, still heavy and stinging with exhaustion. The room was dark, and shadows danced in the corners. I startled, thinking something was staring at me, only to realize it was my coat. I sighed; I needed more rest.

"Meeka..." a raspy voice came on a breeze that wasn't there. I jumped up into a sitting position, squinting wildly around the room, my heart pounding. But it was just me, alone in the small room. I must still be dreaming.

I stayed alert for some time, unable to fall back asleep. I bit my fingernails, staring at the door. Where was that darn prince?

After a while, I decided I made the whole thing up in my head, half asleep as I was. The voice had just been resonance from a dream. I lay back down, getting as comfortable as I could under the rough covers.

"Meeka..."

This time I was too awake to pass it off as a dream. I jumped up and grabbed my coat and hat. I didn't have a weapon on me, but I crouched ready to fight as I leaned down toward my bed. I counted to three in my head then quickly pulled up the bed skirt, exposing the contents beneath. There was nothing there. I grazed the room, but once again found it empty.

"Meeka..."

The voice came from farther away this time. I sprang up, slamming my head against the nightstand. Ouch, bloody nightstand. I rubbed my head.

My heart pounded with adrenaline. I looked at the small window. It was closed. I crept toward it, apprehension squeezing my insides. I pulled the curtain an inch back to peek out into the night.

There was a small barn in the distance, and I thought I saw a figure slip through the door, just as I peered out. The door rattled on its hinges, but in the dark it was difficult to tell if my eyes were playing tricks on me.

The rational part of my brain told me not to follow, but I didn't often listen to my rational side. I tightened my hat, pushing my crimson locks underneath, and slipped into the hallway.

I tiptoed my way to the stairs, taking care not to let the wood creak beneath my weight. Light from the fire below flickered on the walls as I crept down to the tavern. There were still a few patrons about – the prince and his uncle being two of them. They were huddled in the corner deep in conversation.

If I stuck to the shadows, I could probably make it out the door without being noticed. I took my time, willing myself to be silent, until I finally reached the exit. As I was about to push the door open, I heard a loud bang from the prince's direction. I froze, panicked. He would think I was running away.

I took a deep breath and turned, expecting to find him glaring with anger. Instead, I realized he had slammed his fist down hard on the table and was proceeding to have a hushed but angry argument with his uncle. I was intrigued but could not make out their words.

I knew I shouldn't linger. I pushed my way into the night, taking advantage of the prince's distraction. The cold stung my cheeks. I took a deep breath, letting the frigid air sear my lungs.

The snow was thick, and with every step I felt a weight pulling me down. It was as if the hand of fate was reaching up, trying to keep me from getting any closer to the barn. The wind howled and the barn door creaked on its hinges. It opened suddenly and then shut with a bang. It's just the wind, I told myself.

But I had seen someone enter from my window. I was sure of it.

When I was a foot or so away from the door, my heart began beating furiously.

"Hello?" I spoke, my voice coming out in a squeak, "is anyone there?"

There was no response. I grabbed the metal handle of the barn door. It hadn't been properly shut, which would explain why the wind made it bang open and shut, rocking the decaying wood on its hinges. I slowly pulled open the door and entered the barn.

It was frighteningly dark; I could see basically nothing. The hair on the back of my arms stood up, even underneath my heavy coat. This was a bad idea.

"Hello?" I said again to the dark.

I thought I heard a rustle in the corner and turned toward the sound. I squinted but couldn't make out anything or anyone.

"It's me, Meeka," I said to the dark. I shook my head. What was I doing? Was I insane? Either there was no one here and I was seeing things, or someone was waiting for me in the dark, which would mean coming here was the stupidest thing I had done.

"Meeka," the raspy voice jolted me out of my thoughts. Chills rushed down my spine as my heart accelerated to dangerous levels.

"Who are you? What do you want?" I turned about, searching for the voice.

"I've been waiting for you, Meeka." Just then a hooded figure peeled itself from the shadows. The man or thing or whatever it was, was standing only feet in front of me. In the darkness it was too difficult to make out anything other than a dark cloak. The thing was a shadow incarnated.

"Don't come any closer. What do you want?" I backed slowly away toward the door, bracing myself in case I needed to flee.

"I want you, child. And in return I can give you everything you could ever want. Fame, fortune, glory." His voice sounded like a knife slicing against a glass plate. It made me cringe.

"How could you do that?" I asked, the door now at my back.

"All you have to do is serve me, and I will grant you all the world's delights." He inched closer to me, extending a robed arm.

"I serve no one," I replied in a whisper.

"Everyone serves something, my dear. You will have to make the choice soon. I will come again for your answer." He stopped moving toward me and instead stepped backward, once again fading into the shadows.

"Wait. Why me?" I asked the shadows, but there was no reply. Spooked to the core, I needed to get out of the gods-forsaken barn.

I turned, flinging the door open, and began to run - straight into a looming figure.

# CHAPTER 18

I screamed, caught amongst the fabric of the figure that had captured me in a rough embrace. I flailed my arms, pushing, trying desperately to break free.

"Shh, Meeka, it's me." The figure was calm but my mind was reeling from the contact with the shadow.

"What do you want?" I cried.

"It's only me."

I finally recognized the prince's voice and stopped fighting.

"What are you doing here?" I asked pulling myself together.

"When I went to our room you weren't there. I came looking for you. What were you doing?" He asked searching my eyes.

"Nothing, I-" I took a deep breath willing myself to be calm, "I couldn't sleep so I thought I'd take a walk."

"In the middle of the night in the cold?" He asked clearly not believing me for a second.

"Yes," I replied without meeting his eyes.

"You told me you wouldn't run away," the prince stated.

"I wasn't, I promise," I sighed.

"You seem spooked," the prince held me at a distance now, looking skeptical.

"I went to see what was in the barn, but it was too dark. Then you snuck up on me, that's all. Don't do that again by the way," I barked out annoyed.

"You really are a bull-headed pain in my-," he shook his head and let go of me, mumbling the end of his sentence.

"Oh, now who is the mumbler?" I closed my eyes, willing my heart to settle.

"Would you like to know what I think, Nameless?" He raised his eyebrows in challenge. I ground my teeth and shook my head. "I didn't think so."

"Let's just go back to bed. What were you doing up so late anyway?" I asked as we walked toward the inn.

"I was seeing my uncle off," he replied, running his hand through his hair.

"Off? Where is he going?" I asked, curious.

"He is riding ahead, to let the court know we will be returning soon. They will need to prepare for our arrival," he sighed.

I narrowed my eyes but didn't ask any more questions. I knew I wouldn't get any answers.

I pushed the prince as I walked past him, making my way to the inn.

Once back in our rooms, I took off my heavy jacket and removed my hat. I glanced at the prince, who was staring at my hair flowing across my shoulders and down my back.

"Soon, you won't have to cover that hair," he spoke quietly.

"I guess that will be one perk of being your captive," I fumed.

He just rolled his eyes and grabbed one of the pillows off my bed. Settling on the floor, he pulled his fur coat over himself as a cover. I stared down, debating if I should give him my sheet, but decided not to be kind. I turned toward the wall and quickly fell back asleep.

I awoke in a sweat, panting. I had dreamed of the shadow figure, and for a minute I wondered if the whole night had been a dream. But then I turned to see the prince lying on the floor tangled in his fur and realized it had not.

I felt my cheek, where the cut from my Pa had scabbed over. I hoped it wouldn't leave a scar. But all wounds left a scar one way or another. It may heal; it may no longer be visible on the outside, but the wound in my heart would last forever.

Sun peaked through the window, and I realized we had overslept. I knelt on the floor where the prince lay sleeping. I poked at his arm to wake him, but he was deep in slumber. I got on my knees next to him and bent over his body, shaking both his shoulders.

"Wake up, prince," I whispered, continuing to shake him. Nothing. Darn prince. I gave him a few light taps on the cheek but instead of waking he rolled toward me, grabbing me around the waist and pulling me on top of him.

He murmured in his sleep and pulled me close. I tensed my body, covered in his warmth, unsure what to do. I wasn't strong enough to shrug out of his embrace.

"Prince, hello, princey, princey," I tried to get his attention, but he swung his leg over me, wrapping my body against his. This was not what I had intended.

I could feel his hot breath against the top of my head and his heart beat against my ear where my body pushed up against his chest. He was so warm it was hard to deny how comforting it felt to be in his arms. He seemed vulnerable in his sleep, happy almost. But this would not do.

I squirmed but he brought a hand to my face, stroking the hair back from my cheek. Suddenly his eyes flung open, and he met my awkward stare. He jumped up alarmed.

"What are you doing?" He said disoriented.

"Me?! I was just minding my business trying to wake you up, when you all but tackled me in your sleep," I retorted defensively.

"You were cuddling with me," he said unemotionally.

"I was not. You were cuddling with me. I assure you I had no say in the matter," I huffed, crossing my arms. He looked at me doubtful.

"If you wanted to sleep with me, you could have just asked," he narrowed his eyes.

"I did not – you infuriating-" I punched him in the arm, but he just began laughing.

"Ok, ok. I'm sorry. I must have been having a good dream," he gave me a wicked grin.

"You can't just go about embracing people who are just trying to wake you up. It's rude. I thought you were a prince." I stood, straightening my clothes and grabbing my coat and hat.

"I may be a prince, but I told you before I was no gentleman." He licked his lips clearly enjoying my frazzled state.

"You are a rogue," I replied heading for the door.

"That, I can't deny," he grinned but followed my lead, gathering his things.

Together we headed for the tavern. When we arrived, Leacher and Demetri were already up and waiting for us at a table by the hearth.

"How'd you two lovebirds sleep?" Demetri gave a lewd smile as we joined them at a table to break our fast. The prince smacked him on the back of the head.

"Far apart," I declared even though I could feel the heat rising on my cheeks, "did you and Leacher enjoy snuggling together?"

The prince snorted and Demetri choked on his juice.

"I suppose the uncle was there to chaperone?" I laughed. Demetri grabbed a handful of pickleberries and threw them in my direction. I ducked, grabbing a sausage and throwing it back. It hit him right on the nose. He gave a look of mock offence and grabbed it off the floor, shrugging, and taking a large bite.

"You are in a feisty mood this morning, my lady," Demetri sat back in his chair, but his face was full of amusement.

"I didn't sleep well," I countered.

He raised his eyebrows.

"No, not like that, you deviant." I looked toward the prince who seemed to be enjoying my blundering.

"We'd better get going. We're late already," Leacher cut in.

We ate quickly then made our way to the stables, where the men had secured horses for the remainder of the journey. I tried not to groan at the thought of getting on a horse. For some reason or another, the creatures had never warmed to me. Nor I them.

"How much longer will this little kidnapping journey last?" I asked as Leacher helped me on a horse. The horse whinnied and moved about, not too happy with me.

"Relax, Nameless," the prince came to the beast stroking its mane and calming it, "if you are restless, the mare will be restless."

"You say that like it's easy," I murmured.

"Would you rather ride with me?" His lips curled into an impish half smile.

"No," I blurted, "thank you, but no." I felt the heat rise on my cheeks again, remembering that first day we met, riding between his powerful thighs.

"Suit yourself," the prince left me to be with the temperamental mare.

"It's about three more days, if we're quick," Leacher chimed in.

"Three days on this creature," I groaned under my breath. I would not be enjoying this. Although if I was honest, a part of me felt exhilarated by the thought of getting closer to the Old Country. I had no idea what to except, and yet I felt pulled toward my old home.

It almost felt like destiny.

# CHAPTER 19

We spent most of the day riding, my horse and I reluctantly obeying each other. As the air began to warm, I could tell we were nearing the border. The snow on the ground didn't fall quite as heavy. Small sprouts and saplings sprung from the earth looking so fragile yet hardy enough to defeat the cold.

We stopped for supper as the sun grew heavy in the sky. The men had packed several meals in satchels from the inn.

"When my family fled the Old Country, it took us weeks to get to Innesbrown," I mused while munching on a chicken thigh. The men around me stiffened.

"I thought you didn't remember anything, my lady?" Demetri asked. I caught him giving the prince a hesitant look.

"I don't. I just know it took us a long time. Longer than you say it will take to get there," I shrugged.

"I assume you came on foot, and we are going by horse. Besides, we know a short cut to the capital once we cross the border," the prince replied, preoccupied with his meal.

"I suppose we were slow since there were so many of us little ones. Six of us actually. My Ma told me we lost two before we made it here. I was the youngest, only eight years, and Timtim wasn't born yet," I reflected, "most of them are dead now."

"That's an awful lot of death to be surrounded with," Demetri spoke softly.

"I'm used to it," I shrugged, "not much time has passed since Ma died."

"You and the prince share that," Leacher nodded his head in the prince's direction. He was staring at me with an emotion I couldn't decipher.

When the prince came for dinner that night, my Pa said the King had died. The prince had flinched when Pa said it. Now, it made sense. It was the prince's own Pa.

"I wasn't there when he passed. I've been in the North for a while now," the prince looked down. I wasn't sure if it was anger or sadness that made his brows draw together.

"Oh, that's right. Searching for me." I couldn't help biting out the remark. How long would this bitterness sit heavy on my tongue, I wondered.

The prince's head snapped up. He narrowed his eyes at me.

"Let's keep going. We still have a couple hours of sun before we need to make camp," the prince said, standing and shaking off crumbs.

"Fine," I stalked over to where my horse should be. The mare had trailed off through the trees. I suppose I hadn't tied the rope properly to the branches. Of course, I would get the wandering one.

I shuffled through the snow between the thick trees grumbling to myself about the nuisance of large animals. Finally, I spotted the mare at the bottom of a small ditch, where it stood drinking from a stream.

I slid down the drop to the bank but caught my foot on a bramble and tripped. My hat fell from my head, and I sat up huffing, pushing the hair away from my face.

As I made to stand, a hand clamped around my mouth.

I struggled, trying to scream, but the hand prevented me from doing so. I brought my leg up and kicked the knee behind me as hard as I could. The man dropped, falling and clutching at his leg. I made to run and shout for help, but only a squeak came out before another man jumped on top of me, tackling me to the ground. He pushed my face into the mud, drawing my arms behind me. I groaned as my shoulders yanked from their sockets.

"Don't say a word. And don't move or I will break both your arms," a stranger's voice spoke from where he now pressed a knee into my back.

I tried to break free but his hold on my arms only tightened. I sucked in a breath to shout, knowing the prince and his men were right over the ridge, but all I got was a mouth full of mud. I spit and sputtered, but to no avail.

"You're coming with us, princess," the man spat out triumphantly.

Princess?

The other man limped over at this point, pulling out a dirty cloth and lifting my head. He wrapped the cloth around my face and into my mouth, gagging me before I got the chance to call for help.

Carefully the two men pulled me up, first tying my ankles together and then tying my hands behind my back. They carried me as if I were hunted game being brought home to slaughter.

The strangers carried me awkwardly as I continued to kick and flail. They walked in the water to cover any tracks. Downstream, they found their horses waiting in a clearing. One man threw me over the steed's mane, hopping on behind me. We took off immediately. The other man followed suit.

My head flopped with each gallop, and I knew I would get a fierce headache. If I had been bitter about the first kidnapping, I was furious about this one. Who did these men think they were, taking young ladies without their permission. They would need a lesson on manners.

First chance I got, I would give it to them.

If only I had a bloody weapon.

# CHAPTER 20

We traveled with great haste, not stopping when the sun dipped low, and the sky grew dark. My stomach turned at the endless bouncing and I wondered if I would throw up. Even if I spilled the meager contents of my stomach, I didn't think it would be enough to stop these men who seemed to be in a great hurry.

First, I was taken by the prince and his men, and now these fools. But with each kidnapping, I grew less afraid. If this many people wanted me, then I must be valuable. And men didn't kill valuable things.

We finally stopped at dawn. I was exhausted and my head hurt from the endless whiplash of riding. The men didn't dare a fire so instead they sat on the ground, their horses within reach, eating a quick meal. They did not offer me any food. They did, however, remove me from the horse, though I was still tied up and gagged.

We sat in silence, mine involuntary, while the men quickly ate and watered their horses. I glared daggers at them anytime they came near me, but I was mostly ignored.

I wiggled my arms back and forth to see if I could loosen the ties. I couldn't. Luckily, I was flexible and repositioned myself so that I could reach my ankles even with my hands tied behind my back. I was cautious not to make any sudden movements, but carefully I reached for the ties at my feet and began to pull at them.

A knife would really come in handy, I thought. I pulled and fiddled with the rope, but the knots would not yield. I tried to speak to get the men's attention, but with the gag in place my voice came out in muffled grunts.

"I think the girl's trying to talk," the man gestured to his partner. They both wore all black, their hoods pulled low over their brows with scarves tied up around their mouth and nose, making it difficult to tell what they looked like. This one had dark brown eyes and was shorter than the other. Besides that, they were almost identical.

The taller one just grunted but stood up and sauntered in my direction. He bent down, crouching next to me, studying my face.

"I suppose she must be hungry," he scratched his head. I nodded my head yes, hoping they would take the gag out of my mouth.

"I think she can go a little longer without food," the shorter one stood now making his way toward me. They both stared at me, narrowing their eyes, the only part of their bodies not hidden from both me and the cold. I continued to subtly pull at the ties on my ankles that were tucked beneath my knees trying to keep them concealed from the men. Hope flared as they began to loosen just the smallest amount.

"Are you hungry, little fox?" The taller man asked, bending low and running a finger down my cheek. I shook my head from side to side trying to avoid his touch. I attempted several curses, but the gag prevented the words from finding home.

These bloody ties were taking too long. I reared my head back and then slammed down as hard as I could into the man's nose. He fell backward, swearing, holding his face where blood now gushed. I hoped I had broken his nose.

The other man slapped me across the face, reopening the wound from Pa. Blood trickled down my cheek, dripping on to the forest floor.

"You'll regret that," the man I headbutted spit out from where he sat clutching his face.

I highly doubt it, I thought. I glared at him with hatred and gave him a sweet smile. What I would do for my machete.

The shorter man who had slapped me strode to his friend, helping him back up.

"We should be going. We've lingered too long." He gathered up their things. His partner stared at me, hatred in his eyes, but I didn't flinch. He didn't scare me.

"We should be to the river shortly. Once on the other side, we'll be back in Skirsgard," he continued. That seemed to appease his partner who nodded reassuringly as if Skirsgard would protect them.

I finally got the ropes at my feet to loosen, kindling a kernel of hope. I still couldn't untie them, but at least they were beginning to give way. I just needed more time.

"Grrrmmm…" I gestured that I needed to relieve myself, though it came out as a muffled groan.

"Sorry, princess, can't hear you," the taller man wiped at his face but wouldn't even look in my direction. The shorter one came toward me, throwing me across his shoulder like a sack of grain and slinging me back over the horse. Gods, this was infuriating.

I hated feeling out of control. I spent my whole life hiding from who I really was. I had found small ways to be defiant – sleeping in the woods, learning how to live off the land, trying desperately to depend only on myself. It was my own way of controlling my life when I had so little control of the greater things. Now, tied up, mute, and treated like an object, my anger surged. These men would not dictate where I go and what I do. I would decide that for myself.

The men leapt on the horses and took off. The sun was just rising over the horizon. There was a warm breeze on the air. Soon we would enter the Old Country.

We galloped through the woods until the trees opened to a large valley filled with plateaus and rolling hills. It was beautiful. A long river flowed through the center, carved deep into a gorge. We followed a path along the edge, dancing dangerously close to the cliffs that plummeted into the river.

My stomach ached from the bouncing, and my head throbbed, but this would be my only chance. The men had said once we were across the river, we would be in Skirsgard. This must be the river they spoke of.

I shimmied slowly so as not to throw off too much weight. The men, in their haste, neglected to tie me to the horse. The rider kept one hand against my back to keep me in place but was more preoccupied galloping quickly than with my positioning.

During the trip I'd been wiggling my feet, working on the small progress I'd made loosening the ties. The rough twine bit into my ankles tearing at the flesh, but I didn't care, I continued to force my way through.

Eventually I felt what I had been waiting for – a release. The ties snapped. I was careful to keep my ankles crossed not to alert my captor.

I took deep breaths through my nose, waiting for the perfect moment, counting the seconds. When the path narrowed, and the drop looked less daunting, I curled up my knees, pushed with all my strength, and flung myself away from the steed and off the cliff.

# CHAPTER 21

I flew through the air, not allowing panic to sink in until I hit the water. It was by some miracle I didn't hit a rock or the side of the cliff, but when the water slammed into my body, the wind was knocked from my lungs, and I was jolted by a searing pain.

I flailed around, my arms still tied and the gag still in my mouth. Luckily, I was a good swimmer, and my legs were now freed from the restraints. Still, I had trouble staying on the surface, the rapid water pulling me down in intervals making it difficult to get a full breath. I flattened out, letting the current pull me downriver.

I didn't dare look up at the cliffs where I knew my captors would be anxiously pursuing. The river moved quickly, and I could only hope they had lost me among the churning waters.

I struggled to get my bearings with only my legs to keep me afloat, but after some time the waters began to calm, and I was able to float down the river without fear of drowning.

I steered myself as best as I could toward the opposite bank. Seeing no one on either bank, as I floundered toward the shore. I was drenched now, but luckily the land here was no longer submerged in snow, instead warmth from the sun permeated my wet clothing.

A jagged rock erupted from the water's edge, and I backed toward it, using it to saw the ties at my hands until finally the rope fractured and snapped.

Gods it felt mighty good to be free. I tore the gag from my mouth, finally taking a deep breath, which turned into shallow coughing and sputtering as water from the river made its way forth from my lungs.

I didn't want to linger by the shore in case my captors had followed me down river – as I was sure they would. So far, I hadn't seen anywhere to cross, but the men seemed to know where they were going, and I was certain there would be somewhere to ford the river nearby.

The cliffs weren't so steep on this side, and after a time I found a spot to climb out. It was difficult and painful as I scraped my way up the bluff using branches whose roots dug into the side of the earth like a ladder. But I was forged from this land, I would use it to my advantage.

When I made it to the top, I collapsed in a heap. My eyes closed on their own volition and exhaustion took hold.

*Wake up.*

Peeling my eyes open, I rubbed at my throbbing temples. Had I passed out?

Confusion took hold as reality snapped back into place. Oh, right. I escaped. The river. I'd crossed the river and passed out. I was back in the Old Country. How long had I been asleep?

*Welcome home.*

That voice again. Was I dreaming? I looked around to see where it was coming from but saw nothing.

I crouched down low, using the brush as cover while I took in my surroundings. The soil here was rich and the hills were covered in moss and wildflowers. Large oak trees dotted the land and smaller bushes filled in the areas that weren't blanketed with tall grass. It was breathtaking to see land not engulfed in snow.

Though it was warmer here, the chill from my wet clothing sent shivers down my spine. I needed to get out of these soaking rags and warm myself, though I was reluctant to start a fire. If I made it to the hills in the distance, I could look for a hidden inlet where a fire wouldn't serve as a beacon. That would have to do.

*Good thinking.*

I spun around but no one was there. I must have hit my head on a rock during the fall. I shook off my confusion.

I spent the next hour or so creeping between bushes and trees, slowly making my way to the foothills, counting my steps as a distraction.

My clothes had dried somewhat during the trek, but they were still damp, and I felt the cold sinking into my bones as the sun grew lower overhead. My stomach growled with hunger and my lips were chap with thirst, but I could not dwell on that now. My first thought was to get warm.

As I continued to climb to higher ground, my thoughts became distracted. The events of late were overwhelming, as though each was a parasitic creature living inside me. Ma's death, Yesimia's marriage, the kidnapping, and the realization that I was truly in Skirsgard, my homeland - it all hit like a punch to the gut. Breathing became difficult. Or maybe I couldn't breathe at all.

I took in deep rasping breaths, falling to the ground, panic setting in. I thought too much about the way my lungs filled with oxygen, what if I didn't take my next breath? What if my lungs stopped filling and my heart stopped beating?

I dropped to the soft grass. I closed my eyes and let the sun beat down on my eyelids, trying to soak up the warmth. I could do this. I could exist in this world. There must be somewhere I belonged.

*Don't be ridiculous. You are made for this.*

I jumped up, rubbing my eyes. Someone was speaking. But again, I saw nothing.

"Hello?" I spoke to the air, caution making me tense.

But somehow the voice was fortifying, almost as though it had come from a lost part within me.

I was strong. I had always been strong. I could conquer the darkness. It was my way.

I gathered myself, the cold seeping through my damp clothes, numbing my fingertips. I stood. I was at the foothills now and would find a spot to hide a fire.

I weaved through the brush around several bends and dips before coming to a small cave in the hillside perfect for hiding. I slipped through the entrance but stopped short when I saw a flicker of flame and heard voices up ahead.

I tiptoed across the cave's entrance. The voices began again, and recognition struck.

"The part I still don't understand was how she leapt off the horse," the prince's uncle's voice was seething.

"Sir, we had no time to tie her, she was getting too...aggresive." I recognized the voice of one of the men who had kidnapped me.

"She gave captain Fintir a blow to the face," my other captor said.

I smiled at that.

"You're telling me, this young girl was too much for the two of you to handle? Even before you crossed the border. Pathetic." The prince's uncle groaned. "Did the prince see you?"

"No, sir. We were disguised. She won't recognize us either." This must be captain Fintir. I may not recognize him, but at least I now had a name. And I wouldn't forget their voices.

"Did she use her powers?" The prince's uncle scathed.

"Not that we saw, sir, though the way she flew off that horse..." captain Fintir trailed off.

"It's no matter now, you fools. We must beat Ajax to the capital. We shouldn't linger here." The creaking of twigs and sounds of movement brought me back to reality. I took it as my sign to leave.

I scurried out making as little noise as possible. Climbing farther up the hill hoping to stay out of their sight, I came to a small clearing with a large, knotted tree. I had never seen anything like it. It did not look natural.

Branches twisted and protruded at abnormal angles. The size alone could have housed a small cottage. Leaves gathered at the top branches, yet the trunk was barren and rotting. In the center there stood a hole, as though the tree's maw was opening wide.

I heard voices approaching and swore to myself, praying to the gods that my captors hadn't spotted me and followed me here. I ran and ducked behind a fallen log peeking through cracks in the rotting wood.

The two kidnappers and the prince's uncle strode into the middle of the clearing. They glanced around the space but did not notice me. The three of them reached around their necks, pulling off the chains holding rings like the one the prince wore, and discarding them on the ground.

The prince's uncle placed his hand on the rough bark. The two men each put a hand on his shoulder and closed their eyes. The prince's uncle muttered a few words, and the three of them disappeared through the opening.

# CHAPTER 22

The rotting log crumpled under my fingers as I stood, staring open mouthed at the now empty clearing. My eyes had not deceived me; the men disappeared.

I walked over to the large tree, afraid to touch it. I circled it, taking in its rough appearance. Underneath the bark, a curious substance shone like a pit of black tar. The material rippled as though it was pliable, and yet its solid mass stood before me unscathed.

The sun dipped below the hills and with it came darkness and cold. I couldn't stay here in the open clearing. I needed to get warm.

I climbed back down the hill to the cave. Trepidation settled deep in my core as I entered, but as I continued forward, I found it empty, only the remnants of the men's fire remaining.

I bent down and blew on the smoke, but the fire would not come back to life. I swore, frustrated, as I continued to wave and blow trying desperately to bring back the warmth I needed. I closed my eyes and rubbed my face. I let out a grunt of frustration.

"You infuriating fire - just come back to life!" I shouted in exasperation at the dark pile of sticks. I clenched my fists and clapped my hands, wanting to hit something. I closed my eyes, trying to pull it together.

*Calm down.*

I opened my eyes to see who spoke, but to my amazement, an ember glowed. I quickly blew on it, and soon it became a roaring flame.

After adding more twigs, which were plentiful on the cave floor, I stripped off my damp clothing laying them out to dry and sat shivering over the fire, rubbing my hands back and forth for warmth. I allowed the fire to seep into my bones warming me for the first time in hours.

Sometime between dusk and dawn I finally fell asleep while the fire kept the cold at bay.

I awoke to a nudge at my foot but was too tired for my brain and my muscles to work together.

"Go away," I murmured kicking back against the creature I assumed was some sort of mouse or squirrel.

"Ahem," someone grunted.

I sat up abruptly, the blood rushing to my head causing stars to swarm my vision.

I blinked, unseeing, until I realized my vision was blocked by a large cloak.

"Who's there?" I asked tense. Looking down, I saw I was only wearing my thin linen undergarments.

"You might want to get dressed." That voice.

"Prince," I clenched my jaw and grabbed the coat wrapping it around my body like a blanket. It smelled of moss and crisp rain, musk and rich earth. "How did you find me?"

"It's nice to see you too," he smirked.

"Well, as you can see, I am perfectly capable –" I began.

"Yes, yes, I know. You are perfectly capable on your own," he interrupted, "believe me, you have made that clear." He rolled his eyes.

"What's that supposed to mean?" I scoffed.

I should be grateful to see him, and in truth I was. I had no real plan and no way of knowing how to get to the nearest city on my own. I had no food or water, and soon I would need them both if I wanted to survive. I knew how to live off the land in the North, but things were different here.

I would never admit to the prince the relief I felt at seeing him now.

"We followed your tracks but lost you somewhere around the river. It was by luck you were here." The prince's lip quirked up in a wicked half smile, "I might add my extra luck in finding you thus exposed."

I picked up a small rock and threw it at him as hard as I could. He caught it before it could find its mark, chuckling. I scowled.

"I jumped in the river, that's why I'm drying my clothes," I explained.

"I see. Get dressed. Don't worry, I won't look." He turned around.

"How did you know I didn't run away?" I asked while tugging my tunic over my head.

"You promised you wouldn't," he responded flatly.

"And you believed me?" I scoffed.

"Believe it or not, trust isn't so hard for everyone." The prince reproved.

"Well, I was taken...again." I sighed.

"Did they hurt you?" something between anger and concern pierced his tone.

"No. I told you I can handle myself," I seethed and finished getting dressed. I put on my own jacket and hat, then handed back the prince's coat. "Here."

He turned and took hold of the coat, stepping close to me. He searched my face then ran his eyes up and down my now dressed body.

"I'm fine," I ground out, "no thanks to you, by the way."

He narrowed his eyes at me and opened his mouth to respond. Before he could, Leacher and Demetri came into view.

"Meeka, you little minx, there you are," Demetri strolled up and scooped me into a hug, lifting my feet off the ground. I was so surprised I clenched awkwardly in his arms. Demetri laughed then put me down.

"We were worried about you," Leacher chimed in looking relieved and glancing at the prince. I followed his gaze, but the prince looked quickly away.

"I'm fine," I repeated to the men. Even though I had only known them such a short time, it was hard not to like them. I wanted to put them at ease.

"We should get moving. We're already late," the prince spoke. Demetri and Leacher nodded, smiling fondly at me. "And quit googling over Meeka, she told you she was fine."

Demetri and Leacher moved out of the cave, but the prince lingered, looking me over once more before finally turning and exiting the cave. I followed.

We made our way up the hill and into the clearing with the mysterious tree. The prince strode toward the middle.

"Wait, don't -" I shouted, "Don't touch that. I know it sounds crazy, but I saw those men touch it, and they disappeared."

"You saw them? I thought you escaped?" the prince asked looking confused.

"I did escape down at the river, but I followed them here and they touched that tree and disappeared," I pleaded with the prince to believe me, but he seemed to be focusing on all the wrong parts of my story.

"Did you recognize any of the men?" The prince asked.

"Well, yes..." I hesitated, "the two men who captured me met up with your uncle. One was named captain Fintir."

"Hells," Demetri swore next to me. The prince gave him a pointed look but there was no shock written on his face. I wondered if he knew his uncle had been plotting.

"We will sort this out at the capital," the prince told Demetri. "Now let's go."

The prince, Demetri, and Leacher, pulled out chains around their necks, also containing matching rings. They tossed them to the ground, then stepped toward the tree.

"What are those rings? Your uncle and his men had them too," I questioned, curiosity getting the better of me.

"We wear them to keep our memories in the North," Demetri explained.

"Huh?" I furrowed my brow.

"I'll explain later," the prince huffed out.

"You don't believe me, but they really did disappear when they stepped through that opening," I spoke urgently now to the prince.

"Yes, Meeka, I know," he tilted his head studying me, "you better come here and hold on tight to my arm."

"What do you mean?" I asked nervously.

"Remember I told you we knew a shortcut to the capital? This is it." He gave me a wolfish grin, pulling me close against his side. Demetri and Leacher grabbed hold of his shoulders. The prince placed his hand on the bark.

He winked at me and leaned down close, whispering in my ear, "shamesh shamesh candora."

Everything went black.

# PART 3:

# THE SOUTH

# CHAPTER 23

My body stretched and tore apart. My stomach turned upside down as the darkness morphed into light. Shapes came and went in a wispy kaleidoscope. Figures started to form before my eyes, and I realized I was standing back on solid ground. I vomited.

"Give her some space." It was the prince's voice.

"I'm fine," I lied.

My vision swam and I couldn't quite make out where I was. There was cold stone beneath my feet and large pillars surrounding me. "Where am I?"

"You're in the palace in the capital city, Tyev, of Skirsgard," the prince responded, sounding calm.

"How come you don't sound like I feel?" I asked feeling woozy, my vision not quite right. "I can't see anything."

"I'm used to traveling through the trees and having my magic. You are not used to either. It will get better, I promise." The prince was so sure of himself, but I thought everything he said sounded convoluted.

I closed my eyes and pinched the bridge of my nose taking deep breaths to steady my rolling stomach. When I opened my eyes, the world around me cleared.

I was standing in a large forum. The ceilings were at least four stories high, held up by massive marble pillars with intricate trim work winding its way from top to bottom. The floors were likewise marble, but the stone here consisted of bright colors forming a mosaic of patterns.

There was a large tree in the middle, comparable to the one in the clearing, only this one was a dark purple. A giant fountain stood on the far end of the room, the sound of rushing water now filling my ears.

"I think I need to rest," I tried to take a step forward but stumbled, falling into Leacher, who grabbed my arm, steadying me.

"Of course. I'm sure this is a lot to take in. Trafi will take you to your room," the prince gestured to a young woman who looked down at her velvet shoes. She was wearing a flowing purple dress and an apron. She would not look at me.

I tilted my head down, my fiery red hair spilling over my shoulders. I must have lost my hat. I found Trafi's eyes, but she squeezed them shut and looked away.

"Trafi, I'm Meeka. It's ok, you can look at me," I tried to tell her.

"She is trained not to look at her superiors," the prince explained.

"That's ridiculous. Trafi, I am a prisoner, I am not your superior, and even if I were you can look at me all you want." I looked at the prince, eyebrows raised, challenging him.

*You will find things different now.*

I whirled around, but that voice still had no owner. Maybe I was going mad.

"It's the way of things, Meeka. Let her be, or you will only get her in trouble," the prince sighed.

"Aren't you the one in charge of 'the way of things?'" I argued, squeezing my eyes against the ache and the voice in my head.

"Not yet. Trafi, take her to her rooms, and see that no one bothers her. And send someone to clean up this mess," the prince turned to leave.

"That's it? No explanation?" I demanded, frustration bubbling inside.

"Go rest, then we will talk. I have a few things to take care of first," the prince continued to walk away, his footsteps echoing off the walls. Demetri and Leacher followed, the latter at least gave me a pitying look.

"Lead the way, Trafi, but I'm telling you now, if you refuse to look at me, I am going to be mighty annoyed," I huffed.

Trafi looked frightened, she was not much older than a child. I sighed but let her lead me to my chamber.

We walked through several hallways as tall and imposing as the previous room. Whoever built this place really liked pillars, they were everywhere. The walls were bare but judging by the dirty outlines, it seemed there had been a time when the walls were adorned with paintings.

"Where did all the pictures go, Trafi?" I asked.

"I'm sorry, your – miss -, I am not supposed to talk to you," Trafi continued forward, cheeks reddening.

"You can't look at me and you can't talk to me...this is maddening. I am not a rock, Trafi." I said frustrated. It wasn't Trafi who I was upset with, I had to remind myself. It was the lack of information and the lack of consideration.

A vase on a nearby pedestal began to tremble. Trafi pushed me aside just in time as it came flying toward us, shattering on the wall to my side.

*I'm mad too.*

"What in the hells?" I panted, righting myself and meeting Trafi's eye before she quickly turned away.

"It's your opeki," she shook her head, clearly knowing I didn't understand, "your magic, miss. It will return now that you're back in Skirsgard," she spoke in a squeak of a voice. There was no surprise, no shock, in her simple words.

For Trafi, the statement had been straight forward, but in my ears the words coalesced without reason.

"I didn't make that vase move. I have no magic," I tried to explain, tried to convince myself.

"Then how did the vase come flying at us?" She asked with a small smile.

"I don't know," I offered no explanation as I had none. She just shook her head still smiling.

"Here we are," she used her hand to gesture to a set of double doors on my left – my chambers I presumed.

I stood in front of the large wooden doors, gilded in gold. My head stung and I had to grab it, squeezing my eyes against the sudden rush of pain.

I stood here before. Something like a memory tugged inside me, but it was too fleeting to grasp. I didn't know what to do, what to say. Why did I know this place?

I remembered nothing, and yet in my heart I knew I had been here before.

Trafi opened the doors, and I lost my breath. The room was large and circular. There was a giant four post bed, a sitting area around a large hearth, and a table for dining. On the opposite side, there were floor to ceiling windows looking out over a huge garden. It was breathtaking.

"This is my room?" I asked flabbergasted. I wished Yesimia could see this.

"Does it not please you, miss?" Trafi asked bowing her head.

"Trafi, it pleases me very much," I walked to the center of the room going in a slow circle, taking in my surroundings.

"Would you like a fire, miss?" Trafi moved toward the giant hearth.

"Yes, but I can start it myself-" I began but Trafi bent down and snapped her fingers, a spark igniting among the wood. She snapped a few more times until there was a full fire blazing. I stood openmouthed.

"There miss, if that will be all, I'll be leaving you now. A bath has been drawn in your bathing chamber beyond that door," she gestured to a door at the side of my bed, "and clothing has been laid out. I will send for food, as well, but try and get some rest." She bowed to leave.

"Wait, Trafi," I shook my hand in front of her face, but she continued looking down at her feet, "how did you start that fire?"

"I snapped it. I know I'm not as quick as some, but that's because my opeki is weak." She gave me another small smile looking at her feet.

"You snapped it? You used magic?" I asked astonished.

"Of course. Welcome to Skirsgard," she curtsied and hurried out of the room, leaving me alone with my wonderstruck thoughts.

# CHAPTER 24

I paced around the room trying to steady my thoughts. A lot had happened in the past day. I was in Skirsgard. The thought rocked my core. I knew my homeland was different, but I never knew quite the extent. Not only had I been born in this mysterious country, but it seemed there was magic everywhere.

My Ma used to say little comments under her breath about magic, but I always just thought she was a little lost in her head. I never realized a place like this existed. I was caught off guard by how very little I knew about anything.

To the side of the massive bed there was a small door. Trafi said it was a bathing chamber so I decided I would wash up, take a nap, and then find answers. When I entered the room, it took a moment to come to my bearings. The floor to ceiling was once again covered in colorful marble. Large windows overlooked the gardens just as in the bedroom, and I thought I may be a bit too exposed to the outside world. In the middle of the room stood an enormous golden tub, filled to the brim with steaming water. Rose and eucalyptus scents wafted from within, filling me with a sense of peace.

I striped off my dirty clothing and got in the bath, soaking away the aches from the journey of the last several days. It felt beyond luxurious. I closed my eyes and sighed. Now this I could get used to.

I stayed in the bath until my brow began to sweat and my fingers started to prune. It was with effort that I got up, leaving the water much dirtier than it had been when I entered. I found a robe and put it on, not bothering to look through the clothing that Trafi laid out.

I walked to the bed in a daze, fell on top of the opulent covers, and fell quickly asleep.

I startled awake. The room had grown dark, and I felt panic rising inside. I looked around but it felt different. The bedding wasn't quite what I remembered. I thought it had been a grey silk but looking down I found my hands wrapped in a luxurious purple. My hands looked smaller, younger.

There was angry knocking at the door, and I rose to open it. But before I reached the handle, a young woman came out of the wardrobe holding a bundle of furs.

"Put this on, Meeka," she said with dread. I grabbed the coat from her and wrapped it around my shoulders. "We must go, quickly." She looked at the window where the curtains were drawn. I walked over and pulled them back. The gardens were on fire.

"Meeka, now!" She pulled me away from the room, grabbing me fiercely. I recognized her now. It was Serafina. My oldest sister.

But she was dead.

I woke with a jerk, sweat dripping down my back. It was a dream. It had only been a dream.

My breathing came in gulps as I took in my surroundings. I was in the same room – the room from my dreams – only now it was painted differently. The curtains were a solid white and the bedding grey. It was as though someone had stripped it of all its color.

This was my bedroom. The same room I lived in as a child.

My nightmare was not a dream – it was a memory.

I clutched my head and shook it. No, this didn't make any sense. I needed to get dressed and find the prince. I needed answers.

I went back to the bathing room and grabbed the clothes Trafi had left me.

You've got to be kidding me, I thought. These were not clothes. The silky dress clung to my skin, exposing too much. My whole back was practically open. And while there were sleeves, the way the silk draped over my curves left little to the imagination. This dress was about as impractical as they came. I found a pair of slippers next to the bath and slipped them on my feet. These would have to do.

I would have called for Trafi and demanded something a bit more concealing, but I was in too great of a rush. The time for answers had come, and I was in no mood to wait.

Unlike my dream, it was still light outside, the sun just beginning to dip down. I'd slept most of the day.

I barged through my chamber doors into the hallway with no idea where to go. Leacher stood there, presumably guarding me. Whether he was keeping people out or keeping me in, I wasn't sure, but when he tried to protest, I gave him a murderous look.

"Where is the prince?" I demanded.

"The prince wanted you to wait here, my lady. He said he would come soon." Leacher looked frightened. Good, he should be scared. I was in no mood.

"I don't care what the prince wanted. I am going to find him. You can point me in the right direction, or I can spend the evening searching." I gave him little choice.

"I will take you to him," Leacher conceded but looked very concerned.

We walked for longer than I could have imagined, and it made me realize just how massive this place was. There was a vague familiarity about it all, but when I tried to grasp on to why, it slipped away leaving me with a headache.

After several more twists and turns, staircases, and long hallways, I realized I would indeed have gotten very lost if I tried to find my way on my own. Eventually we stood in front of two large double doors guarded by soldiers.

At the sight of Leacher, they moved aside, but several of them stared wide eyed at me, unable to keep the shock from their faces.

The doors slowly screeched open, and I found myself standing at the exterior of a large throne room. There was one long carpeted center aisle, and on either side stood hundreds of whom I supposed were Skirsgard's nobility.

The women were all dressed in vastly different outfits from my own. Their long flowing dresses were an array of colors, but all were made of a gauze like fabric with lace edging and various patterns. The style consisted of a tight fitted bodice with a long skirt, nothing like the flowy silk dress I wore. I looked down at myself, and then at them all. The men wore funny coats which dipped longer in the back and appeared very formal. Something was off.

The door clanged shut and all eyes turned in my direction.

The prince stood on a dais in front of the crowd, an empty throne behind him. Even from the distance I could see his eyes widen and feel the fury radiating off of him. He was not happy to see me.

# CHAPTER 25

I walked slowly down the aisle, lifting my chin with a confidence I did not feel. I paid no attention to the murmurings and whisperings of those around me as I made my way toward the prince. Several shocked gasps erupted, as well as a few outraged complaints. But I only had eyes for the prince, and he for me.

I stood tall, not wanting to cower to these people and their grumbling. My hair spilled down my back in waves, and a part of me wanted to smile at the exhilaration of letting it down so boldly. For the first time since I could remember, I didn't have to hide.

As I reached the dais, the prince walked down the stairs to meet me. He slowly took me in, glancing from my head to toes and back up, but he didn't say a word. Anger simmered in his eyes, but something akin to satisfaction lingered as well.

He grabbed my elbow and leaned in, whispering in my ear.

"What are you doing here?" He spoke through clenched teeth.

"Well, if you hadn't hidden me away in that room, you wouldn't have to ask," I spoke loudly so that those closest could hear. Several people leaned in trying to listen, and others whispered to each other behind their hands.

"This is not a good time. Go back to your room, I will meet you there soon." The prince released my elbow, pushing me back toward the doors. I didn't comply.

"What's this about?" An older man with a droopy white mustache stepped forward. "Who have you been hiding here, Prince Ajax? If I didn't know any better, I'd say that's..." He leaned forward pulling out a singular eye glass, looking me over. His eyes went wide with shock, and he stumbled backward.

He whispered to a portly woman bedecked in jewels standing at his side.

"But how?" She gasped out.

The prince looked at the couple and then at me, a vein ticking in his jaw. He nodded to Demetri, who I only then noticed had been standing next to him on the dais.

"Deal with this," the prince commanded Demetri, gesturing to the crowd. He then grabbed my arm and practically dragged me out of the room.

The murmurs as we strode back down the aisle were louder now, with mutters of "could it be?" and "is that really her?" sticking out in my ears.

As soon as we left the throne room, I turned on the prince.

"What is going on?" I demanded. "Who am I?"

"That was dumb of you to come barging in like that. Don't you know anything about patience?" He seethed.

"Patience?" My voice reached the highest octave, "are you kidding me? You've taken me from my home, brought me here, I have been given no explanation, no common decency, nothing!" My anger boiled. I had never been a very patient person, but I felt like I deserved the title after the last week.

"And what are you doing out and about in your nightgown? As if the sight of you alone wasn't enough to stir up court drama," he huffed, ignoring my outrage for his own.

"My nightgown?" I looked down at the silken dress. No, this was not a dress, of course. My cheeks flushed from embarrassment.

"Not here," the prince looked around then once again pulled me down the hall. If he wasn't so strong, I would have fought him. Nevertheless, his grip, though firm, didn't hurt. Instead, the weight of his large hand warmed me through the thin silk of my sleeve.

We passed several doors until he pulled me through one, shutting and locking the door behind us. It was a small room, much less imposing than the others I'd seen so far. The walls were adorned with bookcases, stacked high with leather bound books. It was the prince's study.

A fire roared in the hearth, and a mahogany desk stood in the middle. Above the hearth was a worgel, mounted as though leaping through the air.

"Is that the same worgel?" I asked, open mouthed.

"I told you I sent it home," he stated.

I looked down at where the prince still held my arm, the silk bunching below his sizable fingers. I sucked in a breath, it suddenly felt very warm in here.

"You don't really need a fire going, when it's already so warm," I muttered, looking into his green eyes. He still held my elbow as if he was reluctant to let go.

"Am I making you hot, Meeka?" He smiled but it didn't meet his eyes, anger still simmering, making the green darken to emerald.

"You're making me mad," I retaliated.

He looked at where his hand wrapped around my elbow. Slowly letting go, the tips of his fingers gently brushed down my arm before dropping away. I felt the cold rush in at the absence of his touch and was hypocritically thankful for the fire, as shivers rushed down my spine.

"What's going on?" I demanded pulling away, letting my anger resurface.

"Think, Meeka." The prince strode to his desk, pouring a glass of amber liquid for us both. He handed me a glass then sat atop his desk.

"I don't want to think anymore, it hurts my head," I told him as I took a sip and then began coughing, "what is this stuff, it's nasty."

"It's plum brandy, a couple sips will help your headache, but I'd stop there." He downed his in one sip.

"You must have a mighty headache yourself," I raised my eyebrows at him. The side of his lip turned up.

"Has your magic returned?" He asked abruptly.

"I don't know anything about magic. I didn't even know there was magic. How could I have any?" I whined, stroking my face frustrated.

I leaned back against a bookshelf but hit it a bit too hard. A loosened book from a top shelf promptly fell, hitting me right in the head. "Of course, just my luck." I rubbed at where the book hit, sliding down to my knees and sitting on the floor.

*You deserved it.*

I sat up wide-eyed looking around, but again I was only hearing things.

The prince suppressed a low chuckle but came to my side, sitting next to me in the corner.

"Meeka," the prince grabbed my chin and turned my head toward his.

"Prince," I ground out.

"Call me Ajax," he looked at me with pleading eyes. I had never said his name. "Please," he added.

"No." The name would feel like a claim on my lips, but I didn't know what I was claiming. I wasn't ready to say it out loud. The prince's green eyes sparkled with an intensity that was hard to resist. He looked disappointed. He gestured to my hair.

"Have you still not remembered who you are?" He asked, reaching out and tucking a tress of my hair behind my ear. I tried not to lean into his hand.

"Can't you just tell me?" I implored, trying not to think of the way his touch made me want to close my eyes and lose myself.

He stood and I sighed. I didn't trust this man. He was a liar, I reminded myself. He had taken me from my home. Not to mention, he was the future king of a nation I knew little about.

The prince walked to his desk and took a key out of the top drawer. He turned toward another bookshelf and fumbled along the side until he came to a false set of books. He pulled back the spine on a large green tome, revealing a keyhole. He unlocked the secret box and pulled out a stack of papers.

After rifling through a few, he returned to where I sat on the floor. He handed me an oversized thick sheet of paper. No, it wasn't just any paper, it was a portrait.

I held the portrait in my hands taking time to look over each face. The memories hit me all at once and I closed my eyes against the rush. I felt dizzy.

Here was a portrait of my family. Not just Ma, Pa, and my siblings. No, here was a portrait of my whole family, my aunts and uncles, my cousins, my grandparents. But we weren't just any family. My Grandpa stood at the center, in full regalia, hair the same fiery shade of crimson as my own. My Grandfather – the king of Skirsgard.

That's right. A memory can never really die.

"Do you remember now, Princess?"

# CHAPTER 26

I stood up suddenly pointing my finger at the prince.

"You," my voice was thick with accusation, "your father was the late king. That means he led the revolution. He killed my family."

"The revolution killed your family. Unfortunately, my father was a part of that, yes." The prince was calm, too calm.

"But then why, why do you want me now?" Bile rose in my throat.

I remembered. I had been only a child, so the memories were blurry, but we had escaped in the night. The rest of my relatives weren't so lucky. My Pa, he was from the North, he knew a way out. Serafina hadn't escaped, neither had Alexendir. My grandparents, the king and queen – the revolutionaries killed them in the town center the day we fled. Ma told us my cousins were burned alive, that my aunts and uncles were brutally slaughtered with magic and acid. Only Pa and Ma got away. They took as many of us as they could.

"Meeka, the council discovered where your mother had been hiding all these years. The North has long been a refuge, as it stifles magic. It was only a matter of time until someone found you." He stood up and poured himself another glass of brandy, swallowing it down.

"So, that's why Ma was killed. Not because she slapped little Jimmy Horner." It made so much more sense.

Events began snapping into place, everything in my life – hiding my hair, living remote – it all made so much more sense. And yet I didn't feel the weight of his words, I didn't feel like royalty.

"Yes." The prince's voice was barely audible.

"And do you mean to kill me too?" I breathed.

"No, Meeka." He shook his head.

"Why did you take me? Why not my siblings?" I demanded. It didn't make sense. I wasn't the oldest. I wasn't even the youngest.

"You're the only one with red hair," the prince stated as if it explained anything at all.

"So?" I was growing tired of guessing. The memories had returned in a flood; it would take some time to sort through them all; to make sense of all that was happening. I rubbed my face.

"You must have been too young to remember the way of things in Skirsgard. The royal title was only passed to the one born with crimson hair. It meant the gods had chosen you," the prince explained.

"You mean to tell me-" but I couldn't finish. My breathing became shallow, shock settling in.

"Yes, Meeka, you are the rightful heir to the throne." The prince ran his hand through his hair.

"But you are the prince now – you are the heir. I don't want it." And I meant it. I didn't want anything to do with this life, this country. But then again, in my heart I didn't want to go back to the North either. I didn't belong there. But it didn't feel like I belonged here either.

"Whether you want it or not, many people in this country will still see you as the heir." He leaned back against the desk, crossing his legs and his arms.

"You should have killed me." I would have killed me. I was his enemy. I was the reason that he may no longer inherit the throne. I was the living challenge to his reign.

"I couldn't." He shook his head, emotions I didn't understand passing across his face.

"Your uncle wants me dead, doesn't he?" I asked, understanding now why he was trying to take me in the woods. Although, I wasn't sure why he didn't kill me outright.

"My uncle and the council see you as a threat, but I think there are other options." The prince looked up at the ceiling and sighed.

"I hardly blame him," I said sinking back down to the floor. It was true, I understood why they would kill me. I was the only one left to challenge the new regime. But I wish they could all understand I didn't want to rule. It had never even crossed my mind.

"Don't talk like that." The prince glared at me. He narrowed his eyes as if he were trying to read my mind. He looked puzzled.

"What will you do with me then?" I asked. If he wasn't going to kill me, what was left?

"Well, I'm trying to figure that out, but I think I have a solution." He continued to stare at me gauging my reaction.

"And what about what I want?" My eyebrows rose in challenge as I crossed my arms.

"You don't have that luxury." He shook his head again, annoyance in the lines of his face. "Don't you see? I took you before they could kill you."

My heart dropped at this truth. He had saved me in his own way. But was I safer here? I was a lamb brought before wolves.

"And will you tell me this solution of yours?" I asked under my breath. I wasn't sure what he would choose to do with me, but it felt like no matter what, I would be some sort of pawn in a greater game of kings and queens.

"You will find out soon enough." He ran his hand through that thick hair again.

"So, what am I supposed to do in the meantime, just wait?" I asked, indignation making my arms flail.

"Try not to die. You've already made yourself known at court barging into the throne room earlier, so it may be slightly more difficult than if you'd only listened to me." He pushed himself off the desk and walked behind, sitting in the leather chair.

"Well maybe if we'd had this conversation sooner, I wouldn't have done that," I argued.

"I was trying to let you rest. I wanted you to remember who you were on your own. I thought maybe if you stayed in your old room the memories would come on their own accord. I hoped it would be less of a shock." He put his feet on top of the desk, leaning back.

"I think you were just scared, prince," I snapped.

"I think you are the scared one, princess," he growled back.

"So, I'm just supposed to trust you? You killed my family, you kidnapped me, and still you keep me in the dark about what you plan to do with me," I huffed.

"I didn't kill your family. I was just a child back then, too. Besides, I have no fond feelings for my late father, trust me." There was pain in his eyes. Maybe his childhood hadn't been so easy either.

"I don't know what I'm supposed to think," I spoke truthfully.

"You are forgetting one very important thing." The prince gave me a pointed look.

He stood up from his chair and walked to where I still sat on the floor. He reached out a hand, offering it to me. I hesitated, but this time I was too tired to fight. I grabbed his hand and let him pull me to standing.

"And what am I forgetting?" I sighed.

"That fiery hair of yours, the hair that names you heir – it means more than just being next in line to the throne." He gave me a weighted look.

"What else does it mean, then?" I narrowed my eyes.

"It means, Meeka, that you are extremely powerful."

# CHAPTER 27

The prince walked me back to my rooms in silence. I was too lost in thought and memories to speak. I needed some food, and some time to sort through all this information.

Looking around the palace now, I was struck with the familiarity struck, but the images were still hazy, the palace had looked different back then. Portraits and tapestries had adorned the walls, there had been children's voices and laughter floating through the space. Now everything was dull and grey and serious. If this had once been home, it no longer felt that way.

When I returned to my rooms, I shut the door and closed my eyes breathing in the heartache of my past. My family had survived the revolution, but not my aunts and uncles, my cousins, and not the king and queen. The rebels had killed them all. And I couldn't remember why. I had been too young. Once we escaped, no one had talked of our time in Skirsgard. The Old Country had become more myth than reality.

Had my parents forgotten as well when they went North, or did they pack that time so far away in the recesses of their minds?

I was struck with an image of the prince and his men taking off the rings around their neck before traveling through the tree. So we don't forget in the North. Ah, so maybe the North made everyone forget. Maybe those rings were a way of protection.

It didn't even matter. Ma was dead. Ma with her red hair, which meant she had been next in line to the throne.

Now here I was, back in Skirsgard for what purpose? Was I in as much danger as the prince feared? I never thought I would, but I missed the simpler days when my only worries were getting food in my belly.

I'd never given much thought to my future, only that I didn't want to be stuck in that small town, living the same boring life generations after generations. I had wanted adventure – and wasn't that what I was getting now? I sighed inwardly. I suppose I would just play the game while I decided what it was that I wanted. Prince Ajax could go to hells for all I cared. He thought it was his choice what became of me, but only I would choose my fate.

*Aren't you forgetting something?*

I whirled around. This voice was driving me crazy, but it could only be from within my own mind.

"What do you want?" I grabbed my head, squeezing my eyes shut.

*Have you always been so dramatic?*

Just then Trafi entered the rooms. Seeing my state she rushed to my side, though still didn't look me in the eye.

"What's the matter, miss?"

"This voice," I started but then realized I must sound crazy, "never mind." I clenched my jaw and took a deep breath trying to gather my bearings.

"Is it your opeki? Has it returned?" Trafi asked, a touch of excitement in her voice.

"I don't know what an opeki is, Trafi." I tried to place the word from my memories, but once again, I was too young when I'd been here last, my memories too green to comprehend.

"Your magic, I mean, your opeki gives you magic." Trafi helped me up, steadying me, while looking at her shoes.

"I don't know what you mean, I'm just hearing things." I shook my head.

I couldn't stay in this room any longer. Too many confusing memories threatened to consume me. I needed something to eat.

I took off the silk nightgown. I didn't have any other clothes except the ones I had traveled in – but those would have to do. I adorned the pants, boots, and dirty tunic, thankful they were still in the bathing room. I didn't wear my fur as it was far too warm for the heavy southern air.

I opened the door to my chambers to find Leacher had been replaced by a different guard.

"Ah, prin-" the guard began.

"Don't you start with me. I'm going to get some food," I interrupted him, sticking my finger in his face.

"Yes, I suppose you would be hungry. I was going to inform you the prince is waiting for you in the dining hall," he spoke out in an elegant voice. I gave him a look over.

"What's your name?" I asked.

"Captain Bellamoni, head of the prince's personal guard," he bowed in my direction.

"If you are head of the prince's guard then why are you watching me?" My eyebrows rose, waiting for his response.

"Prince's orders," he replied simply. He had a friendly smile and was dashingly handsome. His hair was the color of rich honey, and it flopped over his brow. He was tall and muscular. A good-looking captain. I approved. I smiled and nodded.

"Lead the way," I gestured for him to lead.

"The prince wanted you to see if you could remember your way around," Captain Bellamoni stood waiting for me.

"He did, did he?" I murmured with annoyance. I had only been eight years old when I left the palace and the prince assumed I could find my way around? Well, I didn't back down from a challenge so I supposed I would try.

"Tell me about your prince," I asked Captain Bellamoni as he followed me through the imposing palace halls.

"What would you like to know?" He replied, not correcting me when I opened a door to a large ballroom. I was going the wrong way.

"What's he like?" I continued down a different hallway, trying to look for any signs to spark my recognition. Everything looked the same with no adornments.

"I'm his sworn guard," Captain Bellamoni stated.

"Obviously," I gave him a sideways look, "But can you tell me if he is nice? Is he mean? does he have any weird habits or violent tendencies I should be worried about?"

"It would be well advised to fear him," Captain Bellamoni chuckled, "he once went in the wrestling ring with a lion. The lion didn't make it out alive."

I frowned. I wasn't sure what to think of that.

"Is he cruel then?" I asked.

Captain Bellamoni laughed.

"The prince is a man of action. The revolution toughened all those who survived. None of us in Skirsgard are soft. But he is not cruel, no. He bears a heavy weight on his shoulders." Captain Bellamoni slowed behind me as we came to a large, gilded door.

"This is it then?" I asked half giving myself credit for leading us in the right direction, but also reluctantly knowing the captain had helped steer me. He simply nodded.

"I like you, Captain Bellamoni," I smiled at him. He beamed down at me with equally open affection.

"Shall we go in?" The captain asked.

"I suppose we must," I shrugged. The captain stepped in front of me and gestured. The door opened at his silent command. Magic.

I wasn't sure what I had expected – but it hadn't been this. There were so many people in the room. It was not just one dining table, but several. I groaned.

"This is too many people to enjoy one's meal," I whispered to the captain.

"Would you rather I called your meal to your rooms?" He asked sincerely.

"No. If the prince can enter a lion's den and survive, so can I," I winked at him and strode into the room.

# CHAPTER 28

Of the many tables lining the room, one stood out larger than the rest. Prince Ajax sat in the middle, looking bored. He didn't notice me enter, or if he had, he paid no attention.

He was leaning against the back of his chair, one arm holding a glass of wine, the other strewn across the seat next to him. In that seat sat a woman - a young woman who was exceedingly beautiful. Her long black hair flowed past her waist as she leaned across and whispered something in the prince's ear.

His eyes snapped to mine. I turned quickly away.

I spotted Demetri by a table in the opposite direction and headed that way. Captain Bellamoni followed.

"Ah, Meeka, there you are!" Demetri exclaimed meeting me halfway across the room. I was very aware of the murmuring occurring throughout the room as others noticed my presence.

"Demetri," I nodded to him. He looked down at my dirty clothes, holding in a smile, but was perceptive enough not to comment.

"Would you care for a drink? I see you've wrapped Captain Bellamoni around your finger – that didn't take long," he gave the captain a wink.

"The captain is my escort on the prince's orders and yes, we get along fine even if I am a prisoner here. And I would like a drink. What is that?" I gestured to the purple liquid Demetri was holding.

"This is no drink for a lady," Demetri took a large swig then winced, "its elderflower liquor, and it is not for the faint of heart."

"Luckily my heart is strong," I grabbed the drink from his hand, "I'll have yours."

I took a sip too enthusiastically and started coughing. The liquid burned down my throat. Demetri and Captain Bellamoni both started laughing. "Never mind, you're right. That's disgusting." I handed the drink back to Demetri.

"Easy tiger," Captain Bellamoni laughed, "I'm supposed to keep you alive, don't get me in trouble now."

"No promises," I smiled up at him.

Demetri chuckled.

"That hair isn't the only fiery thing about you, that's for sure," Demetri put his arm around me, "Come, let's get some food, and relieve your protector for a time." Demetri steered me away from Captain Bellamoni who nodded and retreated to the corner of the room.

We made our way to a table that was overflowing with decadent amounts of food. There were birds in cream sauce, shredded meat with pickled beets, various breads and pastries, cooked vegetables in lemon, and other dishes I'd never seen before.

"Do you always eat like this?" I asked, stomach growling.

"Fortunately, yes." Demetri grabbed a plate, handing it to me then took one for himself. "Pile your plate as high as you'd like."

"I've never seen this much food at once," I was all but drooling. "At least that I remember," I added.

"Well, get used to it, princess," Demetri patted me on the back, but I winced at the title. He didn't seem to notice.

Demetri walked down the table, pointing at foods which moved on their own accord to his plate. I tried not to be shocked at the casual use of magic but instead used my fingers to place the delicacies.

We found a table and sat, eating in silence. Demetri must have been hungry from the journey, as well. I knew I was.

I ate until my belly was beyond full. The amount of food was excessive, but I couldn't complain.

"Didn't the revolution occur because the people were upset with such opulence?" I asked Demetri. He looked up at me in surprise.

"Well, yes," he said slightly ashamed, "have your memories returned then?"

I nodded, "I'm still making sense of them all," I sighed.

"And your magic?" He asked, leaning slightly away from me.

"I still don't know why everyone thinks I have any," I took the last of my bread and used it to wipe my plate clean. "Although I seem to be hearing voices."

"Ah your opeki," Demetri stated matter of fact, "your magic is returning then."

"I suppose we shall wait and see." Of the memories that had surfaced, there wasn't anything about magic. I don't remember ever using it, having it, or learning about it. I still didn't know much about this country – what the magic here even was or who possessed it, but I would learn.

"Does everyone in Skirsgard have magic?" I asked curious.

"Most do, some stronger than others. Some especially strong," he glanced at my hair.

"Then you have it?" I questioned.

"Of course," he stated, "do you want to see some?"

I nodded eagerly. Demetri pushed his seat back a bit and brought his hands below the table, hiding them. "The council doesn't like us using our magic, unless it's for basic conveniences," he explained.

"How come?" I asked confused. What was the point of having magic if you weren't allowed to use it.

"The old regime was very opulent with their uses. Now there are a lot of laws surrounding who can use their magic and when," he shrugged.

"That doesn't seem quite right," I mused.

"Besides, they think the opeki are beneath us. Anyway, watch," Demetri smiled as he held his palms out. He flexed his fingers, and a tiny little world appeared on the inside of his hand. First, he created a pool of water, then added a tiny mound of earth, which sprouted with green herbs before my eyes. Next a flame appeared, burning it up and causing the water to sizzle. The water steamed, turning purple, then became a rolling bubble of liquid which he poured into his glass. Elderberry liquor.

"Did you just make wine?" I asked laughing.

"Shh, don't tell anyone, it's against the law," he winked at me, grinning.

"So, you are one of the stronger ones with magic?" I wondered.

"Not so much, that was just a trick, though I'm not half bad," he took a sip of the liquor, "oh, stop complaining."

"I'm not complaining." I scoffed, affronted.

"No, not you. Baylor – my opeki." he sighed.

"Your opeki? Your magic?" I tried piecing together what Trafi had called her magic. "Magic is a person? You can talk to it?"

*What do you think, I'm just some psychotic delusion?*

*Well, yeah*, I thought to myself.

Or maybe I thought it to whatever this thing was that seemed to be in my head. I really was going mad.

"I forget how little you know," Demetri pursed his lips, "your opeki isn't a person, it's more like a guardian. A little piece of the gods assigned to give you magic – and sometimes to annoy the heck out of you." Demetri laughed and rolled his eyes.

"So, I'm not crazy..." I mused.

"Is that what you thought?" Demetri sat up straight.

"I thought I was going mad." I laughed but felt unsettled at the thought that this creature could be inside my head.

*You'll learn to love me.*

"So, people with strong magic have strong opekis?" I furrowed my brow.

"Pretty much," Demetri shrugged taking another sip of his elderberry wine. "Since they are from the realm of the gods, we believe the gods have blessed some more than others. That red hair of yours – that means you have a very strong opeki. Strong enough to rule."

"And the prince? Is his opeki strong?" I looked to where the prince still sat next to the lovely woman. His head was thrown back in laughter. I narrowed my eyes, trying not to be bothered. Demetri followed my line of sight then looked at me with eyebrows raised. I ignored him.

"Yes, Ajax has the most powerful magic in the country. Well, he did at least," Demetri glanced again at me, curiosity alight in his eyes.

*And the most powerful thighs.* I spit out the water I was attempting to sip.

"You ok?" Demetri eyed me.

"Fine," I murmured.

*You can't say things like that,* I tried mind-whispering to my opeki. It felt weird but oddly natural.

"His family killed mine," I stated without emotion. It was a fact, and I didn't know how to feel about it. Demetri sat forward suddenly looking serious.

"Meeka, it was war. But the war is over. Try not to blame us too much," he spoke softly.

"Then whom do I blame?" I whispered.

"The idealists," he scoffed. I wasn't sure what to make of that answer.

He wasn't entirely wrong about the war, though. I knew bad things happened during war. It was hard to put the blame all on one side. My family had been the ruling family – they would suffer the results.

Now two young children on opposite sides found each other grown up and tangled together. It was a mess.

"And was the revolution successful? Did they get everything they wanted while my family suffered the consequences?" I asked swallowing hard, not sure if I wanted to know the answer.

"You can decide for yourself," he said cryptically. I scoffed. More half-answered questions.

I looked again toward the prince, debating if I should go talk to him. He was still deep in conversation, and my food suddenly wasn't sitting so comfortably in my stomach.

"I think I will go to bed," I told Demetri.

"Goodnight, princess," he sighed at the scowl on my face. "Find Captain Bellamoni, he will take you back to your rooms."

*You're no fun.* My opeki sighed.

I ignored it.

"So much for the lot of you being any help," I stood to find the captain.

"Meeka," Demetri's voice was somber.

"What?" I turned back toward him.

"There is something else you should know," he looked as though he was warring with himself as to whether he should continue.

"And what is it? Spit it out," I told him, perturbed, bitterness sitting heavy on my tongue.

"The prince," he glanced sideways at me, "is soon to be married."

# CHAPTER 29

The next morning, Trafi entered my room with a tray piled high with more food than I could possibly eat. She set it down on the table by the hearth and briefly left. She reentered the room with an armful of dresses.

"Your highness," she stared at her feet, "Price Ajax told me to burn your clothes."

"I'm sure he did," I grumbled, getting out of bed, trying not to wince at the title. "I'm surprised the prince even noticed what I was wearing last night."

"It was hard to miss," Trafi pointed out, shrugging.

"I suppose he doesn't want to see me in that attire anymore. Nothing to remind me of the North," I grunted.

"No one wants to see you in those anymore," Trafi asserted.

"Hmph," I groaned. For one so meek as Trafi, she didn't suppress her opinion.

"Besides, I don't think the prince misses anything you do," she said cryptically.

I sat at the table, popping a cinnamon pastry into my mouth.

"This is delicious," I exclaimed.

"It's Prince Ajax' favorite," she smiled. Though she wouldn't look at me, I could see amusement in the corner of her eyes.

"Right," I fumbled with the pastry then put it on the plate. "What's on the agenda for today, Trafi?"

"Agenda?" She asked perplexed.

"Yes, what am I supposed to be doing all day?" I tried not to sound on edge, even though I felt like I was standing on a precipice.

"Oh," Trafi began laying out dresses on the bed, "well, nothing."

"You mean I'm just supposed to sit here all day?"

"Well, there is a council meeting, but I didn't think you'd want to attend." Trafi glanced at me but looked away before I could meet her eyes.

"I will attend," I stated.

"Then here," she gestured to a particular dress. It was made of a dark green silk layered with chiffon. Attached was a corseted bodice with capped sleeves. There were tiny daisies embroidered into the bodice of yellows, reds, and golds. It would make my fiery hair stand out. "This is perfect."

I was reluctant but nodded to Trafi in agreement. "Very well."

The dress fit snug, emphasizing my figure, while flowing out until it met the floor. I was slightly uncomfortable, but I took a deep breath mustering courage. If I was the lost heir of Skirsgard I needed to look the part.

Captain Bellamoni met me outside my rooms.

"Take me to the council meeting," I demanded with a small smile.

"Look at you, one day a princess and already commanding armies," Captain Bellamoni chuckled.

"I'd hardly call you an army," I brushed my skirts down.

"You should see me fight," he winked.

"Are all Skirsgard men this arrogant?" I teased.

"Of course," he quirked his lip but gestured for me to lead the way.

"I don't know where to go," I confessed.

"Right. I'll lead." He bowed slightly then marched down the hall. I followed.

I took a steadying breath. The thought of confronting the council made my palms sweat, but they couldn't deny that I was here now and alive. I couldn't hide forever.

No matter who I had been in the North, in the South I was the heir to Skirsgard, whether they wanted me here or not.

"You ok?" Captain Bellamoni queried.

"Oh, just contemplating if they will kill me now or later," I attempted a smile.

"Ajax will protect you." He stated with a confidence I didn't feel.

"Or is he the one I should be afraid of?" I mumbled.

Captain Bellamoni didn't answer but looked at me quizzically.

"What?" I questioned.

"I wouldn't worry about Ajax, your highness." Captain Bellamoni rubbed his chin.

"I suppose he hasn't killed me yet. I should be grateful," I grumbled.

"He saved your life, princess. If you don't mind me reminding you." He raised his eyebrows.

I shrugged, pushing off the feeling of guilt. My emotions were so mixed when it came to the prince, it was easier to shove them away.

Instead of admitting to the captain that he might be right, I inquired how much longer it would take to get there.

"It's the next hall to the right."

We stopped in front of the doors leading to the council room, where the only portrait I'd yet to see in the whole palace stood imposingly large on the wall.

"That's prince Ajax' father, the late King." Captain Bellamoni explained.

He was a striking man. Handsome, like his son. But there was a vicious gleam in his eye that looked inhuman. I shuddered.

"Let's go in."

"I'm afraid I'm not allowed in, your highness, but here," the captain gestured to the doors, which opened with his magic. I nodded in thanks and entered.

The room was smaller than what seemed to be the norm in the palace. Instead of marble, the walls were adorned in a rich wood that reminded me of the trees we traveled through, and I wondered if it was the same.

A group of men, mostly in soldiers garb sat around a large circular table.

"But marriage? Now? Is that really the best thing-" the man addressing the room broke off as all heads turned. "Your highness," he mumbled awkwardly, glancing at his peers as he took a seat.

"Princess," an old man stood slowly, "allow me to welcome you. My name is Lieutenant Barrow. I knew you as a child." He trudged along, hunched over, to where I stood still in the doorway. He bowed deeply, his hand across his chest.

I stood there uncertain what to do, staring down at this man who bowed before me. There were a few murmurs around the table, and I looked up to meet a table full of men staring. I glanced at each of them. There were twelve in total.

My eyes landed on the prince. I was surprised to see him looking amused.

"Continue," I waved off Lieutenant Barrow, who sauntered back to the table taking a seat.

I found a chair on the outskirts of the room and picked it up, dragging it toward the table. A hand on my shoulder stopped me, gently pushing me away and taking the chair from my hands.

"That won't do, your highness. Let me." A young man met my eyes, a gleam there I recognized instantly, matching the voice I knew only too well. Captain Fintir, my captor.

"Have we met?" I faked a smile.

"We've not had the pleasure," his eyes held a note of defiance as he brought my hand to his lips and kissed my palm. "Captain Fintir"

"You look very familiar, Captain, but I can carry my own chair." I grabbed the chair back from him, dragging it along the floor. It screeched in the silence of the room.

"As I said, continue?" I asked looking at the man who had been speaking when I entered the room.

"Ah, yes, Colonol Yntil, at your service." The man stood, giving the prince a glare before continuing. "Like I was saying before, we do not need to rush into any hasty agreements."

"Colonol," the prince jumped to his feet, "let's move on to other matters." He glanced at me and I glared back.

"Very well. There is of course the issue of the coronation. Now that you are back from your escapades." Colonol Yntil sat down gesturing to the prince's uncle to take over.

"It should be soon." He stated coldly.

The council erupted in argument. The prince sat back and sighed.

Lieutenant Barrow pounded his fist on the table. The room silenced, waiting for him to stand. "There is a matter we all seem to be ignoring."

"And what is that?" The prince's uncle asked.

"With the princess back, will the people even support prince Ajax' rule?"

# CHAPTER 30

I spent the next several days avoiding the prince and trying to remember the ins and outs of the palace. My memories were slowly piecing together, and with them a new confidence.

"Trafi, I'm going out, but I need something to wear that isn't so...regal." I looked down at the opulent dress Trafi had made me wear.

"Riding clothes, miss?" She asked as if I knew what riding clothes were.

"Sounds delightful," I smirked. It wasn't so much that I minded wearing the dresses, but it wasn't something I was used to. In the North, we dressed for warmth. Here, the ladies dressed to show off. But where I was going, I needed something less noticeable, so I could move with ease. Hopefully these riding clothes would be the answer.

"I'll return shortly," Trafi bowed and left.

While waiting for Trafi, I went about the room, opening cabinets and drawers, searching not out of necessity but out of boredom. I had already gone through all the cupboards and wardrobes several times, and once again concluded that no one had been occupying these rooms for some time, as they were completely devoid of anything.

*What are you looking for?*

Ah, so now you speak. Where have you been the last few days? I spoke back in my mind.

*Why would I have spoken with you? You've done nothing.*

*I suppose you could have helped me by offering some information. No one else seems to.* I scoffed.

*I don't owe you anything.*

*But aren't you mine?* I asked.

*Yours? I don't belong to you, and you don't belong to me.*

*Then why are you in my head?* I frowned.

A noise like a laugh echoed around me.

*I'm not in your head. I'm a bodiless power. I can come and go wherever I want, whenever I want. In your head...how vain.*

*I just assumed...* I murmured slightly embarrassed. *So, anyone can hear you?*

*Only you and the other opeki.*

*Why me?* I questioned trying to keep up with its logic.

*Because that's the way the gods have willed it.*

*And what are you?*

*I am a Queen of my own right.*

Trafi returned carrying several different outfits. I rifled through them, until I came upon a black linen dress. The dress flowed generously, had no sleeves, and ended above my knees. This would have to do. How any of these dresses were riding clothes made no sense, until Trafi left and came back with several pairs of black linen pants. Aha.

"Thanks, Trafi, these are better," I smiled at her, though she still wouldn't look me in the eye.

*What do you think?* I asked the opeki but got no response. It was a fickle creature.

I put on the black linen shirt dress, the pants, and then my boots, which hadn't been burned with my other clothing. I tied back my hair with a strip of leather, then frowned. If I was to go into the city, I would need to hide my hair. If I had learned anything, it was that the red hair would stick out here just as much as in the North.

"Trafi, I need a scarf," I stated. She nodded, left, then came back with an array of scarves. "The black one I think." I grabbed a black silken scarf from her pile, then dismissed her before tying up my hair.

There was a mirror in the bathing room, which had taken some getting used to. I stared at myself now, not quite recognizing the young woman I saw starting back. I tucked in a few loose strands of crimson then nodded; this would do.

A guard would be stationed at my door, and I wasn't sure I was allowed to leave the palace grounds. I would climb through the window, down the wall, and into the gardens. I was confident it could be done with ease.

The window proved more difficult to open than expected, but once I figured out how to twist the metal mechanism, the glass sprang free. I wiggled out onto a small ledge, then scooted across the outer wall until I came to a rose vine growing up the side of the palace.

I looked out around the gardens, careful not to be seen, but the gardens were empty. Luckily the palace was made of dark grey stone, and the black of my clothes blended in with the wall.

I shimmied down the vine as quietly as I could. My head pounded and I had the distinct feeling it was not my first time scaling these walls. I lost footing a few times, scraping my hands against the thorns. Blood dripped down my forearm where a thorn penetrated my skin.

I was almost to the bottom when I heard voices drifting through a nearby window. I could make it to the ground, go my own way, and be out of the palace for the day, or I could shimmy over to the window and eavesdrop. Curiosity got the better of me, and I shuffled my feet along a small ridge.

"-is almost up if you don't bring it soon." A scratchy voice grated against my ears. I had heard that voice before. The hair on the back of my neck stood up. I couldn't peak into the window without being seen, so instead I crouched to the side, trying not to breathe.

That voice – it sounded like the shadow I had met at the inn.

"She's here now; it will be done." It was the prince's uncle speaking, that sneak. I clenched my jaw. I knew he wanted me dead, but this was something else entirely – and I had a dreadful feeling the 'she' they were speaking of referred to me.

"Do it quick and your debt will be paid," the shadow seethed.

Footsteps approached the open window, and I froze. Panic flared deep within my core. A hand reached out, grabbing the handle on the glass, pulling it closed.

I let out the breath I'd been holding, grateful that I hadn't been spotted. I was too afraid to move for several minutes, but eventually my limbs slackened, and I was able to shimmy back to the vine and make my final descent.

Do you know what that thing is? I asked my opeki, but got no response. I sighed and continued.

It was relatively easy to navigate through the gardens to the outer wall of the palace. I kept low to the ground, dodging between bushes, but other than the random guard here and there, I saw no one.

When I arrived at the outer stone wall, my shoulders slumped. The stone was too slick to climb. I ran my hands along the surface, hoping to remember something from my childhood that would help me now.

I continued along the wall, stroking the cool dark stone. I felt a few notches here and there, but nothing big enough to make a good foothold. I looked to my side at the tall silver birch jutting skyward. There was something familiar about this tree. I had played here before, I knew it. There would be a patch of clovers a little way ahead, and a small stream that trickled through the grates into the city.

That was it. The stream, if my memory was correct, I could squeeze through the grates and escape.

I continued walking along the wall, until I heard the trickle of flowing water. Sure enough, there was a stream up ahead. A grate pressed into the outer wall, allowing the water to pass out of the palace grounds. Only, there was no way in the hells I would be able to fit through the bars. Maybe when I had been a small child, but now - impossible.

I waded into the stream and knelt, holding the cool metal of the grate in my hands. My boots repelled water, but even so a small bit trickled its way down my ankle, cooling my toes. I sighed. If only the grate would open. I closed my eyes and leaned my head back. I was a prisoner in my own palace.

Metal groaned beneath my fingers. I snapped my eyes open in surprise to find the grate had broken off its hinges.

I threw the metal down, climbing through the small tunnel and into the city streets. The grate must have rusted over to pop off so easily, but I wasn't complaining. I was free.

*You're welcome.* My opeki finally spoke.

# CHAPTER 31

The city of Tyev was nothing like I remembered. In truth, I only had vague recollections of riding through the streets in a horse pulled carriage. Large, imposing buildings lined wide avenues made not of dirt and hay as in the North, but stone and gravel. There had been an enormous fountain in the heart of the city with a statue of my grandfather in the center.

A vivid memory surfaced – children played in the fountain while I stood across the street on the steps of the opera house as my grandfather gave a speech. I didn't listen to what he was saying. I watched the children splashing and laughing, wishing I could join. But I wasn't allowed; I was never allowed to do normal things. I shook away the memories.

It was an unnerving phenomenon to suddenly know whisps of a past life. My adolescence had not been shaped by those experiences. Rather it felt as though there were two of me. I did not know how to reconcile them both.

I shrugged off the nostalgia and ducked across the street encircling the outer wall of the palace. I made sure my scarf was pulled tight around my hair while advancing through a series of alleyways before spilling out on a main thoroughfare. I didn't know where I was going, but if this was supposed to be my city, surely, I couldn't get lost.

In my vague memories, the city was full of life and color. Looking around now, all I saw were grey buildings, some falling apart, with shops in various states of disarray.

Citizens roamed the streets in tattered clothing, beggars gathered on the corners, and trash accumulated along the walkways. This was not the city I remembered as a child.

After wandering for some time, my stomach growled but I realized I hadn't brought any centiar – not that I had any to bring. I spotted a line of people wrapping around a corner up ahead, the smell of onions wafting in the air.

"What are you waiting in this line for?" I asked a man near the back. He looked me up and down, his shadowed eyes casting a wary gaze.

"Food, miss," He turned back toward the line, looking down at his feet. His toes poked through the holes in his boots.

I didn't wait but followed the line, turning the corner. There was a table with several servers dishing ladles of a stew-like substance. The people shuffled along, grabbing a chunk of bread and a soggy bowl of the mush. I wouldn't eat with them. Not that I thought I was too good to be among them - I had spent my fair share of time starving - but I was able to eat at the palace and would save the food for those who needed it more.

"I'll be back tomorrow."

I started at the familiar voice, ducking behind a group of women who shot me irritated glances, but I ignored them. I knew that voice.

I peered out around one particularly thin woman's shoulder, keeping my head low. Prince Ajax stood tall amongst the other servers. He was removing an apron, speaking animatedly to a few of the workers. I narrowed my eyes, confusion settling in. Did these people know their prince was among them? Or maybe here he was Johnny Pullver once again.

Taking several steps backward, I did my best to flee without being spotted. Making sure my scarf was still tight, I hurried away before being caught.

Not knowing where else to go, I decided I'd find the fountain from my memories.

I wandered through streets and alleyways, keeping my distance from others while quietly observing the conditions of the city. There were lively pockets, flags of the revolutionaries strewn across the streets, shops still swarming with customers. But overall, there was a sadness weighing down over the city like a cloud. It was a heavy weight, as though these people were carrying too much pain on their shoulders.

I didn't know anything about what happened after the revolution, though I couldn't help but think this heaviness was related. A pain emanated from my chest, concern blossoming where I did not want it.

As I grew closer to the center of the city, the buildings grew in grandeur. Larger stone structures with columns became the norm as the streets grew wider. It was a beautiful place, but I wasn't sure it was mine.

The buildings gave way to an open square, and whether it was muscle memory or simply the inevitability of reaching the center, the fountain I'd been searching for loomed tall in my sight, drawing me toward it like a compass. Only now, no water flowed, and no statue of my grandfather stood in the center.

Derelicts roamed the square, some sleeping on the lip of the fountain. The opera house still stood across the street in all its glory, except now the steps were littered with vagrants and pestilent birds looking for food. The city and its people had fallen into neglect.

I would have some choice words with the prince. But then I remembered him feeding the poor. I shook away my line of thinking. It was dangerous to care.

I had seen enough. It was time to get back to the palace before my absence was noted – though no one seemed to care very much about my activities or lack there of in the past days.

Turning around, I went back the way I came. Or at least I thought I did, but after a few wrong turns here and there, I found myself down a darkened alley I hadn't previously transited.

"For a centiar I can read your heart's desires?" A thin man stepped out of the shadows, blowing out smoke. I shook my head, trying to hurry past.

He brought forth his hand, puffing a cloud of fire and smoke on his palm. It was difficult to tell if this were true magic or a trick.

"The only thing my heart desires is for you to leave me be," I stated, walking quickly away.

As I traveled further into the alley, more doorways opened offering everything from trinkets and indulgences to services I'd rather not know existed. I wanted to get away from this place. A hand grabbed my wrist turning me forcefully.

"Girl-" a man yanked me vigorously into an alcove, "I recognize you." He narrowed his eyes and yanked the scarf off my head. His eyes went wide, and he dropped my hand, backing away slowly. "What – it can't be."

Before I could respond and make up an excuse for my hair, I was yet again firmly pulled away, this time through a door in the wall.

Stumbling forward, the door clicked shut behind me. A burly woman, dressed in all green quickly turned the lock.

"You have returned," she stated. She looked at me expectantly, her eyes darkened with kohl.

"I don't think I've ever been here before," I mumbled in reply.

We stood in a small apartment, wood floors marred with scratches and dents from repeated use, wallpaper hanging from the ceiling in tatters. There was a small stove in the corner and a washbasin on a stand. A round table stood in the middle of the room, with four bentwood chairs.

"Sit," the woman gestured, "I will make you tea."

"Do you have any cookies?" I asked optimistically, my fear giving way to hunger as soon as I knew this lady was offering refreshments. I bit my lip as she gave me an incredulous stare.

"Cookies?" she chuckled, "goodness, no, child. But I have some potato pita, I will prepare it."

"No, no, that won't be necessary. Tea is fine. And if you don't mind telling me exactly who you are and what you want with me?" I tried not to sound rude, but I'd never liked potatoes.

I was thankful she rescued me from that man, though, so I supposed I owed her a thank you. Then again, she had pulled me into her home with no explanation and could be as big a threat for all I knew.

"In time, child. I will first bring the tea." She turned toward the small stove and began soaking the leaves.

I fiddled with my fingers while bouncing my knee, not sure if I was in danger, but the woman seemed kind, so I would do my best to be trusting. However, that did not prevent me from devising an exit strategy in my mind.

A small door creaked open to the side of the stove and a thick, hairy, man emerged.

"Thanks, sweetheart," he spoke to the woman, kissing her on the cheek. He grabbed a coat hanging on a hook next to the door then turned back toward the woman "oh, I almost forgot. Here," he threw her a centiar and left the apartment. My eyes went wide at the exchange.

"You're a woman of the night?" I asked, surprised.

"You think I live like this by choice?" She asked, amused. My cheeks flushed, but she only chuckled and brought a tea pot, setting it on the table.

"So, you have returned," she said as she poured us tea.

"I don't know what you mean." I took a deep sip of the green liquid. It tasted like grass, but I held my tongue and swallowed.

"Your family fled, but now the princess has returned," she stated. I almost spit out my tea, which would have been to my benefit if it didn't feel impolite.

"How do you know who I am?" I asked.

"It's not difficult to recognize you." She gestured to my hair, amusement alight in her eyes. "What do you plan on doing now that you're back?"

"I don't know," I replied honestly.

"Will you fight for the crown?" She looked genuinely interested.

"I would rather not." I took another sip of the tea trying not to gag.

"It's been ten years since the revolution. It hasn't served the people. The old way didn't work either, though," she mused.

"And what do you expect me to do about it?" I sighed, the pain in my chest flaring. How could I care about these people? And yet, how could I not?

"You are the rightful heir." A statement not a question.

"A fact I only just learned. The prince has been groomed for the role; he can handle it alone." I thought of the prince among his people, laughing with the servers earlier today.

"Can he?" A bemused smile. I narrowed my eyes. I didn't like the sense that she could read me so easily.

"Well, he won't be alone. Soon, he'll be married." I tried to mask the disappointment I didn't want to feel in the first place.

"Interesting." She sipped her tea, dark eyes analyzing.

I felt a slip of something pass through my mind. She was using magic.

"Are you using magic on me?" I asked affronted.

"Just a small amount," She shrugged as though it were not an intrusion. She had been playing on my emotions this whole time. I stood abruptly, angered.

"The tea was disgusting." I slammed the cup down, leaving the small apartment in a rage. She didn't stop me.

Fuming, I wiped sweat off my brow as I continued down the dark alley, desperate to reach a main road. I turned the corner and crashed into a hard wall, falling to the ground.

Only it wasn't a wall. It was a child.

"Sorry," I stammered, unaware how this small figure sent me toppling to the ground.

He flicked out a knife and held it to my chest.

"Don't move," the child's voice was deep and rough, the voice of a man not a boy.

"What the-" I began as the boy/man undulated, turning into a large serpent. The thing coiled as if ready to strike. I backed away frantically.

I covered my head with my arms, waiting for an attack that never came. I blinked my eyes open, but the serpent was now lying on the floor unconscious. No longer a serpent, the limp body was in the form of a pockmarked man with a thin greasy mustache.

Above the man, brick in hand, stood prince Ajax.

# CHAPTER 32

"Did you hit him with a brick?" I asked stunned.

"It does the job," he walked toward me and held out a hand. My fingers slid into his as he pulled me to standing.

"Demetri said you have the most powerful magic in the country. Why didn't you use it?" I brushed the dirt off my clothing.

"Demetri should mind his own business," prince Ajax ground out.

"Well, why didn't you? I've yet to see you in action," my eyebrows rose, questioning.

"You'd like to see me in action, now, would you?" He had a wicked gleam in his eye as he stepped closer. My heart raced, but instead of continuing forward, he threw me a scarf. "I hate to have you cover your hair, but it's probably a good idea until we get back to the palace."

I didn't argue as I tied the crimson tresses back under the purple scarf, which wasn't a scarf at all but the sash the prince had been wearing around his waist. I tried not to blush as the fabric caressed my face, thinking of where else it had recently touched.

"I'm not lost, by the way," I let him know as he steered me back toward the palace, "I know perfectly where I was going. How did you find me?"

The prince snorted, not believing my words for a second.

"I followed you after I saw you in line with the hungry. Have they not been feeding you at the palace?" His eyes glared playfully.

"Of course they have. They feed me too well. What do you do with all that leftover food, anyway?" I asked changing the subject.

"I'm not sure," he glanced at me sideways.

"You should probably find out. You can give what's left to some of your citizens, so they don't have to starve. No one wants to eat that nasty mushy stuff every day." I shrugged trying to keep disinterested but so many ideas were starting to form in my mind.

"Noted," he scanned my face, "if I didn't know better, I'd say you sound like a princess."

"Thank the gods you know better then," I couldn't help the tug of my lips.

"What were you doing out here? If you wanted to explore the city, you could have just asked." He turned to me; there was a note of concern in his eyes before he blinked it away.

"I thought I was your prisoner," I mocked bitterly. I couldn't forget what he was to me. My captor.

"Meeka-" he started but I cut him off.

"The city has fallen in disrepair. You need to do something about it," I chastised.

"I agree," he looked thoughtful, "would you help me?"

I stared at him, the question catching me off guard.

"Me?" I asked, not sure how I could be of much help. Was this his solution? Asking me to help? It was better than being murdered at least.

"You are smart and brave. You can join my council." He put his hands in his pockets and shrugged but kept moving toward the palace. I didn't know how to respond, compliments made me uncomfortable.

"Is this a 'keep your enemies close' type thing?" I narrowed my eyes.

"Can you really not believe I might actually have your best interest in mind?" He took a hand from his pocket and rubbed his hair.

"No one has ever looked out for my interests but me," I whispered.

"Well, maybe you should start letting someone." He stopped, turning toward me.

"Do they know it's you?" I asked suddenly curious, needing to change the subject as a flush rose up my cheeks, "when you go and serve the people, do they know it's their prince?"

"No," he looked at me, his green eyes sucking me in.

"Why not?" I asked, my intrigue unfeigned.

"What would be the point? It would become a show if they knew who I was." He ran his fingers through his hair again.

"But don't they recognize you?" I asked confused.

"I don't usually make public appearances," he clenched his jaw. There was a bitterness to his tone, and I suspected it had something to do with his father. I still didn't know much what had happened between them, except he had mentioned there was no fondness.

"What was that thing in the alley?" I changed the subject, nervous by my sudden desire to know everything about him. How easy it would be to tell him all my secrets and hopes, and to keep all of his in return.

"It was a proteus. A magic shifter. They can take on different appearances but never for very long. Dangerous if you're unaware, but not so difficult to deal with if you know what to expect," he shrugged.

"Easily handled with bricks." I muttered.

"How many times have I saved you now? I should start keeping score," he chuckled and nudged my shoulder as we walked side by side. I pushed him back lightly unable to contain my grin.

"Yes, but you've also been the source of most of my problems, so you're going to have to subtract a few points from that score card." I bit my lip but glanced sideways at him. He was looking back at me, assessing.

"At least I made you smile," he put his arm around my shoulder drawing me in close as the palace came into view, "come on, let's get some real food."

I tried not to melt into his warmth or read too much into the way his body was claiming mine. I tried to act casually like he did, but I felt every contact where his strong arm was draped against my skin, and I couldn't prevent my body's traitorous actions as my heartbeat surged, and my stomach fluttered.

"You mean you aren't going to ignore me as you have the past several days?" I tried to sound playful, but it came out bitter. I needed to work on this bitterness, I did not want it to fester. I wanted to move on.

"You've been staying in your room by choice. I thought you wanted some space to," he gestured his free hand around in the air, "I don't know, remember your childhood, deal with your new life, that sort of thing."

"And if I wanted to return North, could I?" I turned toward him before we made it to the main gates. His arm fell and the absence lingered. He looked at me, all amusement gone.

"You want to return to a father who beats you?" I flinched at his words, and he looked as though he immediately regretted them. "That is, yes, if you truly wanted to return, I would help you. But I don't think you would live peacefully. There are those from Skirsgard that will always try to find you." He didn't add 'and kill you,' but the unspoken words were implied.

"Well, can I at least write my sister? Let her know that I'm ok?" I asked. I knew he was right. My life had changed forever. There was no going back.

"I'll have writing tools sent to your room as soon as we return." Guards motioned to stop us from entering the gates, but as soon as the prince turned toward them, they sputtered, lowering their spears, and letting us pass.

"Are they in danger?" The question had been weighing on me ever since I found out who I was.

"Your family?" The prince asked. I nodded. "I sent a small contingent of guards North. They will stay out of the way; your family won't even know they are there. But they will make sure no harm is done."

"Do you trust these men?" I asked, a weight starting to lift from my shoulders.

"They are loyal to me. Yes, I trust them with my life." The way in which he emphasized himself made me wonder, but I kept it to myself.

"Would you eat with me?" He asked looking hopeful after we were back in the palace.

"No. I'll have Trafi send a tray to my room." It sounded harsh, even to my ears, but I wasn't ready to share a meal with him alone. His family had been the cause of mine's deaths. And yet, I was starting to enjoy his company, and I didn't know what to think of that.

He clenched his jaw, a vein ticking in his forehead, but nodded.

"Very well," he spoke quietly as he turned to leave. "One more thing," he turned back. Part of me was hoping he would demand I join him. If he pushed, I would say yes, and maybe I would allow myself to stop fighting.

"Yes?" I said expectantly, taking a step closer. But he didn't ask again.

"There will be a masquerade at the week's end. I have an announcement, and I would like you to be there." He left before I could respond.

An announcement. My first thought was of the woman he so enthusiastically talked with the other night at dinner.

I remembered Demetri's look as he told me the prince would soon be married. I groaned. I did not want to go to the masquerade.

# CHAPTER 33

The next day, sunshine beat through half-opened curtains stinging my eyes in a pleasant sort of way and expelling the foul mood that hovered from the previous night. I wasn't generally bothered so easily, but the prince made me react in ways I couldn't quite control.

After breaking my fast, I decided to wander the palace grounds.

The masquerade was approaching, but I wouldn't worry about that today. Today, I would put my worries behind and continue to explore.

I wore my hair down in flowing waves. I chose a light pink, linen dress to wear, one that flowed casually with small, embroidered flowers around the edges. Though it was more traditionally southern in design, it was soft, and the linen was more suitable to the heat.

I stood in the palace gardens, soaking up the fresh air and the warmth. I remembered hazily running through these gardens as a child. The memories felt frayed at the edges when they struck, almost as if they weren't my own. They felt too distant, too contrary to the life I knew. But they were mine, and I could no longer hide from the truth.

The gardens had not been properly kept, I noted. Another item I would add to my growing list of things the prince must work on once he became king. Regardless, the grass was thick and I took off my slippers to feel the softness beneath my feet.

"You're looking rather comfortable in your new home." The prince's uncle strode forward as I stood among brambles of overgrown roses. His hands were drawn behind his back. "Or shall I say old home?"

"I never got your name," I stated, fed up with referring to him only as the prince's uncle. He had barely spoken to me in the time since leaving Innesbrown.

"General Alexi Nikandr Vissarion," he held out his hand. I reluctantly shook it.

"And what would you like from me, General?" besides my head, I wanted to add.

"The prince seems to have grown fond of you," he declared.

"And?" I took a deep breath, steadying my anger at this man who wanted me dead.

"I knew your parents, were you aware?" His gaze was shrewd.

"What does it matter now? Ma is dead. And my Pa-" I cut myself off. He had been there the night Pa had tried to kill me.

"Your Pa served in the military with me," he spit out, "he was a lowborn outsider, not a royal like your mother. It was quite the scandal when they married."

"Do you have a point, General?" I was growing annoyed. He was trying to provoke me.

"You, on the other hand," he looked me up and down, "are half outsider and half royal, both by blood and by experience."

I narrowed my eyes at him, what was he getting at.

"I've worked very hard to get where I am today," he sighed, "the prince may be fond of you now but don't expect that to last long. You won't ever belong here. Not fully."

"Is that a threat?" I hissed.

"Make it what you want. But be careful, princess." He patted me on the shoulder using more strength than necessary.

I fell sideways and caught myself on a rose bush. A thorn pierced my skin and the blood trickled down my wrist.

"How clumsy." He took out a handkerchief and wiped the blood off my arm then stashed it into his pocket. I narrowed my eyes glaring at him, but he only nodded in dismissal, leaving me alone in the garden with my thoughts.

He made me uneasy. I knew he was the one who ordered those men to take me during our journey here. The prince knew it too, yet nothing had been done. There was a bigger game at play here, I was sure of it.

*I don't like him.*

*That makes two of us.* I agreed.

*Something is off, his opeki...*

*What is it?* I asked.

*I'm not sure.*

*The other day he met with that shadow figure.*

*I may need to leave for a while. I need some answers.*

*Where will you go?* I asked.

*Another realm. Goodbye.*

*Wait. What is your name?* I hadn't thought to ask until now.

*Hofsdora.*

I passed the remainder of the day exploring the palace grounds, trying not to think too hard on the conversation with the general or with my opeki, Hofsdora.

I met several groundskeepers, all who reluctantly told me about how the palace was run. I even met one old woman who had known me as a child.

As the sun lowered and my belly grumbled, I decided I would have my meal with the rest of the nobility. Hopefully Demetri would be there for entertainment. He wasn't the only one I hoped would be there, but I tried to push that away from my mind.

I found Trafi back in my rooms with a serving tray piled high with food.

"Trafi, I'm going to eat in the hall tonight," I told her. She still wouldn't look at me, but I didn't miss the slight annoyance that passed quickly across her brow.

"Yes, miss," she stammered, picking up the tray, "do you need help dressing?"

"No, I'll do it myself," I sighed, "and Trafi, enjoy that food. You can eat in here."

A look of delight crossed her face, and for the first time I caught her eye before she hastily looked away, cheeks reddening.

"Trafi, you are not my slave. I'm not going to eat this food. Indulge my peace of mind and eat it. And for the love of all that is good, you can look me in the eye." I threw up my hands exasperated.

I didn't wait for Trafi's response, and I didn't change my clothing either. Instead, I left the room before she could argue, hoping she would heed my request.

Captain Bellamoni was waiting outside my door, but this time I made it to the dining hall without his help, quickly having remembered the lay of the palace by piecing together memories with my earlier exploration.

Noise wafted from the hall as we approached the large doors. I took a deep breath and entered.

The room was filled with the same assortment of people as the dinner I'd attended previously. Dignitaries, nobility, and all the general stuffy types you would expect at a palace function lined the room. I found it hard to believe the revolution had accomplished much besides replacing one ruler with another.

The prince was sitting at his usual spot, but I didn't approach him. I was here to eat and to show these people that I was not afraid of them. They may have overthrown my family, they may want me dead, but I would not cower. No one had outright killed or imprisoned me yet.

"Ah, there she is," a thin, older man approached. He was decorated in medals stitched along the breast of a long woolen coat. His hair was slicked back with too much lard, as was his moustache, which twisted into points on either side of his mouth.

"Sir," I nodded to him.

"I'm so very pleased to finally meet you," he tipped his head in a small bow. "You are looking quite marvelous this evening, I see you've replaced your usual garb."

"And you are?" I tried to ask patiently, but my patience was thinning.

"I am compatriot Neriai, Lieutenant of the Southern forces," he put his hand over his breast in a salute, "I welcome you back to court, princess, many of us thought never to see you again." He made a flourishing gesture with his hand and produced a red rose out of thin air.

"Well, here I am," I shrugged, not quite knowing what to say as I awkwardly accepted the rose.

"That prince has made it very difficult for any of us to get close to you," he mused, giving me a pointed look.

"What do you mean?" I furrowed my brow.

"To think a member of the royal family is among us, and we've heard barely a word about you," he smiled down at me, but the condescending tone was not lost.

"And what would you like to know?" I asked, smiling prettily.

"What do you intend to do now that you are back? Do you wish to take the throne?" He spoke in a friendly tone but moved his hand to rest on the hilt of the sword strapped to his waist. He didn't dance around words.

I kept my composure, reining in the insult that wanted to burst forth. He was threatening me. I wasn't sure how to respond, so instead I only shrugged and made my way further into the room.

I passed several groups chatting, mostly talking of small things, but a few whispered conversations clearly about the princess' return, and others on talk of the coronation. With the King's death, the council had taken over control, and still no one had decided on a date for the prince's coronation.

"She's practically feral," a young woman sneered to her friends, glaring in my direction. The words were spoken in a tone which, though hushed, was clearly meant for my ears. I smiled prettily back and winked.

I recognized the young woman the prince had sat with the other night – his betrothed, I assumed. Unafraid to meet her eyes, I looked her up and down trying to find her plain, even though her beauty was undeniable.

This was the woman the prince would marry. The one who would become queen – my birthright. I didn't want that life anyway, I reminded myself.

She sneered at me and used her magic to lift her drink, presumably to her lips, but instead hovered it a bit too near my dress, spilling its contents across the bodice.

I didn't mask my anger. She took a step back, afraid at whatever she saw on my face, as she tripped into her friend. I grabbed her arm and pulled it close, biting her. I left a mark but didn't pierce her skin.

"I'm not 'practically' feral. I am feral. Don't forget it," I tilted my head and smiled at the look of shock on her face.

"She bit me!" The young woman remarked, holding her forearm, mouth open in alarm.

"Close your mouth, you look like a fish," I curtsied and left the group standing there speechless. Maybe I really had gone mad.

On the way to the refreshment table, I was accosted several times. Strangers interrupted with pleasantries, reluctant introductions, and sometimes downright resentment. It was clear no one was quite sure how they were supposed to treat me, just as I wasn't sure how I was supposed to react.

I did not fit in here. I was supposed to die in the revolution, tying up all the loose ends nicely. But now I was a reminder of the country's past and the lengths it took for those in this room to attain power.

"Meeka, join us," the prince lightly touched my shoulder as I was piling food on my plate. I flinched. His jaw tightened, but he waited. I hadn't seen him approach.

"I'd first like to get some of those puffed meat pastries at the end, those are my favorite," I continued to walk down the table.

"Very well," the prince shook his head a smile tugging at his lips.

When my plate was so full there was no possible way I could add anything else, I joined the prince at his table.

"Sit here," he gestured to his right. There were a few mutterings and pointed looks in my direction, but no one outright complained. I noticed the prince's uncle, General Alexi, glaring in our direction from a few seats down, but it wasn't toward me. He was staring daggers at the prince.

"I think your uncle may hate you as much as he hates me," I whispered to the prince as I sat.

"You have no idea." The prince met my eyes.

I frowned at his cryptic remark.

"Or maybe they are all just trying to ignore the wine spilled all over my dress." I sighed, taking a bite of food.

The prince looked me up and down, questioning. I shook my head. I didn't want to explain my momentary insanity.

"Are you excited for the masquerade?" I asked then cursed inwardly. I didn't want to know how he felt about his upcoming announcement.

"I am..." he paused, "hesitant but hopeful." The dubious expression in his eyes had me frowning deeper.

"Did they decide on a date for the coronation, by the way?" I asked changing the subject. A few men at the table cleared their throats, looking around as though I asked something offensive.

"You were at the last council meeting," the prince answered.

"Oh right, I seem to be the problem with that," I tilted my head, leaning conspiratorially close.

"You apparently leave a wake of problems." He leaned in. "You look lovely tonight, by the way," he whispered.

I couldn't help the blush that rose to my cheeks. The council members at the table openly stared.

"But I have the perfect solution," the prince sat up looking pointedly at the men, his answer appearing more for them than myself.

"Boy, you know where we stand on this matter. The monarchy was never meant to continue, the military should control this great land," Lieutenant Neriai postulated.

"Funny, Neriai," the prince continued, "now that my father is dead, you have no problem inserting yourself. A word of advice - perhaps control that tongue, treason is unbecoming."

"Is that a threat, boy?" Lieutenant Neriai spit out, the medals on his coat shaking with his growing displeasure.

"Call me boy one more time and find out," the prince shot him a murderous grin.

"Now, now, the council will meet again after the masquerade," General Alexi interrupted, glaring at the prince. "We will remain civilized while we consider the next steps for our great country."

"Excuse me, I am needed elsewhere," the prince abruptly stood. I looked around at the men. They were giving each other sideways glances, some even going as far as rolling their eyes. There were a few, however, that looked equally as put out as the prince.

I stared down at my plate still piled high with food. I had only managed a few bites. I looked up at the door where the prince had hastily disappeared. I shouldn't go after him. I should sit here and fill my belly.

I sighed, standing up and leaving both my food and the odious men to themselves.

# CHAPTER 34

I found the prince in the gardens. The sun had long since set, and the moon hung high and full in the sky lighting the gravel pathway.

"It appears arrogance is a requirement of the ruling class," I spoke softly, taking a seat on the stone bench where he sat, head in his hands.

"I shouldn't have run out," he shook his head back and forth but looked up, meeting my eyes. There was an intensity in his gaze that spoke to me.

"If I were you, I would have flipped the table." I smiled softly. I shouldn't comfort him, but I felt the need in a deep part of me. A part that didn't connect with my brain, but my soul.

"Of course you would have. You are impulsive and rash." He dipped his hands in his pockets and swayed back.

"I am not," I protested.

"Oh really. Says the girl who traipses through the woods, dances to the fiddle, jumps into rivers, sneaks out of palaces, and bites people." The prince shot me a sideways look.

"You saw that?" I flushed, slightly embarrassed.

"I'm sure she had it coming." The prince chuckled.

"But isn't she-"

"Meeka, I've always had to do what I was told, even when I didn't want to," the prince interrupted, "I see your impulsion as a strength, though sometimes misplaced."

"Oh." I didn't know what to say. My cheeks burned and I wasn't sure why.

"Don't look so put out. You can't take a compliment, can you? Anyway, I think you would make a great leader." He stretched out. I couldn't help but notice the tautness of his muscles as his chest expanded.

"I don't want to be a leader. I've thought a lot about what you said. And maybe I can help you. Though I'm not sure how much help I'll be." I said sheepishly.

"Do you mean it?" He sat up, serious.

"Well, if I haven't totally ruined your chances becoming king." I looked up at the numerous stars in the night sky.

"It isn't just you. There are some who want my uncle, the General, to rule. They want the military in control of the country. They say it was the intention of the revolution before my father claimed power." The prince ran his hands through his hair.

"Is that why you've done nothing to punish your uncle for capturing me?" I asked, though it felt selfish in the moment. He glared at me.

"I thought you could take care of yourself?" he scoffed.

"I can, I just thought-" I stammered.

"Meeka, I have gone through great lengths to keep you protected here at court, I promise. Including appeasing my uncle. Trust me, if politics weren't involved, I'd have sent him to meet his maker long ago," he took a deep breath.

"Want me to do it for you? I'm skilled with a machete." I raised my eyebrows, questioning.

"You are not at all what I expected," the prince turned toward me, green eyes gleaming.

"And what did you expect? I suppose when you kidnap someone you hope they will be docile and easily manipulated?" I challenged him.

"Gods, you're a pain," he shook his head, but a smile tugged at the corner of his mouth, "sometimes you just need to shut up."

I turned my face toward his to protest but he suddenly grabbed my cheeks in his hands, and all my objections vanished.

He pulled me close, my body going taught but not fighting. His hands were so large. They covered my jaw and brought warmth and fire to my body, rushing down to pool in my middle.

He leaned in and kissed me.

It wasn't gentle, but it wasn't rough either. It was perfect.

I melted against him, but too quickly he pulled away. This was dangerous.

"There, that ought to shut you up for once," he grinned wickedly, a sparkle of amusement in his eyes.

"I- what-" I stammered but no coherent words would come forth.

"Exactly," the prince chuckled.

I shook out of the reverie and stood, fuming.

"You can't just go around kissing people!" I shouted, my face scorching against the heat rising to my cheeks.

"You didn't seem to mind," he shrugged as though it were nothing.

"You're engaged!" I glared.

The amusement drained from his face.

"Actually, I've been meaning to talk to you about that-" he began before I cut him off.

"There is nothing to talk about. You are a scoundrel!" I stormed off but he grabbed my arm, turning my body to face his.

For a moment, neither of us said anything, lost in each other's gaze. Then slowly the prince dropped my arm, looking over my shoulder.

I turned, following his stare. General Alexi was watching us.

"Prince Ajax, a word," the general scowled.

"This conversation is far from over," the prince whispered down at me. He nodded at his uncle, then left me alone in the gardens.

I sat on the bench, confusion, anger, and giddiness all warring for dominance inside my muddled mind.

I touched my lips. The feel of the prince still lingered. I closed my eyes and took a deep breath, pushing all thoughts far away until only the feel of Ajax's lips remained. My stomach flipped.

"Meeeeka," came a low wispy voice. My eyes flew open as I sat up straight, alert.

"Meeeeka," the voice came again from deeper in the garden. A voice I had heard before.

I stood, almost involuntarily, and walked toward the shadows. The garden grew unruly the farther I went, brambles and vines winding overhead and knotting over the ground. I ducked beneath a particularly large branch, almost banging my head in the dark.

"We meet again," the shadow man stepped from behind a low hanging tree. My heart beat furiously but I was alert and ready for a fight. I would not shy away.

"What do you want?" I demanded.

"I come again to offer you the world," he spoke cryptically.

"The world is not yours to offer," I spit out.

"Oh, but it is, the world is my domain. I can give you fame, fortune, glory. I can give you the greatest magic." His features were hidden beneath his hood, and yet I could make out a sly smile on pale lips. I cringed.

*Hofsdora, are you with me?* But I received no answer.

"And what do you want in exchange for this world of yours?" I asked with disgust.

"Your service," he replied.

"I will never serve you," I hissed out.

"Think on it. The time approaches when you must make a choice," he wheezed then turned back into the shadows.

I was left there shaking, feeling like spiders crawled against my skin. Twice now he had offered me the world and twice I had denied him. How many more times could I look forward to him popping up out of nowhere. I shuddered.

Then I remembered the prince's uncle. The General had met with this shadow man as well. They spoke of an unpaid debt.

General Alexi must have made a bargain with the shadow. But what did it have to do with me?

# CHAPTER 35

Soon the day of the masquerade arrived. Since the garden incident, the days had passed quickly in a whirl of preparations. Hofsdora was fickle when she answered me at all, and I could only assume she had gone to another realm, whatever that might mean. I was beginning to think there was so much I would never understand.

Trafi made me a dress for the occasion, even though I told her it was unnecessary. But as I stood staring in the mirror, my new gown flowing luxuriously around me, I couldn't help but be pleased. I thought of Yesi, and how I had mocked her when she tried on her wedding dress, a fact I now regretted.

Oh, Yesi. Since the prince had sent writing tools to my room, I had written Yesimia to tell her I was safe, though I couldn't find the words to explain everything that had happened. There had yet to be a reply, and I could only hope that my letter had reached her. She was happy and safe, married and well taken care of, I reminded myself. There was no need to worry.

"Trafi you're a wizard," I exclaimed, "How did you make this?" I looked down at the luxurious black fabric. The dress practically melted against my body, accentuating the curves I had grown from the lack of starvation since arriving at the palace. It was simple yet elegant. Flattering yet comfortable. Threads of crimson wove through the skirts, playing off my hair and making the dress flow like fire.

"No, I told you I only have very rudimentary magic, my opeki cannot often be bothered," Trafi squeaked out in response.

"Oh, never mind. It was supposed to be a compliment," I groaned.

"Yes, your highness," Trafi bowed, "you look very pretty."

"Thanks to you." I smiled in the mirror. I wore my hair down and flowing, still unaccustomed to the fact I no longer needed to hide the fiery tresses. I didn't wear any jewelry or makeup; I didn't want to. The dress was the focus. The dress and my hair. No one could deny who I was now.

"I heard a rumor the prince was getting engaged tonight," I tried to sound nonchalant, covering the fact that the question alone made my heart hammer.

"Yes, miss, that is the rumor going around," Trafi responded giving me very little information.

"And is it true?" I stiffened.

"I heard not only will he get engaged, but that the ceremony will take place at the end of the night," Trafi gossiped.

I gasped before I could help myself.

"That can't possibly be true. That's too fast," I whirled on her, but she looked away. I tried to push down the feeling of mounting panic that threatened to consume me.

"Does it bother you?" She asked, and I thought I heard amusement in her voice.

"No, it's just fast, that's all," I mumbled. "Anyway, I'm ready." I nodded my head, taking a deep breath and filling myself with confidence.

I could do this. I could face the prince again after everything that happened in the garden. Even though he would be engaged tonight.

But married? Tonight? Surely, Trafi had to be wrong. I clenched my jaw. I might be sick.

"Your mask, miss?" Trafi asked.

"I'm not going to wear one." What was the point, my hair identified me easily. Besides I was tired of hiding.

"Prince Demetri is waiting to escort you outside your room," Trafi nodded to the closed door.

"Prince Demetri?" I asked shocked, turning toward Trafi.

"Yes, Prince Ajax's younger brother," Trafi looked confused.

"Demetri is the prince's brother?" I glared, mouth open. How did I not know that? Now thinking back, it had been so obvious. And they did share many features.

"Of course," Trafi furrowed her brow, looking down at her shoes. I scoffed and marched out of the room.

Just when I was starting to think I had things figured out, I remembered there was so much about this place, these people, that I didn't know.

"You little liar," I seethed at Demetri as soon as I opened the door. He held two hands up in surrender but laughed at the look of rage on my face.

"Easy there, you animal. Don't bite me or anything," he backed up in mock terror.

"So, everyone apparently heard about that," I muttered, "don't change the subject, you're a prince?"

"Oh, that," Demetri had the decency to look abashed.

"You and Ajax are brothers," I narrowed my eyes, "which means it was also your family that killed mine."

I remembered back to the words he spoke, Meeka, it was war. But the war is over. Try not to blame us too much.

He had not just been speaking of the prince, but of himself.

"Ajax and I were just children," he reminded me, but a look of sadness and regret crossed his brow.

"I know," I ground out. And it was true. I did know they had just been children, they were not to blame, not really. They hadn't been the ones to kill my grandparents. But their families had. Did the blood spilled by your kin stain your own hands? I wasn't sure I knew the answer to that. And if it did, what did that make me?

"I wasn't purposefully hiding it from you, Meeka, it just never came up," Demetri shrugged giving me a small smile.

"I can't believe I didn't know. It's so obvious now. You're both so annoying," I glared at him but sighed.

"Forgive me, Meeka, please. You and I work better on the same side," he gave me a pleading look, sincerity behind his smile.

Forgive him? Was it that easy? It was hard to stay mad at Demetri, I had to admit. There was something just easy about him. Something naturally likeable.

"You and your brother are the same. Full of smug charm," I gave him a warm smile, accepting his apology. He smiled back, genuinely looking relieved.

"Ah, so you think I'm charming." I spun around to find the prince, the other prince.

"I meant it as an insult," I replied haughtily.

My heart flipped in my chest as I took him in. He wore black fitted trousers and a crisp white tunic. A long coat with tails rested on his shoulders, clasped together with a gold pin at his collar bone. My eyes went wide as I came to rest on his face where he was watching me closely, hunger in his deep gaze.

"Ajax," I nodded to him.

He stared at me, focused. The world paused and my breath hitched at the eagerness in his eyes.

"Say it again," he demanded.

"What? Ajax?" I breathed.

"You called me by my name," he reflected.

"Well, now seeing as there are two of you princes, I suppose I can't call you 'prince' any longer. And since Johnny Pullver was a lie, Ajax is all that I have left," I rolled my eyes.

"Ah, so you finally figured out we are brothers, I was waiting to see how long it would take you," the prince's lips tugged upward.

"How typical, you told me nothing," I bit my lip holding in a scowl.

Demetri looked between Ajax and I, clearing his throat.

"I will let you escort her, brother. I assume you have much to talk about," he gave Ajax a pointed look, bowed, and then left.

Once Demetri was out of sight, Ajax stepped closer drinking me in, shamelessly looking me up and down.

"Remind me to give Trafi a raise," his lips twitched upward.

"Oh, shut up," I swatted at him, trying to cover up the blush rising to my cheeks.

"You know how to make me. That method I taught you in the garden - it works both ways," he winked but chuckled as I pushed him again.

"I bet you shut up all the ladies that way," I muttered under my breath with irritation.

"What was that?" He leaned in.

"I said you're a pig," I glared.

"Come on let's go," he held out his arm, eyes twinkling with amusement.

I grabbed his elbow clenching my jaw against warring emotions as we walked through the palace. When I was with him, everything felt so right. But he was going to be engaged – possibly even married – tonight. And that felt so wrong.

"You aren't wearing a mask," I pointed out.

"Neither are you," he countered.

"Will anyone actually be masked at this so-called masquerade?" I asked genuinely curious if anyone followed the rules.

"It depends if they come with their husbands or lovers," the prince chuckled impiously. I dropped his arm and stepped away. "I'm joking, Meeka."

"That's not funny," I grated my teeth. "I happen to take faithfulness seriously, unlike you." I thought of our kiss when he was promised to another. It made my stomach knot in all the wrong places. Once again, I thought I may be sick.

"Meeka, so do I. I was only joking," he looked confused.

"It didn't seem that way in the garden," I tried to be angry, but I couldn't keep the hurt out of my voice.

"What are you talking about?" He shook his head and ran his fingers through his hair. "You continuously irritate me. Speak plainly."

"I know about the engagement," I blurted out.

But it was too late. We had arrived at the double doors as they opened to announce that the prince had arrived. Ajax's eyes went wide with concern, but before he was able to speak, he was pulled forward by a military man dressed in tails and medals.

"Prince Ajax," a trumpeter announced as the prince was sucked into the ballroom. He looked back at me with pleading eyes, and I could tell he desperately wanted to say something, but there was no time.

He was paraded forward, and I was left behind.

# CHAPTER 36

After several elderberry wines, my head felt light, and it was hard not to smile. I felt good. Hells to the prince, I wanted to dance.

I stumbled toward the dance floor but ungracefully fell into a couple of men blocking my way. No, not a couple men, just one. My vision swarmed. Too much elderberry wine I chuckled to myself. Yesi would kill me if she were here, I smiled.

"You, sir, make a better door than a wall," I slurred.

"Meeka?" the man looked down at me, concern in his eyes.

"Leacher? Is that you?" I grabbed his face with one hand, pinching his cheek. "Little Leacher, cute as a button. Why are you so scared of our prince? He is a loaf. A loaf of bread. Butter him up and toast him. Or toast him and then butter him up," I giggled.

"Are you ok, Meeka?" Leacher looked nervous.

"I'm brilliant. Just hungry with all this talk of bread. Shall we get some food?" I stumbled but Leacher steadied me. "Good point, Leachy, a drink first!"

"No more drinks for you, Meeka," Leacher wiped his brow. Was I making him sweat? Silly Leacher. I patted him on the head.

"Why don't you sit, and I'll bring you some food." He plopped me down at the nearest table while he went for refreshments.

I stared out over the ballroom, sighing. I wasn't the only one having too good of a time. There were several others stumbling around, one lady had even broken her glass on the dance floor, cutting her feet as she continued to dance in delight across the broken shards.

There were several in masks and several without, the difference only in those who wanted to be known versus those who did not. Now that the prince had put the image in my mind, I couldn't help but think all the masked couples were secret lovers.

"Bah," I scoffed aloud thinking of the prince. I didn't want to think of him, why did my mind keep going back to him.

A man sat next to me, breaking through my thoughts.

"Leacher, where is the food?" I asked looking up in his face, but it wasn't Leacher. "Who are you?"

"Your highness," the man took my hand and kissed it.

"Yuck." I pulled my hand back, wiping the lingering wet on the tablecloth. The man looked affronted for a minute before plastering on a fake smile.

"I heard you were charming," he smirked.

"Charming I am not, hungry I am. Shoo," I flicked my wrist trying to shoo him away.

"Your highness," he began again, "I'd like to introduce myself. I am compatriot Lexim."

"Are you food?" I asked rudely.

"Am I? What – no," Lexim blustered.

"Then I don't care," I rolled my eyes at him, "be off. Shoo." I tried again to shoo him away.

"You know, princess, I came over here to be polite, but my manners have fled," he paused, nodding to the dance floor, "your prince sure looks happy dancing with my sister, doesn't he?" Lexim growled under his breath then left abruptly.

I followed to where Lexim had gestured to see the prince gracefully dancing with the same girl I had bitten. His fiancée.

Leacher chose that moment to sit with a large tray of food, but I had lost my appetite.

"Nope, sorry, Leacher, party is over," I stood causing my chair to fall backward. Those around us stared with displeasure.

"Shall I walk you to your room?" Leacher asked.

"I can make it on my own." Leacher looked doubtful but didn't press. My head swam dizzyingly. I needed to get out of here.

A glass began to clink.

"Attention, attention, everyone." General Alexi, stood at the top of the center dais, hitting his glass with a knife. The room quieted. "Our prince has an important announcement to make."

Prince Ajax dropped the hand of the lady he was dancing with. He turned and looked at the crowd, taking everyone in, almost as if he was searching for something, for someone. He sighed and walked toward his uncle.

I backed into the shadows making my way toward an exit. I did not want to be here. I did not want to witness Ajax's engagement. It shouldn't matter, I had only known him for a short time. But I couldn't deny the pain that raced through my chest.

"As you all know our law," the general continued as Ajax stood beside him, "the crown prince must be married in order for the coronation to take place."

No, we do not all know that law, I thought to myself. But it was clear now why the prince was getting married - so, he could be king. Hells. Was this the way he appeased his uncle? Getting married to a snobby member of the nobility? Just so he could get his precious crown?

"As you also know, this last year several candidates have courted our young prince here, in hopes of joining his side-"

"No!" We don't all know that either. Scoundrel, I thought, except I had accidentally shouted the 'no' part.

Several heads turned in my direction giving me irritated looks. I shrugged innocently, holding my hands up in defeat before sinking further into the wall. The prince looked like he was attempting to find the source of the voice, but the crowd was shifting and making way for several young ladies who came to stand below the dais.

"Moving on," the general continued looking disgruntled in my direction, "the prince will now choose his bride among the suitors." Excitement erupted around the dais, clapping and giggling, as the four young women fanned their faces with giddy excitement.

I had to get out of here.

"Pst."

I turned to the side; Demetri was bee-lining to where I stood halfway behind a draped curtain. "There you are. We've been looking everywhere for you"

"I'm just admiring the linens," I said stroking the rich velvet fabric. "But I need to go - too much elderberry wine, you know how it goes." I floundered toward the nearest exit.

"Meeka -"

"Demetri, just let me go." He grabbed my arm, and I tried to wrestle out of his grasp.

"Meeka-"

"I don't want to talk right now," I argued.

"I didn't say anything." I turned toward Demetri who nodded up at the dais.

"Meeka."

Again, my name. But it wasn't from Demetri's lips. It had never been from Demetri's lips.

I glared up at Prince Ajax, my eyes finally meeting his.

"I choose Meeka."

# CHAPTER 37

*What.* I glared up at the dais where Ajax' stare blazed in my direction. The room had erupted into gasping and muttering. Slowly Ajax smiled. A smile that could melt the world, that could destroy nations. He was enjoying the chaos that ensued.

I needed to leave. The wine was causing a headache and whatever games Ajax was playing at, I wanted no part of. I tore my eyes away from the prince and sprinted toward the exit.

"Stop her," Demetri shouted to the guards at the doors. Traitor. The doors shut in my face.

I was in no mood. Sighing deeply, I threw open my arms.

*Hofsdora, a little help.*

*All you ever had to do was ask.*

The doors burst open.

Whether it was my loss of inhibitions from the wine, the overload of emotions from the night, or simply the basic fact that I asked – suddenly magic was at my fingertips, obeying my command.

I laughed to myself without true humor. After so long without, I could feel the magic stirring within, as though it had been there all along just waiting for me to say hello. I looked back at the prince who glared now, annoyance coating his gaze as I smiled sweetly then turned and ran out the doors that answered my command.

I dashed down the hallways, leaving shocked murmuring behind. I needed to be in the gardens, in the fresh air, where I could breathe. Had the prince really just announced his betrothal – to me?

A ripple of emotion slithered down my spine. How could he announce that in front of everyone without bothering to ask me first? I hardly even knew him. Marry him? Impossible. But why was it so impossible... my traitorous mind whispered. It made sense, the old heir and the new coming together. But no, no that was not what I wanted. I didn't want any of this, did I? I didn't know what I wanted.

I finally made it on the terrace overlooking the garden and gulped the warm air in panicked heaves. Sweat coated my brow, and I suddenly felt an overwhelming need to escape this place. This may have been my home once, but not anymore. I didn't have a home. I didn't belong anywhere.

I sucked in a breath and brought my hands to my face, wiping the sweat away. I lengthened my arm, twirling my palm around, remembering the magic that had willingly answered my command.

*Hofsdora, is the magic now mine?*

I flicked my palm, bringing heat to mind as a small flame erupted in the center. It didn't burn my flesh, and yet it gave off heat. I splayed my fingers and tried again, willing a rose to bloom on the dead vine hanging off the terrace balcony. Three yellow flowers opened brilliantly. Interesting.

It felt so natural to wield. I smiled. This could be rather fun.

*I can give it, and you can receive it, but the magic is neither yours nor mine. It belongs to a greater power.*

The doors to the terrace banged open and I turned, whipping my hand as a burst of wind flew toward the man now striding angrily toward me. Prince Ajax. He used his own muscular arms to shield against the spiral of wind, as though it were nothing.

"Meeka, let's talk." Prince Ajax strode in a predatory way, making his way too quickly toward me. I backed up but had nowhere to retreat. I bumped into the terrace balcony and threw my arms behind me, clutching the stone balustrade.

"I don't want to talk to you," I glared at him, meeting his stare.

"You must marry me. There isn't another choice for either of us. I've gone through every possible scenario." He reached out as though he would lay his hand on my shoulder, but instead clenched his fist, dropping his arm.

"How romantic." I turned away from him, not wanting him to see that his words had stung. Not wanting his words to sting in the first place.

"When we first arrived, they were going to kill you. There have been riots and rebellions in the countryside. The council worried if news spread of your arrival there would be civil war. We cannot risk that. You have no idea how hard I've worked to keep you safe." He ran his hand through his hair.

"So, you decided to marry me? So that I could be a pawn in your rise to power, pushed out of the way so as not to cause you any trouble? You may as well have killed me." I clenched my jaw against the anger and hurt that threatened to boil over.

"I convinced the council that this was the smarter arrangement," he sighed.

"Again, how romantic." I turned back toward him, fixing him with an evil glare. His eyes bore into mine, unmoving. Unblinking.

"Understand this, your choice is marriage or death." He moved ever so slightly closer. Only an inch, but I could feel the heat radiating off his body.

"Then I choose death," I spat out, anger and hurt mixing together. All those times I thought that maybe we were connecting, maybe something special was growing between us, I was wrong. He had only ever been after the crown. He was just using me, placating me, so I would be his wife.

He stepped closer, caging my body against the balcony resting his arms on either side of me as he leaned down. He brought his mouth toward my ear, his breath caressing the side of my neck.

"Very well," he breathed into me, our bodies almost touching.

I closed my eyes, shivers running down my spine. I tried willing myself to turn away, but my deceitful body answered, tilting forward.

My eyes flew open as I was lifted up, up, up, and thrown over his shoulder, just as he had done that day in the woods.

"What are you doing?" I kicked and punched him, thrashing against his powerful arms.

"We marry," he ground out, "tonight."

# CHAPTER 38

Ajax strode back into the ball while I kicked and screamed. Gasps and horrified murmurs rippled through the room as we strode toward the dais, which had already been turned into an altar of sorts.

"Uncle?" The prince shouted out to the crowd, searching.

"I'm here," the General strode forward, and I raised my head to see a look of pure disgust cross his eyes before plastering on a fake smile.

"The magistrate?" The prince asked, sounding equally annoyed as I felt.

"He has been sent for and should arrive any moment." The prince made a huffing sound.

"Trafi?" The prince asked again.

"She is behind you." The prince spun, whipping me around.

"Ah Trafi, it will be the alternate plan," Prince Ajax breathed in and out deeply, I could feel his lungs expand against my chest, where I rested on his shoulder.

"Yes," she took a deep breath. She nodded at the prince, her face hardening.

"Good." The prince set me down but kept a firm grip on my arm. "If you run now, Meeka, I will kill Trafi."

"I hate you," I glared at him with all the evil I could muster.

"What's new?" He looked bored and turned back toward the crowd.

A portly man, sweating profusely, inched his way through the crowd, holding a handkerchief and intermittently wiping his brow. His nose was red and overlarge, and he was surrounded by a general air of panic.

"Ah, Percil," Prince Ajax helped the poor man up the dais. "Good evening, everyone. Tonight, not only did I invite you to this ball, but to my royal wedding." The prince bowed to the crowd, who stood open-mouthed. Some seemed to be enjoying the spectacle, others seemed repulsed.

"Magistrate, if you will," he gestured to the magistrate to begin.

I stood there, the prince's arm firmly holding mine, as time slowed. I looked around at the crowd who whispered behind hands, glaring openly, judging. I looked to the prince, but he seemed to look anywhere else but my eyes.

"Trafi," the prince nodded behind me. Trafi put a veil over my head. I turned, pleading with her, but true to character she did not meet my eyes. Would the prince really kill her if I ran? Every time I thought I was beginning to know him, he betrayed me.

Magic stirred within me as the magistrate began reciting lines that were lost in my swirling thoughts. I stood paralyzed in shock or fear, or any other number of emotions I could not quite wrap my head around. This couldn't really be my wedding day. I thought back to Yesi's wedding, the beautiful ceremony and the painting that cried on my shoulder. Had the woman in the fresco known of my fate? Did she cry out of pity or shame?

I tried again to meet Prince Ajax's eyes. The magistrate was fumbling over a few words, then turned expectantly.

"Meeka?" He asked, nodding vigorously in my direction.

"What?" I barely whispered.

"This is where you say 'yes'," he responded.

"I-" I stammered.

"Yes," the prince spoke, his jaw twitching. He seemed to be enjoying this charade even less than I.

He brought his gaze slowly down to finally meet mine. His eyes pierced my soul, and my stomach dropped. A lump in my chest hardened, my heart struggling to beat. But my mind was ever traitorous.

"Yes," I squeaked out, shocking myself and the prince, whose eyes went wide a millisecond before once again steeling themselves.

The magistrate brought out a long silver knife. Grabbing both our hands he cut my palm and the prince's, drawing blood. He brought our two hands together, tying them with a sash, as our open wounds mingled together, joining us in both blood and law.

The prince shuddered at the contact. I felt a tingling sensation go up my wrist and in to his. We were bound.

"You are now husband and wife," the magistrate blew out a deep breath, relief clearly written across his face.

"Wait, no-" I floundered, "I didn't mean that." The prince grunted, the corner of his mouth rising in a crooked smile filled with danger and mischief.

"Too late, wife," he ground out against clenched teeth.

"I wasn't in my right mind; it was a mistake." I shook my head, everything taking on a surreal nature.

"I'm afraid we are bound. If fate's hand had not been upon us before, surely it is now." The prince turned toward the crowd. "My wife," he gestured to me, "your future queen."

I stood in front of the people, my people. They began to clap slowly for me, but I looked at Ajax, hoping desperately that he would pinch me, and I would wake up. This had happened too fast. But once again he didn't look at me, instead he looked over my shoulder, giving the slightest of nods.

I turned, confused, to see Trafi still standing, cheeks flushed. She was so close; she was practically breathing down my neck. I looked into her face, meeting her eyes, preparing for the usual downcast look.

But for the first time she didn't shy away. She met my eyes with a fierceness that both terrified and impressed me.

"Don't worry," she whispered so only I could hear. And then she plunged a knife into my heart.

# PART 4:

# THE THRONE

# CHAPTER 39

First came the darkness. Pure black, as deep and dark as the pit itself, enveloped me, all consuming. Then came the pain. Searing heat raced through my veins, piercing every inch of my flesh. And then the void.

An invisible string attached itself to my lip, pulling me down as my body melted slowly into a puddle. A curtain lay before my mind's eye, and I only need pass through it to get where I wanted. But what awaited on the other side was a vague mystery, and one I was hesitant to discover.

Time didn't exist in this dark puddle. Eons and ages passed, or was it mere seconds? There was no such thing as time. I couldn't tell if I was alone or if I had joined others, forming one mass pool of liquid thought.

My mind was fuzzy, going in and out of consciousness, confusing my self-awareness with a general awareness of the state of all. But centered in the pooling bubble of my mass was a small stone that beat and pulled me inward, sucking me into a congealing form.

"Meeka." That was a name. A name I'd been called before I was here. When there was a before. Now there was an after. A before and an after settled in as time reappeared, founding itself on the knowledge of befores and afters like a story written down on a page.

"I am Meeka." I spoke though there was no voice. I blinked but there was no light or dark. I breathed, but there was no air.

"Meeka." I said again and this time, heard it. I could hear. I blinked again and this time there was light. I could see. The curtain in my mind opened revealing a dark and cramped space.

I sat up frantically as my mind and body came crashing back together. Well, I tried to sit up but couldn't. I was strapped down by some sort of invisible source. I looked around but only made out vague shapes. Was I in a box? No, that was blue radiating down. Open sky.

I blinked several more times, my vision swimming but forming slowly. I was moving, my body bumping up and down, though I could make no movements on my own. I lay rigid in some sort of box, flowers surrounding me forming a bed. Looking up I only saw blue sky. Several clouds floated wistfully above.

I came crashing back to reality. Panic rushed through me, as I realized I was completely paralyzed, but for the movement of my eyes.

I had been killed – stabbed in the heart. But this was not death. No, I was lying atop a carriage. Voices sounded through the air in waves. Not the voices of demons beckoning for my soul, but crowds cheering as I was paraded through the city. No, this was not death, this was a funeral. My funeral.

I tried to look around but could not. Prince Ajax rode atop the carriage in formal attire, waving to the crowds. I could only glance at his back, but his broad shoulders and domineering posture were unmistakable. He did not look back to where I lay.

What in all hell's corners had happened? I wasn't dead, though I should be. And yet I was stuck as though my soul was alive only in my eyes.

I struggled between anger, frustration, and awe as the carriage continued to parade through the streets in what felt like an unending circle of torture. I needed answers, and I wouldn't get them until this ritual ceased.

I took a deep breath. I could breathe, though I felt no movement in my chest. It was like I was under a spell.

*Relax. All will be well.*

*Hofsdora.* Some of the panic dissipated knowing my opeki was with me.

After rattling down the bumpy roads endlessly, the noise of crowds began to dwindle. Overhead buildings gave way to trees and wind whipped the crimson hair cascading around my body. The smells of the city succumbed to the fresher air of the country. The funeral must be coming to an end as the sun began to set.

The carriage stopped and I heard the squeak of rusty metal. We passed under an iron archway, then another screech indicated the closing of a gate. We made our way up a hill until the horses whinnied, and the carriage came to an abrupt stop inside a cold stone room.

"We're here," Prince Ajax spoke as he roughly jumped from the carriage, still not looking at me. "You men are dismissed, take the horses from the stable near the gates. I'd like a moment alone with my wife to say goodbye. Demetri will help me lay her in the family crypt."

"Your highness, that is unseemly, we will stay for the burial," came a rugged voice.

"I will do it myself. Dismissed," the prince snapped in a tone that brokered no argument.

The rugged voice did not return, but I could hear steps retreating on the stone.

Silence permeated the space. Silence I could not break though I longed to spill the questions that overflowed from my thoughts. We waited that way for a while until finally Demetri spoke.

"They've just gone through the gates," he sighed with relief.

"Good. Is anyone else still here?" Prince Ajax demanded.

"No. Just you, Trafi, and myself." Demetri jumped on the carriage and gave me a half smile "There she is," he winked.

Trafi was here. Trafi who had stabbed me and yet not killed me.

I tried to speak but couldn't move my mouth.

"Release her slowly, please. I'm in no mood for a fight," Prince Ajax sighed.

"Very well." Trafi jumped atop the carriage and looked me full in the eyes, "I told you not to worry." I felt a buzzing sensation around my head as my muscles began to twitch.

"What in the mighty hells," I shouted, my voice finally working, though I still could not move my body. "What is going on?"

"Calm down," Trafi said, a sparkle to her I had never seen before.

"Who are you?" I asked trying to sit up, but still not able. "Why can't I move?"

"I'm your cousin," she gave me a large smile then. This was not the same timid girl who wouldn't look me in the eyes, this was someone different, someone with secrets and a boldness that was kept expertly hidden.

"My cousin?" I stammered in shock, straining against the invisible restraints, "release me darn it, let me move!" I shouted, frustration reaching its peak.

"Meeka, before I let her release you fully, I want you to promise me you won't hit me," prince Ajax's face appeared above mine full of mock concern.

"I will promise you no such thing," I ground out, narrowing my eyes in an angry glare.

"Now, wife, there is no need to quarrel," the corner of his mouth quirked upward.

"I am not your wife-" I began to say then remembered the events that had just occurred. I was his wife. My eyes widened and the prince began to laugh.

"Oh, don't look so alarmed. It was necessary." He waved an arm at me.

"Please release me from whatever spell you've got me under." I ground through clenched teeth, trying to remain calm.

The prince nodded to Trafi who cracked her neck, closed her eyes. She took a deep breath. Pins and needles rushed along my body in a painful tingling sensation as feeling spread out through my chest and limbs. I sat up too abruptly, bumping heads with Trafi awkwardly.

"Sorry," I murmured though I was sorrier for myself as I rubbed the bump on my head. Looking down, I wiggled my toes and swung them around the side of the carriage. I lost my footing and fell, but not before Prince Ajax caught me.

"Easy now, it's been three days since you were murdered," he whispered, holding me and gently rolling me down along his muscular body, setting me tenderly on the ground. He held me steady as I leaned into his chest, feeling his strength embrace me. I took a deep breath, filling my lungs with his air, until I remembered how mad I was and pushed him away.

"You have a lot of explaining to do," I shoved him.

"Hey, no hitting, remember, wife?" His eyes twinkled with amusement.

"That was a shove not a hit. And I made no promises." I scoffed, though it only made him laugh.

"How am I not dead?" I rounded on Trafi, "and why did you try and kill me? And you said you only have rudimentary magic. Why do I always seem one hundred steps behind."

"I gave you the choice between marriage and death," prince Ajax cut in.

"And I chose death, not marriage. And yet here I am married to you and alive." I gave the prince a scornful look before rounding back on Trafi. "And what do you mean 'cousin'?"

"I think we better start at the beginning," Demetri said, interrupting.

"And you," I pointed at him, "I have some words for you as well."

"Hey, I'm just following orders," Demetri raised his hands in surrender, "take it up with your husband."

"He's not my-" I stalked toward Demetri, hands raised.

"Husband," prince Ajax was quicker than I, striding behind me and wrapping his arms around my center, holding my flailing limbs down in place and whispering in my ear. The hair on the back of my neck stood, shivers running down my spine as his breath caressed the back of my neck. "If I remember correctly, I believe you said, 'yes,' to the magistrate."

"I was drunk," I protested.

"They say elderberry wine brings out the truth," he teased. How could he be teasing me at a moment like this.

I took a steadying breath that came out in a rattle as his lips grazed my ear. I turned around to face him, but he didn't release me. Our bodies were pressed together in a rough embrace, and as I looked into his eyes my stomach knotted. I opened my mouth to speak but couldn't. He searched my eyes then dipped his gaze to my mouth.

Demetri cleared his throat, and I pushed prince Ajax away, shaking my head to clear it.

"If you want an explanation, we should be quick. We need to leave soon. News of your miraculous rising from the dead will circulate quickly," Demetri pointed out.

"Is there anything to eat?" I asked, suddenly starving.

"Here," Trafi handed me a sack, which I opened to find an array of sustenance. "Meeka, I was only four when the revolution happened. But you weren't the only family to escape. With some help, many of us were able to get away," she glanced at prince Ajax.

"She's been working with me for a long time," prince Ajax continued, "and together we've been looking for you."

"Why?" I asked, genuinely confused.

"Not everyone supported the revolution," Demetri chimed in. "Not even everyone in our own family. Our mother was not a supporter. She was the one who raised us, but when Father took the throne, he had her killed." Demetri looked down at his feet.

"She spoke out against the new realm - against her own family and husband. My father used her death as a warning to us, but it only ever had the opposite effect." Prince Ajax continued, jaw clenching. I could tell there was pain there, pain he had pushed away – something I knew a lot about.

"And you helped my family escape." I stated, my back falling against the carriage as the pieces fit together. "You aren't the reason my family died; you are the reason they lived."

I met the prince's eyes, seeing him in a new light. He gave me the slightest of nods.

"They were going to burn me alive, but he hid me away," Trafi spoke quietly, "I've remained invisible as his servant ever since, but he has never treated me as such. We've been planning a way to get you back for a long time."

"The council was going to kill you after the wedding, Meeka. They wanted it to take place first, so Ajax could be crowned and be their puppet. But they wanted you dead. You've had too much influence over him and those that would see the old realm reinstated," Demetri explained.

"I told the council I would kill you so they would trust me," Ajax chimed in, "we needed to fake your death. When the council finds out it was all a lie, they will know we are against them. This could mean war."

"And here I am. But you stabbed me, Trafi. How am I alive.?" I whispered.

The prince took a deep breath as he swaggered toward me. He ran his hand through his hair then placed it over the bare skin below my neck. "Your heart is made of stone."

# CHAPTER 40

"My what?" I exclaimed, placing a hand over my heart where the prince's touch lingered.

"You have a stone heart. You are very difficult to kill. It is why your grandparents were burned." Demetri offered in explanation. Prince Ajax began pacing.

"How is that even possible? How do you live with a stone heart?" I shook my head confused.

"Magic," Trafi looked at me and shrugged. "It's been a royal secret which very few know. It is how we were able to fake your death."

"And are all royals stonehearted?" I asked, remembering Ma's lifeless body hanging.

"No," Trafi shook her head.

"And how did you know I was?" I narrowed my eyes.

"The day you escaped, you were found lying on the ground in the gardens. You had a knife protruding from your chest, but you were not dead. Do you remember?" Prince Ajax reflected.

"No," I slid down against the carriage, unable to stand. Visions of fire and death swarmed before my eyes, but I did not remember being stabbed. "What now?"

"Demetri will return to court. He will gather supporters and hope it hasn't come to war. Trafi will rally the rest of your family." The prince explained. My pulse beat at the thought of reuniting with my family. Just how many had survived?

"And what am I supposed to do? Do I just to pretend I'm dead?" I shook my head, "I don't like to lie."

"News you're alive will spread quickly. We needed to buy some time and escape the eyes of the council. They will want to kill us both now. They want a military state." The prince rubbed the arch of his brow.

"Was faking my death necessary? It seems a bit dramatic," I stood.

"It's a delicate situation." Prince Ajax towered over me.

"Come," he grabbed my hand and led me to the front of the carriage, helping me up. "I'll answer any more questions on the road. We need to get to the next town by nightfall."

"We say goodbye again, cousin," Trafi looked up, meeting my eyes with a passion. I was not used to the timid servant turned bold cousin, but I nodded down at her, smiling.

"I like you better this way, Trafi, boldness suits you, no wonder you wouldn't meet my eye," I tilted my head, amused.

"If I had, you would have known it was all a lie," Trafi winked.

"I'm glad to have family here," I said honestly.

"Until we meet again," she bowed and turned away.

"Brother," Demetri nodded to prince Ajax. "Sister," he nodded to me, his gaze full of smug satisfaction. I glared daggers at him but he laughed playfully in response.

"Try not to break his heart, not all of ours are stone," he shouted up before turning to follow Trafi toward the stables.

"As if I could," I murmured reminding myself that this marriage was a lie. That all of this was a political ploy for the throne.

I glanced at prince Ajax, who had taken the reins, but he was paying no attention. Instead, he flicked his wrists, the horses answering the call, as we made our way back through the stone corridor and into the dusk.

At the stables, Demetri hurried on his way back toward the city, while Trafi took off into the woods. Prince Ajax and I unloaded the funeral arraignments from the carriage and packed it instead with supplies Demetri had hidden in the stables.

I was wearing a white silk dress with lace details sewn around the edging – my burial dress. Though there was no time to change, prince Ajax offered a long linen coat to cover my bare attire, promising I could properly change at the next town. The coat smelled of horse, and earth, and Ajax.

We traveled the opposite way from the city, strolling through rolling hills as dusk gave way to dark.

With so many unanswered questions on my mind, I was hesitant to ask the one that plagued me the most. Finally, I worked up the courage.

"Who are you really, Ajax?" I bit my lip

"What do you mean?" He stiffened.

"Sometimes, I feel like I know you. And then you do something so drastically different, I can't possibly understand." I admitted.

"Like what?" He asked, voice soft.

"Well, when you were Johnny Pullver, for example, the way you acted with me. I don't know how to explain. But then that night you took me, you became cold. Intense. Different. The same thing happened at the marriage ceremony." I sighed trying to reconcile the many different sides to this man who now called me wife.

"Sometimes I don't want to do the things I know I must." He shuddered, a look of pain in his eyes.

"I see." My heart dropped. So, it was true. He did not want to marry me except for the crown. He had not even wanted to kidnap me. Maybe I should be relieved, but I just felt sad.

"What's wrong?" He asked, looking concerned.

"Nothing," I sighed.

"Meeka. Whatever you are thinking, you are probably wrong. Tell me." His eyebrow rose expectingly.

"Just thinking about my magic. It seemed to come alive suddenly." I lied.

"Ah, yes, I noticed," he nodded, hesitating, "and why did you not use it to escape our marriage?"

"You threatened to kill Trafi. Would you have?" I stiffened.

"Of course not. We were working together. As you can see the plan was never to hurt you. We were trying to protect you," he sighed grabbing a piece of straw and chewing it.

"Always you say you are trying to protect me..." when really you hurt me more than ever.

"You could have used it before then - on the terrace, when I was carrying you, at any other point before we reached the ceremony." He pulled the straw out of his mouth and tossed it to the ground.

"I-" I tried to come up with an excuse, but he was right. I hadn't fought back at all. I let him lead me to this fate. "Hofsdora likes you, against my better judgement."

It was the only explanation I could come up with. It wasn't as if I had wanted this. Or so I told myself on repeat.

*I do like him.*

"Your opeki?" He snorted, grabbing both reins and kicking the horses into faster gear.

"Yes, but it only seems to tell me these things at the most inopportune times," I grumbled, distracted by the way he wet his lips with his togue.

"And how were you finally able to use your magic?" He asked, looking genuinely curious.

"I guess I was just so angry with you," I glared.

"Ah, so I inspire your magic then, wife?" He teased, nudging me.

"You are so irritating, husband." I said mockingly, but when I looked up at him, he grinned, amusement lighting his eyes.

"So, you finally admit it," he nudged me again.

"Stop pushing me," I nudged him back. He laughed and brought his free arm around my shoulders, his other hand still controlling the reins.

"Since you now admit I am your husband, I will hold you close as husbands should." He tightened his grip around me, pulling me close.

"You don't have to pretend here, we are alone." I knew I should push him away, but my traitorous body leaned into his warmth.

"Who says I'm pretending?" He glanced down at me smiling lazily.

"Oh, stop. Now that I know I can use my magic, I can use it against you, you know?" I threatened yet still did not push him away.

"And yet you haven't," he spoke quietly.

I flailed backward as the horses picked up their pace, grabbing his arm to keep from falling. He glanced at me sideways, eyebrow raised.

"Why the sudden hurry? Are we being followed?" I glimpsed over my shoulder but saw nothing of note.

"I just realized something very important. I don't want to lose another second getting to the inn." He looked suddenly serious making my heart skip in anticipation.

"What is it? What is the matter?" I bit my lip.

He grinned down at me, a wicked gleam in his eye. "It is our first night together as husband and wife."

# CHAPTER 41

We pulled up to the inn on the outskirts of the town, Bellmorne. The night had settled in, yet it was still early enough.

"Should I cover my hair?" I asked prince Ajax as he helped me down.

"No, not anymore. Never again." He grabbed a large satchel from the carriage, then led the horses around to the stable while I followed him. Once our belongings were secured, we went to the entrance of the small stone inn. The roof was thatched, with two chimneys, though no smoke rose from within. No lights shone through the windows, either.

"Is it abandoned?" I asked.

"You'll find they use their magic in the countryside much more...liberally," Prince Ajax just smirked and grabbed my hand pulling me inside.

Once across the threshold, I blinked several times taking in the sight before me. The room was bright and lively, larger than it looked from the outside. No curtains were drawn across the windows, and it was easy to see out, yet when we stood outside it was impossible to see in. It must be magic.

And magic was clearly plentiful here as I gaped at floating plates and pints of ale, invisibly whisking their way across the air to find their owners at the various tables. The tables were full of patrons chatting and drinking merrily. Music played from the corner, though the harp and fiddle moved on their own accord, no musician stood plucking the strings.

We took a step forward, looking around for an empty table when the patrons took note of us newcomers. At first, we were only given a quick glance, before several double takes caused a low hush to befall the room.

A tall, bearded man with round belly and rosy cheeks approached, scribbling on a piece of paper.

"Can I help you?" He asked before looking up. When he did his eyes went wide, his mouth opened in shock. "You-"

At first, I thought it was a response to the prince, until I remembered my fiery hair flowing casually around my shoulders.

"So, it's true, you've returned." He looked around the room, eyes narrowing at his patrons, and I assumed he was looking for the start of any trouble. "They said you returned, then that you were dead, but clearly it was a lie."

"We would like a table and a room," I stated before he could continue. I was not used to being the center of attention in this regard.

"Of course, your highness," he bowed and led us to a table in the corner. I peeked over my shoulder at prince Ajax, who was looking way too entertained by my new role.

"Two ales." Prince Ajax held up two fingers.

"Of course." The man flicked his wrist, and two ales came flying from the kitchens settling themselves at our table. I tried to act casual but couldn't help feeling overwhelmed.

"My name's Mr. Tipero, I'm the owner of this here tavern. Can I get you anything else?" He bobbed his head.

"Cabbage rolls and bread," I blurted out, my stomach growling. The man nodded.

"I will personally oversee that they arrive," he bowed and then left for the kitchens.

I turned to prince Ajax who laughed at my unease.

"You fit in well with your people, your highness." The prince nodded to me in a mock bow, then downed a long sip of his ale.

"And your people seem not to know you at all," I commented, following suit and taking a long sip. It was cool and bubbly, rushing to my stomach in a pleasant sort of way.

"I thought we had already established that I don't make many appearances as the prince. Plus, you are the rightful heir." He leaned back in his chair. I frowned.

"You said once that you had seen battle." I remembered suddenly, thinking of the day in the woods which felt so long ago.

"Hmph," the prince snorted, "that's a tale for a different day."

"Tell me," I prodded. He stared at me a long while before sitting up.

"Very well," he paused, "after my father took the throne, a lot of people in the country rebelled. It was civil war. And as a punishment for my insolence, my father sent me in to fight." He spoke casually but there was pain behind his voice.

"You would have been very young," I commented.

"I was twelve," he sighed.

"You were twelve?" I exclaimed, almost spitting out my ale. He nodded.

"I fought hard, but there wasn't much a twelve-year-old could do. I was captured easily, but they took pity on me. When I returned home, my father sent me to the pits instead of putting me to death. He thought I'd become a traitor." He finished his ale, just as Mr. Tipero came over carrying two steaming trays.

"Your highness, for you I serve these myself." He bowed and set the food before me. "Your companion-"

"Her husband," prince Ajax interrupted.

"Oh my, forgive me," he looked between the two of us clearly flustered, "I did not know, I-"

"It's of no consequence. Now if you wouldn't mind," prince Ajax gestured to their food.

"Why yes, of course, enjoy your meal. I'll ready your rooms," Mr. Tipero sputtered, trying hard to be proper.

"Room," Prince Ajax responded.

"Sir?" The tavern man asked.

"Not rooms, room," prince Ajax emphasized. The tavern man looked to me, and I rolled my eyes. He looked unsure but nodded again and left.

"You're crazy if you think I'm sharing a bed with you," I said after the man left.

"It wouldn't be the first time we shared a room," his eyes sparkled and the mischievous smile reappeared. I glanced around at the nearby tables, whose patrons were trying very hard not to stare at us. "If I recall, last time I woke with you cuddling me."

I felt my cheeks burning but hardened my stare.

"That was not what happened, and you know it," I stammered, "Anyway, do you think it's smart we let ourselves be known?" I whispered looking around.

"Probably not. But I'm done hiding. And you should be too," he gave me a pointed look before digging into his meal.

"I'll admit it feels good to wear my hair down." I shook out my locks, "but won't our enemies find us, and then what?"

"Our enemies? So, we are on the same side then?" He asked, pausing mid bite.

"I suppose so," I finally agreed. If I had learned one thing from this whole ordeal, it was that prince Ajax, though a liar, was not quite the villain I had thought. Perhaps we did want the same things.

"Most of our enemies are at the palace so we have a head start. I'm sure they have spies all around the country but plenty of these folks never wanted a revolution to begin with. We won't find out who our allies are by hiding." He continued to eat.

"So, we trapse the countryside looking for supporters and then what?" I understood his logic, but it all felt too simple.

"We hope there is no war. We find a way to make peace with the council. Then we return to the palace for the coronation." He swallowed down another mouthful of ale.

"But couldn't you have done all that without me? You were already set to be coronated once you were married." I frowned.

"Oh, I don't plan on being coronated," he gave me a pointed look and set down his pint.

"But you said-" I started.

"The crown must be married, that is our law," he took a deep breath, "but I will not be named ruler of Skirsgard."

"I don't understand," I wrinkled my brow.

"We will return to the palace, my dear wife, with a mass of support. We return for the coronation - but not mine."

"Then whose?" I asked bewildered.

"Whose do you think, Meeka?" He leaned forward in his seat, "yours."

# CHAPTER 42

I slammed the door behind the prince as soon as we were in the privacy of our room. Mr. Tipero assured us it was 'the best room in the inn.' But with my emotions mixing in a swirl of confusion, it was difficult to appreciate the tavern man's gesture.

Prince Ajax strolled lazily to the bed, laying down with legs crossed and arms folded behind his head. I stood there clenching both my jaws and my fists, livid. I used my new found magic to lift a pillow, coming down hard to smack the prince in the face, my magic responding to my anger.

*You act like a child. You are to be a queen.*
*Go away, Hofsdora.*
I seethed whirling on Ajax.

"Why do you always have to be a step ahead of me? Why don't you ever just tell me the truth! You think you can just decide my future without permission? You think I want to be the queen of Skirsgard?" I shouted angrily. The prince hastily sat up, swatting the pillow away.

"I think that you, like myself, have little say in your future," he ground out.

"But you pull the strings, and I, your puppet, comply," I accused with derision.

"This is greater than you and me, Meeka. This is the fate of our nation. This is history in the making." He sat up on the bed

"And why do you get to decide the course of history?" I glared.

"I'm only trying to change it," he spoke in a low voice, staring down at his feet.

"And so, what? Once you give me the throne that you apparently don't want, what then? You leave? Or do you continue to pull the strings out of sight so you can never be blamed, hiding away like you do with your people now?" I could feel the magic stirring in me, wanting to be violent, but I held it at bay.

"It's not like that, Meeka," he shook his head.

"Then what, Ajax? You have lied to me every step of the way." My jaw hurt from the strength with which I was clenching it.

"You'll never know how much I love hearing my name from your lips." He looked up at me, his eyes searching mine.

"Stop." I turned away.

"Meeka." He rose slowly to stand before me.

"You have toyed with me in every way," I whispered as I took a deep breath.

"I'm not trying to hurt you." He placed one hand on my shoulder, but I shrugged it off.

"Yet, you don't care when you do, as long as you get what you want." I walked away from him, standing by the small window overlooking the garden below. The moon had risen over the forests beyond, a full moon.

"I have to go. There are a few people I need to meet." He stalked toward the door.

"Of course you do." I turned away, holding in the bitter tears that threatened to spill.

"This is a good thing, Meeka. You need to see that. You are the leader this nation needs, the true heir of Skirsgard. You are the future," he opened the door to leave.

"You only use me for revenge against your dead father." I didn't face him.

"That's not true," he whispered. But I knew in my heart it was.

"Just go," I ground out. I didn't want him to know that I was hurt.

"I may think I've lied to you, but not everything has been a lie," and with that he left me alone in the room.

I was happy he left. I needed time alone, away from him. When prince Ajax was near, everything became muffled, emotions getting the better of me. I needed a clear head to think, to understand, and to decide my future.

Prince Ajax wanted me to become the queen. What a ridiculous notion that would have been only a few weeks ago, but now? So much had changed – I had changed.

I hated feeling like I was being used, like I was a puppet in another's game, but I had been that way my whole life. Since I was born, I was destined for things not of my own choosing. If the revolution had never occurred, it was I who would have been groomed for the throne.

When we fled to the North, I had to hide my identity without even knowing why. Always others had told me what to do and I complied without questioning. But now was the time to question. Could I fight my fate? Or were the hands of the gods at play, the inevitability of the throne a destiny I could not escape?

If this was to be my life, I would not sit back and watch as others defined it. I would take the reins; I would do what was best for the sake of my people, not for the sake of those who played the game.

And what of Ajax? Here I was thinking that he had constructed this whole affair so that he could be King. But I was wrong. All along he had done this for me. Looking back there were signs, but he'd never been forthcoming. This was all too much.

Prince Ajax might have his own interests at heart, but I would think of all my people. I suddenly felt tired. I had been practically dead only this morning, and whatever magic Trafi had used to paralyze me, had exhausted my body.

I grabbed the satchel prince Ajax had brought and pulled out a silk nightgown. I couldn't wear this. Instead, I pulled out a large rough tunic and slipped it on over my head. I went to the bed, pulled down the thick, fluffy covers, then stuffed two pillows down the middle, creating a barricade.

The prince may be my husband to the public, but he was not my husband in body or spirit. The bed was big enough to share, but the pillows would provide an ample wall.

I drifted off quickly, my eyelids heavy with the sting of exhaustion.

Serafina stood before me.

"Sister?" I questioned her.

"Meeka, we need to leave now!" She shouted, pulling open the curtains in my room in the palace where the gardens roared with fire.

"I'm tired, Serafina," I turned over in my bed, rolling the covers over my head. I couldn't muster the energy to care.

"Meeka. Now!" Serafina shouted at me, throwing the blanket off and yanking me by the arm.

I sat up groggily, rubbing my eyes. Serafina panicked around the room, grabbing little things here and there.

"What's going on, Serafina?" I asked, the flames licking against my window not yet registering in my brain. I grabbed the worn stuffed rabbit my mother had sewn and held it close to my chest.

"We are under attack. The King and Queen have been taken. We need to go – now!" She shouted at me again, flinging shoes and a coat in my direction. I took them and placed them on my feet and shoulders. As I did so, the situation finally sunk in. The gardens were on fire. The palace was burning.

"Oh my..." I began but couldn't finish. I leapt to my feet, grabbing Serafina's hand to hurry out of the room. I was scared and wanted my mother. A banging sounded on the door. Serafina looked at me. I had never seen her so frightened.

"The gardens," she whispered.

I nodded, understanding. We would need to go out the window, climb down the palace walls, and escape through the gardens.

Serafina used her magic to pull open the windows. She barricaded the door, throwing any furniture against the heavy wood with her mind. Sweat fell from her brow.

"Serafina, where are the others?" I asked while straddling the windowsill.

"Don't worry about them, Meeka, you are the one who needs to escape. You are the heir." Serafina motioned for me to hurry.

I began the slow climb down the wall, the fiery gardens quickly approaching and heating my brow. My magic hadn't come in yet, my opeki had only recently started to visit me. I was still too young, but Serafina would help make a path through the fire once she hurried down behind me.

I jumped the last few feet to the terrace, rolling upon the impact and screech of pain in my ankle. I stared up at the window, but Serafina was nowhere to be seen. She hadn't followed me down the wall.

Then I heard the screaming.

I ran like a coward, not sure where else to go, heading straight for the flames. I wove through fire and brush, my face scratched and bloody. I heard another scream.

A knot of shame burrowed in my stomach, and I forced myself to stop running. I couldn't leave Serafina, what was I thinking? I turned back toward the palace and ran.

Something pierced my chest.

I looked down to find a knife buried hilt deep, straight in my heart. My head swiveled, searching for the culprit, but all I saw were blurry shapes.

I heard a devilish sigh of relief as a dark figure ran from sight. Then another figure was there, hovering above my face, pulling me up into his arms. His blurry face focused and though he was only a boy, I recognized him immediately – Ajax.

"Stay with me," he breathed.

Then everything went black.

I awoke with a start, clutching my chest.

I was back in the inn.

It had been another dream. No, another memory.

# CHAPTER 43

Prince Ajax wasn't in our room when I woke. I looked around, panic settling deep in my chest. I calmed my breathing, closing my eyes, and focused on what I could smell, what I could touch, what I could feel, grounding myself. There was no danger here.

I looked out the small window to see dawn approaching. Had Ajax come back to our rooms at all?

I tried to shake away the feeling of dread. I shouldn't care one way or another if something happened to him. He deserved it, after all. But regardless, I dressed quickly and rushed from the room.

There were no patrons in the dining room, the hour too late for degenerates and too early for enthusiasts. I pushed through the front door and stepped into the warm air of dawn. A forest lay just beyond the inn, and the trees swaying in the breeze beckoned me closer. I loved the forest, it was where I felt most at home, most at ease, where I had spent most of time as a child, the time at least I remembered best.

I wasn't wearing any shoes, I realized, forgetting to put them on in my haste. I felt the mossy ground of the woods against my bare feet as I ventured deeper and deeper beneath the canopy of tall birch trees, giving way to pines. There was no sign of Ajax, but I was being pulled toward something, and I knew he was like my compass; I was drawn to his location.

Magic stirred beneath my skin, I could feel it crawling, feel it wanting to breath the fresh air as deeply as my soul. This new sensation was both exhilarating and overwhelming. I never knew I possessed this power, and yet it felt as much a part of me as my own mind. I still wasn't quite sure how to use it, but I was growing more confident in my abilities, even if I wasn't sure exactly what they were.

*Hofsdora, what can I do?*

*You can call the elements.*

*Do you need to do it for me, or can I do it on my own?*

*I've given you the ability, you can call it on your own. Though if I die, it dies.*

I threw my hands out now, calling the wind, feeling it swirl around my hands and answer my call. I asked the tree for a branch, and it dropped one in my hand. I held it and swirled it in my palm, smiling joyfully. I told the tree to take it back, and it obeyed, the branch lifting back up and reattaching its fallen limb.

"Neat trick," I swirled around, baring my fists, slapping out at whoever had approached. I connected with rough skin, before looking up to realize I had hit Ajax in the face.

"Don't sneak up on me like that," I shouted at him, pushing him on the arm. He gave me a look of annoyance and scoffed. "Are you hurt?"

"Not from that little thump," he mumbled.

"I could have hurt you if I wanted to," I replied cockily.

"I'm sure you could have. Though not in the way you think." He put his hand to his cheek and rubbed against the mark I'd left.

"What are you doing out here?" I asked.

"I could ask you the same," he replied, eyebrows raised.

"I was looking for you," I crossed my arms over my chest.

"Ah, so you missed your husband." His eyes glinted as he took a step closer. I backed away into a tree, leaning against it. Ajax continued forward, eyes trained on me with a predatory gleam. He placed one arm on the tree against the side of my head and leaned down. I could feel his breath against mine. My heart raced as warmth pooled in my middle.

"I didn't miss you, I just wanted to know what mysterious things you were up to this time," I whispered out, trying not to look at his lips which were much too close to mine.

"So, you were worried about me?" His mouth quirked up in a lopsided smile.

"No, I-" I stammered and pushed him away before I did something I would regret. But the absence of his body felt more like a punishment than a relief. I closed my eyes, trying to regain my thoughts before turning around.

"And are you still mad at me, my queen?" He placed both hands in his pockets and looked at me with eyes drawn. He appeared almost regretful, almost like he truly cared about my feelings. I didn't know what was true and what was a lie.

"Don't call me that," I clenched my jaw. Was he trying to get a rise out of me?

"You will always be my queen," he dipped his chin ever so slightly as in a bow.

"Oh, shut up," I rushed toward him pushing against his chest with both my palms. I was so sick of his games. He was playing with both my mind and my heart. He stumbled back a step, taken off guard, but when I tried to pull away, he grabbed both of my wrists, keeping my hands pinned to his chest.

"Meeka," he purred my name the same way he did in the North, back when he was Johnny Pullver, and I was an ignorant fool. I wanted to pull away, but I couldn't. I was locked into his gaze, locked against his body, pulled by a force I didn't understand.

My breathing became ragged. I was torn between reality and whatever this was between us. My brain told me to stop, told me not to trust this man, this man who had lied to me continually, who wanted things for me that I wasn't sure I wanted myself. But a lump beat against the inside of my chest. The lump reached for him, wanted him, needed him.

"Is it true? Was it you who saved me?" I asked remembering my dream.

"I told you I've saved you many times," his voice was unfocused, his breathing ragged.

"I had a dream, or maybe it was a memory. When I was a child, a fire, a knife in my heart. It was you that picked me up. You rescued me, didn't you?"

He nodded slowly, his breath mingling with my own.

"But why?"

"I told you. You are my queen. Then and now."

I took a deep shuddering breath. I was on a precipice, the tension waiting to snap.

I could see the same wild indecision in his eyes. He searched mine with an intensity that made me shudder. I opened my mouth to speak but no words came out.

"Meeka-"

"Ajax," I breathed out a soft sound through pursed lips.

It undid us both.

I saw the loss of control in his eyes. I saw when his face melted and rugged determination won.

He dropped my hands from his and instead reached up, caressing my face then reaching around to grab my hair in his fists.

He pulled my face toward his and took me.

His lips crashed into mine, a force needing release. The want was so great, I met it with my own. My arms came up his chest and wrapped around his neck pulling him closer and closer, I needed him closer, deeper.

"Ahem," a rough voice interrupted, and I reluctantly pushed Ajax away, wiping at my swollen lips.

I looked at Ajax, who stood panting, hair as wild as the eyes locked on mine. It was almost impossible to look away. A deep frustration shone in his gaze, and I felt the unsatisfaction of the moment down to my core. I wanted more.

"You're early," the voice of the newcomer continued, moving closer. With great effort I peeled my wide eyes away from Ajax to look toward whoever had severed the moment.

"Who are you?" I asked, still too shaken to be concerned with this man. He was tall and regal looking, though he dressed in peasant clothing. His dark hair was slicked back, and a large, slanted nose stood imperiously underneath sunken eyes.

"My name is Tieman, your highness. I'm your uncle and I've come to welcome you home."

# CHAPTER 44

After gathering our belongings from the inn, we rode all day on the horses Tieman brought with him. Ajax and I barely spoke, his lips still too fresh on my own.

I did my best not to complain, though my fondness for horses continued to dwindle. Periodically, I caught Ajax glimpsing in my direction, but neither of us seemed prepared to break the silence. Something had snapped between us. A line that had been previously drawn, now erased. My body burned for him, even as my mind still warred.

My legs and thighs were aching by the time we stopped to rest by a stream on the side of the road.

"Thank the gods," I murmured as I dismounted.

"To think, my very own kin, with an aversion to horses," Tieman chuckled, shaking his head.

"They don't seem all that fond of me either," I grumbled, rubbing my thighs.

"Nonsense." Tieman batted me away.

"How much longer?" I asked.

"A few more hours until we arrive at the village. But we can rest a moment before we continue." Tieman grunted as he pulled out a loaf of bread from his pack.

"Always rushing." I grabbed a chunk from Tieman, taking a seat on a nearby log.

"Enjoy this time, princess, I'm afraid things won't slow down for you anytime soon." Tieman handed Ajax the remainder of the loaf.

I sighed. Tieman was right.

"Did you hear that?" Ajax tensed.

"No," I frowned.

"What did you hear?" Tieman pulled a blade from his pocket.

Before Ajax could answer, a low moan came from the bushes across the road.

I stood abruptly, dropping my chunk of bread on the ground.

The bushes rustled as a man came sauntering out of the brush. He wore ragged clothing that was torn in places. His face was muddy and bleeding. Cuts ran the lengths of his arms. He wore no shoes. This was a man who had been terribly beaten and left for dead.

"What happened to you, man?" Ajax shouted across the road, his hand resting on the hilt of his sword.

"Bandits. Beat me to a bloody pulp. Took off with my horse and all my belongings." The man slurred.

"When was this?" Tieman bellowed.

"Not an hour past." The man stumbled toward us.

Ajax stepped in front of me, shielding me with his body.

Tieman looked up and down the road, eyes narrowed.

"I see no hoof marks," Tieman drawled, unsheathing his dagger.

The man seethed, barring his teeth. "You refuse to help a man who's been robbed?" He spat and sputtered.

"What do you need?" I pushed past Ajax.

"My lady," he bowed slightly though he wobbled on his feet.

"Here," I picked up the bread that I had lost in my haste. I grabbed my water skin from the horse and brought it to the man.

"Meeka-" Ajax cautioned before I interrupted him.

"He's in need, and we have plenty to spare," I glowered at Ajax.

Ajax grabbed my arm stopping me from meeting the man. I whirled on him.

"He doesn't have any eyes, Meeka." Ajax whispered, stopping me in my tracks.

"What-" I twirled back as the man began to hackle.

"Clever, clever, little one," he met my eyes. Ajax was right. Where his eyes should have been, instead rested two opaque and speckled orbs.

I froze, fear pinning me to my place.

The thing jumped, quicker than it had any right to be.

Ajax moved, slashing his sword, but the man used his magic to push Ajax away, sending him flying. He hit a tree and fell to the forest floor. Tieman brought his dagger around, attempting to stab the man, but the man was too quick. Tieman missed and the creature kicked him in the chest. He crashed to the ground with a thud.

I stood there, paralyzed.

"You showed me kindness. Perhaps I should let you live." The man smiled, showing his white teeth in an evil grin.

"What are you?"

"A blemmyes." He lunged and grabbed my wrist, pulling mc in close.

Ajax shouted, struggling to his feet. "Don't touch her."

I stared up into the creature's nonexistent eyes, not knowing how he could even see me.

*Hofsdora, a little help.*

I heard a chuckle in the back of my mind. Bloody opeki, no help at all.

The blemmyesi are an ancient tribe. Their opeki follow their own rules.

"Well, well, it's the little princess, isn't it?" The blemmyes hissed in my face, its breath smelled of rot and dirt. He grabbed me around the waist, squeezing my back against his chest as he brought a long taloned finger against my neck.

Tieman lay unconscious on the ground. Ajax tensed, sword drawn, looking panicked.

"Move and I slit her throat, prince," the creature hissed.

"How do you know me?" Ajax furrowed his brows.

"You fought my kin in the pits," he seethed, "I should kill her just to spite you."

Ajax' eyes went wide. "You dare and I'll-"

"What?" The blemmyes laughed, pushing his talon lightly against my skin, just enough to form a shallow cut. I felt the warm blood drip down my neck. "You'll use your magic on me?"

"Ajax," I whispered his name, fear creeping down my spine. Ajax glanced around in dread.

"What do you want?" Ajax pleaded. It was the first time I had seen his mask of confidence shatter.

"Want?" the creature chuckled, "I don't have your same luxury for wants." His grip tightened.

"Use your magic, Ajax!" I shouted.

*You forget you have magic too.*

This world was still so new to me, I had almost forgotten in my fear.

I whirled on the blemmyes, taking him by surprise. His talon missed my neck, but swept across my collar bone, opening a shallow wound.

I used my magic to fling him backward, the strain of the effort making my muscles ache. It worked briefly until he lunged with inhuman strength, leaping on top of me.

Ajax jumped on top of the creature, throwing him off. The blemmyes whirled on Ajax, kicking him across the road. I struggled to my feet.

Tieman groaned, finally regaining consciousness.

The blemmyes hissed, turning his attention back on me. He leapt again, landing a foot away, but Tieman used his magic this time to create a wall a flame between the blemmyes and myself.

The creature hesitated, and I took a deep breath, willing more power to obey my command. I jumped across the flames and threw my magic at him, pushing him in the air and fixing him to the trunk of a tree.

"I tried to be kind," I growled, keeping him pinned to the tree with my magic.

"It is why I spared your lives." He barred his teeth, the strange lack of eyes making my stomach turn.

"Will you help me?" I challenged.

"What?" Even without eyes I saw the surprise rip across his face.

"If I am to rule these lands, I want all its peoples to be united – the blemmyesi included," I pressed on.

"I don't understand." He strained against my hold.

I sighed, "I'm not going to kill you." I let him fall from the grip of my magic. He looked around in dismay, uncertainty casting a light on his features. "You are free to go. But tell your tribe I've returned. Tell them what I've asked."

He looked around confused, and for a moment I thought he may attack. Instead, he turned, taking off into the forest faster than should be possible.

"Well, that was weird," I crumpled to the ground sitting beneath folded knees, rubbing my face. "What was that thing anyway?"

"The blemmyesi have been troubling these parts for centuries," Tieman offered in explanation.

"It was so fast." I rubbed at my collarbone where the blood was beginning to congeal.

"They have powerful opeki. They are skilled in many things, strength and speed being topmost," Tieman continued.

"They could be useful," I mused.

"You seem to forget that thing just tried to kill us," Ajax grumbled, limping over and shaking out his minor injuries.

"And yet it didn't," I pointed out.

"You are mental," Ajax shook his head.

"You didn't use your magic to help me." I tried not to sound disappointed.

"I don't have any." Ajax came beside me, kneeling.

"You what?" I asked, shock contorting my face.

"I haven't had magic since I was a child."

I looked up into his face and saw a rawness filled with grief.

"You never told me."

"You never asked."

"What happened?" I whispered.

"My father killed my opeki." He clenched his jaw. There was more pain in his words than I could understand.

"How?" I gasped.

"When I came back from the war. Before the pits. He said I didn't need it anymore. I was too great a threat. He made his opeki kill mine." The pain was clear on his face.

*Is that even possible?* I asked Hofsdora.

*Of course. In our world there is death and war as well.*

"I'm..." I couldn't find the words, "I can't even imagine." I shook my head.

"It wasn't your doing." Ajax gave me a soft smile.

"No more lying. I want to know everything from now on." I looked deep into his eyes, pleading. I didn't want anymore secrets between us.

"I promise." Ajax pulled my body close to his, wrapping me in his warm embrace.

# CHAPTER 45

As soon as we recovered enough to ride, we mounted the horses and took off, not wanting to waste any more time in this forest. After a few hours, we finally made it to the small village hidden in a deep valley. As we dismounted our horses in the stables, exhaustion was replaced with a deeply unsettling feeling. I was about to meet my family.

I remembered very little of these people. I had no idea who had survived, and who had perished, no idea where their loyalties lay, or what they had been through in the years since the revolution. And I was supposed to blindly trust them.

"We need to talk," I pulled Ajax aside while my uncle busied with the horses. Ajax glanced sideways and I thought he may refuse but instead nodded and followed me into a nearby stall.

"Are you ok?" Ajax looked concerned by whatever he found on my face, bending down and checking for injuries. But besides the cut on my neck and a few bruises, I was fine.

"A lot happened today," I sighed.

"About this morning-" he began but I cut him off.

"That's not what I want to talk about," I replied hastily, not yet wanting to confront whatever had happened between us in the forest.

"Then what?" He smiled wickedly but looked relieved. "Back for more?"

"You're so annoying," I muttered, turning away to hide the blush that crept up my cheeks. "No, I just, I don't know what to think about all this-" I began but didn't know how to phrase my reluctance. I waved my hands, gesturing to the space around us.

"Don't worry, Meeka. This is your family. You can trust them," he spoke quietly, his eyes softening.

"But I don't even know them," I whispered.

"Meeka, look at me," he stepped forward and grabbed my hands. I looked up into his eyes. "Everything is going to be ok. I am by your side."

"Well-" I let go of his warm palms.

"You still don't trust me?" He stepped back.

"There is just so much I'm trying to process."

"You better start. I am your husband, after all." The muscle in his jaw ticked. "Actually, I wanted to talk to you about something, too."

He ran his hands through his hair. Hair that I had recently touched, my own fingers running through the delicious locks. I shook away the thought.

"Are you two done fooling around?" Tieman cleared his throat from the other side of the stall.

"That's not-" I fumbled, "we are just talking."

"Whatever you say," I could hear a light chuckle, "but it's time to meet the family."

"Talk later?" I asked.

Ajax looked disappointed but nodded.

We left the stables and followed my uncle, walking through abandoned looking streets. Dusk was settling in with a breeze that refreshed my skin after hours of riding. Candles flickered in the windows of straw thatched homes as we passed.

"Where are we?" I asked no one in particular.

"Tysenky, a small village in the west. This has been the home of our people the last ten years," my uncle responded.

I looked around. Some of the homes looked alive and peaceful but sprinkled throughout were homes that had been half burned down, crumpled, or razed.

"What happened here?" I asked.

"This was where the rebel forces held out after the revolution," my uncle sighed beside me, eyeing Ajax, "where the final fighting took place."

"And they haven't come back to finish you off?" I curiously wondered aloud.

"We signed a treaty. We would stop fighting back if they let us live here in peace. Negotiations were carried out by your prince here," he gestured to Ajax.

"Her husband," Ajax interjected.

"About that-" Tieman turned on Ajax, eyes simmering.

"Why don't we wait for the others, and I'll explain everything," Ajax interrupted.

"I thought you went to the fighting pits after the war?" I asked.

Tieman eyed Ajax.

"I did," Ajax ground his teeth. I had the feeling he didn't want to discuss this further, but I pushed on anyway.

"So, you fought in the war, went to the fighting pits, then came back here?" I asked confused.

"Not quite," he murmured.

"We captured Ajax during the war. When we heard he helped rescue you and many more of the family, we trained him. Then we sent him back to find you." Tieman explained.

So, the prince had been working with my family the whole time.

"You trained him then sent him back to the palace?" I glared.

"Exactly." Tieman nodded with pride.

"So, you're the reason he was tortured, the reason he went to the fighting pits?" I asked, anger rising. He'd been only a child when he was sent to war. Then they had captured him and honed him into a fighting machine, only to return him. Because of them, Ajax had gone through hell. It made my blood boil.

"You turned him into a walking target," I seethed.

"We did what was necessary. It worked, didn't it? He found you eventually." Tieman shrugged.

"He went to the pits because of you. His opeki was killed because of you."

"Easy there, princess," Tieman glared down at me, taking my anger seriously for the first time.

"Meeka, don't act like I had no say in the matter," Ajax interrupted.

"Well, did you?" I asked, spinning around to meet his gaze.

"It wasn't all that bad. If they hadn't trained me so well, there's no way I would have survived so long without my magic," Ajax pointed out. His lips quirked up at the sides. He was enjoying my outburst.

"Captain Bellamoni said you fought a lion and won. The blemmyes said you fought his kin. But without magic, how?"

"I fought well," Ajax shrugged.

"You really fought in the pits and killed a lion without any magic? You faced the blemmyes?" I narrowed my eyes.

"Yes. I did." He looked away.

"Wow, my husband is so strong," I bat my eyes at Tieman, who scoffed in return.

"Come on, you. Quit drooling," Ajax shook his head as he hid a smile, pulling me along down the road.

We continued through the various avenues before arriving at a large hall in the center of the village. It reminded me a bit of Innesbrown, which caused mixed emotions to swirl inside me, knotting my stomach in an unpleasant way.

We entered a long wooden building. Tapestries hung from the walls under a row of thin windows. The ceiling was made of a series of crisscross beams, covered in a thatched roof. The room itself was long and narrow, with pews lining either side. These pews were full of people, my kin.

Murmurs and whispers erupted as Tieman led us to the front of the hall. Although these people were my relatives, I was still the only one with hair a fiery red, sticking out from the crowd like a candle in the dark.

Tieman knocked loudly on the pedestal that stood at the front, quieting the murmurs. I spotted Trafi in the third row. She gave me a secretive smile and nodded. I nodded back.

"You can see now why I gathered you here," he began and gestured to me, "our princess has returned." The room fell into a deep hush as though a great intake of breath had been sucked out of the room. I stood there awkwardly, not sure what I was supposed to do. Not sure what these people even wanted from me.

Slowly, one by one, they began to kneel. I looked to Tieman who smiled and then kneeled himself. I turned toward Ajax. I shook my head, begging him silently not to kneel, but he gave me a wicked smile and dropped to one knee.

"Stand up," I demanded, feeling overwhelmingly uncomfortable. Everyone in the room complied. "I-" I began but wasn't sure what to say. Ajax looked at me questioningly and I nodded for him to continue.

"Princess Meeka was rescued from the North as soon as we found out her mother was alive. Unfortunately, her mother did not survive." Prince Ajax looked down meeting my eyes. "Meeka has been through a lot but has been slowly regaining both her memories and her magic."

"And why should we trust you, son of a traitor?" One of the older men in the front shouted.

"Have I not done everything you've asked of so far?" Ajax asked, annoyed.

"Don't forget he saved you, too, Maurice," a greying woman across the halls shouted at the man.

"He's been gone from us many years now," Maurice sighed, "who knows what they've been teaching him."

"I assure you, I am on your side." Ajax ground out.

"He is," I spoke in barely a whisper, but even that quieted the room. It was odd having this sort of power over a crowd. "He is my...my husband."

I looked at Ajax who seemed profoundly amused at my confession, if not a little surprised. The crowd erupted in a fit of grumbling. Some of the younger ones squealed in delight, while the older folk cast wary glances as a suspicious buzzing broke out throughout the room.

"Quiet, quiet," Tieman bellowed, "whether the prince has his own self-interest at heart or that of our future queen, is irrelevant. Regardless, their fates are intertwined, and we must live with that." He sounded drained.

"The rumors have spread of the princess' return," Ajax continued, "and now the rumors of her marriage, and her death will grow – but also her miraculous resurrection."

"A bit of a theatrical touch, I'd say," Tieman cut in.

"That's what I said," I agreed. Tieman grinned.

"It's done the job. Many will support her." The prince argued.

"And you, Prince Ajax? Are you not the one who would become king?" A woman in the front row pointed out.

"You know I have never wanted that. I have been helping support your family for years. Why question my loyalty now?" Ajax sounded exasperated.

"And was a marriage really necessary?" A vein throbbed in Tieman's forehead.

"You know she needed to be married to be coronated," Ajax bit out.

"It didn't have to be to you," Tieman growled. I felt for Ajax in that moment. He had been rejected by his own and fought for my people. Yet here still, he was treated with contempt. Really, it was a lot like my own life.

"I-," Ajax stammered and looked down at me. He placed his hand protectively on my lower back, nudging me ever so closer to his side. "It seemed the best option at the time."

"And what of the council?" Maurice asked.

"They aim to place my uncle as leader of a military regime," he sighed. I glanced at Ajax. "However, the marriage gives both Meeka and I the right to claim the throne." He ran his hands through his hair in the same gesture I found distracting.

"They will know you came here," Maurice shot back.

"Yes," Ajax sighed.

"So, you have brought war to our doorstep," Maurice shook his head.

"War was inevitable," Tieman cut in, "it was only a matter of time when the treaty would break."

I looked around the room at the faces of my kin. These people had been the ruling class once, had been knocked down to nothing, and still, they would fight for my throne. They would fight for me. I took a deep breath steadying the dizziness that threatened to knock me down. Just like prince Ajax, these people had high expectations for my life. I was a symbol, a piece in a game, not a real person with real opinions or thoughts. These decisions were beyond my own. But I was not weak.

Standing there amongst the crowd, I finally realized that it didn't matter. It didn't matter what I wanted, there were greater forces at play. This was about a nation, a whole people that needed stability, needed a ruler who would care for them, listen to them, be there for them. Could I do that? Could I be that ruler? Not if I only cared about what I wanted.

So, I took a deep breath and made a promise to myself. I could do this; I would do this. Not for myself, but for the good of all, I would serve my country.

"I'll do it." I spoke, this time not in a whisper, but with conviction. Even though the people in this room, the prince, and countless others had already laid this path down for me since the moment I was born, I would choose this life.

I would be Queen.

# CHAPTER 46



We spent the next week preparing for the future. A group of volunteers traveled to nearby villages, gathering support. News from Tyev proved our thoughts correct. A military council had taken control of the capital. War loomed on the horizon.

I spent the early mornings training in the woods with Trafi or Ajax. My days were full of lessons on politics and planning for war with my kin. By nightfall I was so tired, I stumbled to bed half asleep.

I woke and made my way to the usual training ground. The morning fog was still heavy beneath the canopy, and the chirping of insects provided tranquil music.

I took a deep breath and closed my eyes. I focused on the world around me, bending it to my will. A force of power swirled around my skin, obeying my command before I blasted it out.

*See it isn't so hard.*

*I still don't understand if it's me doing the magic or you.*

*That's because you don't understand magic.*

*Well then enlighten me.* I huffed.

"What's wrong?" Ajax asked as he entered the clearing.

"My opeki tells me nothing useful. Kind of like someone else I know." I eyed Ajax sideways.

"What do you want to know, Meeka?" He asked.

"How does it all work? Magic and the opeki?" I took a deep breath. "Sorry does it bother you when I ask about magic?"

"It doesn't bother me. It was hard at first, but I've grown used to life alone." He sighed. My heart dropped at his confession, and I resisted the urge to go to him, to comfort him.

"How does the magic work?" I asked instead.

"No one knows how the opeki choose their person but it's believed to be the will of the gods," he shrugged, "the opeki have different of strengths. They match with those who are compatible."

*I told you I am a Queen, like you, where I come from.*

*You really are?*

*Yes.*

*Can I see you?* I wondered.

*Only if I let you.*

"How are there different types of magics if it all comes from the opeki?" I asked Ajax.

"Well, everyone has different strengths and weaknesses. The opeki are similar. Where they come from, there are different abilities. The opeki join with those who share similarities playing off their person's strengths and weaknesses." Ajax continued to stalk around me.

"So, there are those with elemental magic, like me. And that proteus we met in the alleyway. The blemmyesi are strong and fast. Also, Trafi did that play dead thing to me. What was that?" I asked.

"Trafi can manipulate the body. She has some elemental as well – most do," he explained.

"And the proteus?" I asked.

"That's a type of physical magic. A manipulation of the senses. Probably both the opeki and the human are naturally good with deception." Ajax paced.

"Hmm," I furrowed my brow, "and the opeki's realm – is it somewhere we can go?"

"Not in this life," the prince chuckled.

I closed my eyes, trying to picture another realm. Only a short time ago, I didn't even know there was magic. And now I was picturing other realms. How far I'd come.

"And what of my stone heart?" I wondered.

"That's something different," the prince ran his hands through his hair.

"What do you mean?" I looked up at him, alarmed.

"The opeki take an oath to the gods to honor their person and to serve them or leave them – but never to turn them to darkness. Many generations ago, one fell into the shadows and entered this world, vowing to turn others to its side. Your ancestors fought against the fallen opeki, banishing the creature, but not without consequence. A piece of the fallen one entered the slayer's heart, turning it to stone." Ajax looked me up and down.

"So, I have a piece of an opeki within me?" It felt unbelievable yet made sense. I thought instantly of the shadow creature and debated telling Ajax.

"We all have darkness within us. But you have a curse as well. Once that could be used for greatness or evil," Ajax sighed.

"How reassuring," I muttered.

"It's not all bad – it has saved your life a couple times now." Ajax shrugged.

"So, the opeki use their person's strengths and weaknesses?" I mused, happy to lead the subject away from my cursed heart.

"Yes." Ajax stopped pacing and leaned against a tree, one foot propped up against the trunk. "What are your strengths and weaknesses?"

"My strengths - I have a stone heart so am hard to kill. I can use elemental magic. I am weak because...I don't know. Why do I have to be weak?" I huffed.

"Finish answering the question." Ajax folded his arms across his chest.

"I am weak because I still have so much to learn. I am weak because I'm cursed. There, happy?" I always knew

I must be cursed. I just never knew my heart was so involved.

"Having more to learn isn't a weakness," Ajax replied.

"It is to me." I looked into Ajax' eyes. He shook his head.

"And what are my strengths and weaknesses, Meeka?" He pushed off the tree.

"Your strength is lying, and your weakness is me." I gave him a sly smile. He grinned.

"I am very strong in general, and I have no weakness," he stalked toward me.

"I'm not so sure about that," I sauntered toward him with confidence.

Two could play this game. When we were standing close enough to touch, I brought my hand up to his cheek but did not touch his skin. Instead, I glanced at him beneath my lashes, placing my hand against his chest. His heartbeat quickened as I traced my hand down his broad torso. He sucked in a breath, his face moving ever so slightly down to meet mine. I gathered power and pushed. He flew a few feet and landed on his backside.

"See, I am your weakness," I held my hands over my mouth as I laughed wholeheartedly.

"That was foul play, you little-" he jumped up and grabbed me around the waist, lifting me over his shoulder as I kicked and laughed playfully. He put me down and nudged me backward as I bent over laughing. I hit him on the arm, but he grabbed my wrist pulling me in close.

"Maybe I'm your weakness too," he breathed, his air mixing with mine.

"You two seem to be getting along," Trafi stood against a tree at the end of the clearing. I pulled away from Ajax, my face flushing in embarrassment.

"I was just practicing my magic," I said more defensively than intended.

"Oh, sure," Trafi held back a smile, "anyway you're wanted in the hall."

"What do they want?" Ajax asked, sounding annoyed.

"Not you. Just her," Trafi gestured for me to follow her. I glanced back at Ajax who was running his hands through his hair.

"I'll see you at dinner," I told him. He nodded and turned, walking in the other direction.

"So, what was that all about?" Trafi asked.

"What do you mean?" I replied distractedly jumping over roots so not to trip.

"You and the prince seem awfully cozy," Trafi said with a hint of amusement.

"He is my husband, afterall," I murmured, annoyed and embarrassed.

"Not really, though, right?" She glanced sideways at me.

"No, not really," I ground out, confused by the knot of anger in my core. Trafi didn't push the subject further and I was glad.

We made our way through the remainder of the forest and back through town, until we arrived at the hall. Several encampments had formed over the past several days of neighboring men and woman come to support my claim. It was an unsettling feeling, that all these people wanted to follow me blindly. They didn't know me, or even what I stood for. Yet, they would fight for me. They chose me. I could only hope I was worthy of their loyalty.

"Meeka," Tieman spoke, waiting for me at the front of the hall.

"What is it?" I asked.

"We need to talk," he took a deep breath, slowly exhaling.

"Yes?" I asked.

"I'm sorry we haven't spent much time together besides talk of war," Tieman said, "as you know we've all been busy preparing. But I wanted to check in and see how you are doing with this all. Come sit," He gestured to the nearest pew. We both sat.

I appreciated the thoughtfulness of his remark but wasn't quite sure what to say.

"I'm doing ok," I spoke slowly.

"Ajax - is he treating you-" Tieman cut off, looking away, not sure how to ask.

"He's saved my life numerous times." I hoped that would be a good enough explanation. I wanted to change the subject.

"Did he force you into this marriage?" He asked looking down at his feet. For such an imposing man, it was almost comical to see him sheepish.

"Well, yes kind of," I began, but at the way Tieman went rigid I quickly continued, "but also no, not really."

"Is that supposed to make me feel better? We can get this whole thing annulled once you are coronated. We can change the law; a ruler shouldn't need to be married. It's outdated," he blustered.

"He didn't tell me his plans beforehand. But-," I paused, feeling awkward, "I agreed to it. I said 'yes.' And if I didn't, I'm not sure he would have gone through with it." I hadn't thought about it before, but it felt true.

"Hmm," my cousin replied vaguely.

"Don't worry, Tieman," I put my hand on his shoulder, "I'm grown up now. I can handle this. I can handle Ajax," I gave him a smile trying to reassure him.

Tieman only nodded.

"He's not all that bad. Actually, he's been," I struggled to find the right words, "well, on my side."

Tieman eyed me, his gaze boring into my own. Whatever he saw in my eyes seemed to appease him and he nodded standing up.

"Very well then," he smiled shaking his head, "love has a funny way of choosing its victims."

"Who said anything about love?" I choked out.

Before Tieman could respond the door to the hall opened with a bang.

"Tieman, they are here," one of the younger cousins panted, "the military has arrived. They come prepared to fight."

# CHAPTER 47

250

News spread quickly about the military's arrival. They formed a camp a half day's ride from the village, preparing for an imminent war. Panic settled deep into my core. I did not want anyone to die because of me, though I did not see any other way.

The village had been training for this. Not only since my arrival, but since the revolution. Maurice informed me they'd always planned to fight back as soon as my mother or I was found. They never meant to keep faith on the treaty, instead they lay in wait, a snake coiled to strike. Still, men would die, and the blood would be on my hands.

"What's the plan?" I asked Tieman as we collected the children and mothers, loading them on to wagons with provisions to be taken away from the village.

"You need to decide if we go to them, or wait until they come to us," Tieman panted out, lifting a child.

"I need to decide?" I asked in a panic.

"You are our leader – you might as well start now," he gave me a pointed look.

"But I've never fought in a battle," I squeaked out.

"Then I suggest you ask for help," he continued loading children.

I took a deep breath, exhaling slowly. I needed to find Ajax, he would know what to do. At the look of panic on my face, Tieman softened.

"Don't forget who you are, Meeka," he nodded at me.

I nodded back, hardly feeling at ease. How could I forget?

I found Trafi piling crates with potatoes and corn.

"Have you seen Ajax?" I asked.

"Not since this morning," she replied, a question on her face.

"Continue," I waved her to complete her task, trying to sound like I had an ounce of authority over the matter.

I meandered down the lane until I spotted Maurice. He was gathering weapons and handing them out to a line of ragged men and women.

"Maurice," I strode with a confidence I didn't feel, "how many men do we have?"

"About 200 strong," he glanced up at me, jaw set, "we can win this fight."

"And how many men do they have?" I asked. His mask of certainty wavered.

"We don't know," he spoke low, so the others couldn't hear. It wasn't reassuring.

"Well, we better find out. I'll sneak into their camp," I nodded.

"Not you personally?" Maurice looked at me in disbelief.

"And who else? I know my way around a wood better than most," I challenged.

"Bring someone with you, at least. And be careful, Meeka. If anyone needs to survive, it's you," he stared me down. The knot of tension in my stomach only grew.

I left him there to resume preparing the men. I was impressed that everyone seemed to know what to do. I wish I had that same confidence. I needed a plan, and quick. First, I would discover how many men we were up against – and to do that, I hoped to find Ajax. But he was nowhere to be found.

The day passed as I made rounds, checking on everyone's progress, as I slowly began to form a plan of my own. As the sun fell, those remaining in the village gathered in the hall, Ajax' whereabouts still unknown.

I pushed away the knot of worry. Surely, he hadn't betrayed me yet again. But no, things were different now and the trust I was so scared to give, had begun to form anyway. I desperately wanted to search for him, but there were more pressing things at hand. These people were looking to me for answers. I was their leader.

A hush came over the hall as I stood to address the room.

"Before we begin this fight, there are a few things I'd like to say," I took a deep breath steadying myself before continuing, "thank you for placing your faith in me, I don't know if I deserve it, but I will do my best to earn it. I have a plan, and if it goes as hoped, maybe we can avoid a fight altogether. If not, we leave at daybreak. Let's not drag this on."

"Here, here!" Someone shouted from the back.

"I did not choose this life, but I am a fighter and a survivor, and I promise you that I will do my best to serve you if we make it through," I squared my shoulders, "though I will need all your help."

I let Tieman take over, leaving the fighting preparations up to him.

I gestured for Trafi to come to my side. Without Ajax here, I would bring her with me to the enemy camp. We needed to find out how many men we were up against and what kind of weapons they had. We would not go into this fight blind.

"Trafi," I brought her to the side before continuing, "you and I will leave as soon as darkness falls."

"Where are we going?" She asked crossing her arms, "and where is your prince?"

"Don't worry about that now," I said pushing my own knot of worry down, "I think I have a plan."

Knowing we would be up most of the night, Trafi and I took advantage of the evening to eat and rest. I went back to my small chamber in a nearby thatched cabin, and lay down, the weight of the world feeling heavy on my chest.

I thought it'd be impossible to sleep, but before I knew it, I drifted into the world of dreams.

Once again, the fires were all encompassing. I looked up at the window, but Serafina had yet to descend. What was taking her so long? And then the screaming began.

I ran as fast as an eight-year-old could run – but I was strong and fit, I'd been trained all my life. Mother said I would be queen one day. It made me feel special.

Halfway through the gardens I halted. I couldn't leave Serafina. I was a leader. They were counting on me. They told me so, often. I turned back toward my rooms. My opeki was stubborn and wouldn't let me use my magic yet, but all my tutors told me I would be powerful. If it would only surface now, I could save Serafina and put out the fires.

"Pa," I startled. Pa stood in front of me, knife drawn.

"I'm not your Pa, girl," he snarled at me, "you little red devil, time to go back to the hell you came from."

Pa came at me, only he wasn't my Pa, not really. My father had died in an accident years ago. This man was my stepfather, a military man from out of town. He had won over Mother, but all of us kids knew he was hiding something. Mother wouldn't hear of it.

"Pa, what are you doing?" I was afraid. He looked at me with wild eyes, knife focused in my direction.

"What I came here to do all along. Long live the revolution," Pa stepped closer and slammed the blade into my chest.

I woke sweating. I remembered. Pa was the traitor. It had been Pa all along.

# CHAPTER 48

I'd forgotten. How could I forget? Pa. He wasn't my real father. How could I possibly have forgotten. In the North my memories had been stripped. Pa had traveled with us, hidden amongst us as though a friend. As though a father.

I had been so strong for so long. I had held in tears and betrayal, anger and sadness, but this? This was too much. For the first time in years, I cried.

Once the tears began, they would not stop. I cried for myself, I cried for my dead brothers and sisters, I cried for my Ma – my mother who had been trying to protect us, forgetting there was a wolf among sheep. Maybe she had never even known.

Sobs racked my body, spasming as the grief and anger poured out of my soul, the tears cleansing my very core. I stayed that way a while, praying to the gods who had cursed me with this fate.

As my body and mind began to calm, I took a series of deep breaths, stilling myself, finding an inner peace I never knew existed. This was not the end. This was only the beginning. The truth had a way of freeing me from the confines of my past.

I got up, resolving to put the past behind me. My future was to be queen- it was always meant to be this way. And to do that I needed to put my people first. I would be a shepherd among sheep; I would lead them so safety and protect them from the wolves.

I found Trafi asleep in a pile of hay and nudged her awake.

"Time to go," I gestured for her to follow. She murmured something foul but reluctantly got up, rubbing her eyes.

"I was having a good dream," she complained.

"Funny, my dream was particularly awful," I shook away those thoughts.

"Will you tell me where we are going?" She asked, more awake by the minute.

"To the enemy camp, let's see if we can stop this war before it starts." While grief was still fresh in my mind, I felt stronger than before, as though the truth lifted a weight I didn't know I was carrying.

"Lead the way," Trafi smiled, a genuine smile that made her eyes sparkle.

We walked for hours through the woods. Though I didn't know the way, I had been told the general direction the military's camp lay, and I used my tracking skills to my advantage. Trafi and I barely spoke, staying quiet in case anyone else was lurking around, keeping watch over the ominous forest.

"I think we're getting close," I whispered.

"Are you sure we aren't going in circles?" Trafi countered.

"Yes, I smell smoke. There'll be a campfire nearby," I took this opportunity to use my magic, pulling the smells from the surrounding air.

*Something isn't right.*

*What is it, Hofsadora?* I asked, trying not to be alarmed.

*A shadow lurks.*

"What do we do now?" Trafi asked.

"We need to get close enough to see how many men they have," I motioned for Trafi to stop, "then we need to find a way to speak with the General without being killed."

"Sounds easy," Trafi rolled her eyes, "is that your genius plan?"

“Do you have anything better?” I shot her a look of annoyance. She frowned.

*Ajax said his opeki was killed by his father’s,* I spoke to Hofsdora in my mind.

*What are you proposing?*

*I think there is something off about the General’s opeki.*

*And you think I can kill him in my world?*

*Can you?*

*Perhaps.*

We continued tip toeing through the woods until we spotted a clearing where the military had made camp. We had the upper ground, situated at the top of a ridge before the woods dipped into a small valley. From here we could see the sprawling encampment. There were hundreds of them.

“This doesn’t look too promising,” Trafi moaned.

“No, it does not,” I squinted against the dark, trying to count.

“Looks about five hundred,” Trafi inhaled, biting her lip. I nodded coming to the same conclusion.

“Five hundred against two hundred. Peasants with pickaxes against soldiers with horses,” I uttered dejected.

“I thought you had a plan?” She scoffed.

“You aren’t going to like it,” I muttered.

“I don’t like anything about this,” she admitted.

“I need you to go into the camp and find out where the General is. You can manipulate bodies – can you immobilize him then bring me to him?” I looked at Trafi nervous she would fight my plan, but she only slowly nodded approvingly.

“Ok, and then what?” she asked.

“I’ll take care of him. Then I need to meet with the council. I need to convince them I am not the enemy – we can work together.” I closed my eyes.

“You want to work with them?” Trafi asked incredulously.

"Our country wasn't perfect when my people ruled, and neither is it now. We need a compromise, Trafi. We need to work together. Everyone should have a voice, an opinion. This is the right future for our nation – the only way for peace." As I spoke the words, I knew them to be true.

"I'm glad Ajax found you," Trafi put her hand on my shoulder. I wasn't sure how much to read into that comment. Where was Ajax? I hoped he was back at camp, but I couldn't be distracted by that now.

I said my goodbye to Trafi, warning her that if anything went wrong to run. We hugged as she departed, and I hoped desperately that she would be ok. My plan had to work.

I sat down and brought my knees to my chest, waiting. I didn't know how long it would take for Trafi to find the General, if she could find him at all. It was hard to sit and wait. I rose and paced, the seconds ticking by like hours.

"Meeka."

I started at the sound of that voice. Like spiders crawling up my spine, the shadow man was here. I turned to the voice, but it wasn't the shadow standing in front of me, it was the prince's uncle, General Alexi.

I mustered my magic to fend him off, but before I could, I was hit from behind.

*Hofsa, help*, I began, but the world went black.

# CHAPTER 49

I awoke in a dark tent. My head throbbed as I attempted to move, a low groan escaping my lips. My feet were bound and my hands were chained behind my back with some sort of metal. Try as I might, I could not summon my magic nor Hofsadora.

"What did you do to me?" I asked the general as I struggled against my chains.

"A rare metal, but useful in severing one's connection with their opeki," he mused. Upon closer look, I recognized it. It was the same metal as the rings the prince and his men wore around their necks when they went North.

"What do you want?" I ground out through clenched teeth. We were alone. It made my skin crawl.

"What I've wanted since the beginning," he spit out.

"To kill me? Then why chain me up? Why not just do it already?" I shouted, hoping someone would be near enough to hear.

"I never wanted to kill you," he laughed, "why, you are too precious for that."

"Then what do you want?" A feeling of dread infused my body.

"Your blood, of course." He knelt, knife in hand and hunger in his eyes.

He brought the blade down to my wrist, holding it in place as I struggled and screamed. He didn't care, the gleam in his eyes was unnatural – unhuman.

He sliced a cut along my arm, the pain searing as heat rushed to my head and my body threatened to lose consciousness. He bent over and licked the blood dripping down my arm, shuddering in pleasure.

"What are you?" I breathed, horrified, still trying to fight, yet no match for his natural strength. He didn't answer but put his lips against the wound and sucked.

I screamed. The pain was excruciating. Not only blood was being sucked from my body, but my very soul. I was split into a thousand pieces, rebuilt, only to be torn apart all over again. The pain lasted an eternity, and when he finally stopped, I fainted.

I woke a time later to an empty tent. There was commotion in the distance, it sounded like fighting. I tried to move toward the entrance, but between the cut on my arm and the chains, I could barely manage to lift my head.

The flap fluttered open. My heart leapt as hope surged within me, only to be quickly doused as General Alexi returned.

"Ah, you're awake, my dear pet," he smiled sweetly, as though I were a prized horse.

"What do you want with me?" I sputtered, backing into the corner.

"I have..." he paused, thinking, "a curse."

"So, what do you need me for? You're sick," I screeched.

"I only need a little bit more," he spoke low, the same hunger as before filling his gaze. I wanted to vomit.

He rushed forward, knife in hand, slitting open the opposite arm. I cried out in horror, unprepared for the pain even though the memory was still fresh. I screamed as he put his mouth to the new cut, once again sucking with a force no human could muster.

This time I didn't pass out but swung my knee up with my remaining strength, catching him beneath the jaw.

Blood dripped down his chin as he fell backwards. He rose with a crazed look, but instead of anger he began to laugh. His chuckle was manic as he leaned his face toward the ceiling, his eyes rolling back in his head.

The crazed laughing continued as his body split apart. What was once one man suddenly became two. No, not two men exactly. The prince's uncle remained, the shadow man detaching itself from him like a serpent shedding its skin.

General Alexi rocked back and forth, blood still dripping from his mouth as he fell to his knees. The shadow man continued laughing hysterically. I stared horrified.

"You-" I began.

"Meeka," he hissed, smiling at me from beneath his hood. "I told you I would come again."

"What in the hells?" I murmured appalled and in pain.

"I've given him his army and his revolution," the shadow man wheezed. "but we cannot live together much longer, we need your blood."

I sat, mouth agape, not understanding.

"You're the fallen opeki." I had my suspicions before, but knowing I was right only intensified my fear.

"You are a clever girl," the shadow opeki smiled, "where there is evil, I will always thrive. I live off the deceit of men."

"You don't belong in this world," I tensed.

"You are wrong. This world is full of those who lust for power. They are the easiest of prey. They come willingly in exchange for the magic I can offer," he sneered.

"You have no power over me," I spat.

*Hofsadora, where are you?*

"She cannot hear you now," he gestured to my chains. I grunted in frustration.

"What do you want from me?" I scowled.

"You know your offer," he gave an eerie smile.

"You want to give me glory and fame? So, I will serve you? So, you can live off of me like a parasite? Never."

The evil creature hissed.

"I will give you your throne. They'll never allow you to rule without my help," he offered with venom.

"I don't want my throne if they do not choose me," I ground out.

There was more commotion outside the tent. I could hear screaming and the clash of swords. Was it daybreak already? Were we too late?

"He will continue to ask until you give in," the general spoke up, still barely conscious, swaying on his knees.

"I will never give in," I cried, "never."

"He gave me the military, but he drained my soul. My magic – he took it," the general whispered. I looked at him with disgust.

"You gave him your soul because of your greed," I snapped.

"Her blood has restored you, get up," the shadow man hissed. The general met his glare, the hunger back in his eyes as he began to chuckle. He turned his palms around, staring at them greedily as two flames burst forth in his palms.

"It's returned," he gasped, then stood finding his footing before running out of the tent.

"Wait!" I shouted after him, "these chains! Let me out! I must stop this war."

"If you want to stop the war, if you want to save your precious country and your precious prince, you will need to accept my offer," the shadow man sneered.

"I told you my answer. Never. You are wrong. There is always another way. Yours is the way of darkness. I will follow the light." I clenched my jaw, straining against my chains. I could hear the metal tang of swords meeting in the distance. I had to stop this war before too many lost their lives.

"You need me just as I need you," he ground out.

"That's not true." I continued to strain against the chains.

"A piece of me lives in your heart. I can be your opeki, and together we will be whole. You've never belonged, not really. With my magic, your heart will be free," he grinned against the shadows.

"No." I would deny this shadow at all costs. It was tempting, his words. I did want to feel that wholeness, so very much. But there was another way, a way I was slowly realizing as I felt my heart thawing over the last month.

The shadow man rushed at me, but he couldn't touch me.

He passed through me like smoke.

I knew then that he couldn't hurt me. He was only a shadow, a thing from another world, thriving off the pain and greed of men. Without it, he was nothing.

"You can't hurt me," I almost laughed, "you are nothing but a parasite."

The shadow man shrieked, an ear-piercing noise from the hells.

"You have no power here," I continued, "go back to the darkness."

Chained as I was, I still couldn't stand, but I sat taller, overcoming the pain and the fear, giving this thing no power over me. He continued to screech as though he had been struck, wailing until his body shook, disintegrating back into shadows.

I stood panting, alone. The general had fled, magic back intact. The shadow man was gone, at least for now.

Where there was evil, the shadow would stalk. But he had no power over me, and I would give him no power over the future of our country.

Sunlight shone through holes in the tent. The sounds of fighting continued, and I racked my brain for any idea how to escape. I pushed against the chains, but my arms still burned from where the general had drunk my blood.

The tent flap opened, and I braced myself for the General's return. But this time, it wasn't the General who came sauntering inside.

"Where have you been?" I gasped, panic mixing with relief.

"Thank the gods we found you," Ajax breathed out, entering the tent, Demetri following behind.

# CHAPTER 50

"What's happening out there?" Questions circled in my head making me dizzy.

The prince ignored me, rushing to my side, gathering me into his arms. I winced in pain, as my swollen arms pressed against my chest.

"Are you alright? What did he do to you?" Ajax looked ready for murder.

"I'm ok, he - your uncle he -" I paused, unsure how to say the words. "He sucked my blood."

The prince looked horrified. I heard Demetri gasp from behind.

"I leave you for one day, and this happens." Ajax fumed.

"I'm ok, I promise," I tried to reassure them, even as the tears began to flow down my cheeks, "it wasn't just him. A shadow creature was attached to him – an opeki. He said he needed my blood to live. He tried to make me an offer, too. I refused."

"Oh, Meeka," the prince brought my head against his chest, holding me tight. He stroked my hair then planted a kiss against my brow. "You're safe now."

"Let's get you out of those chains," Demetri cut in.

"They block magic and my opeki from reaching me," I whispered, "I couldn't fight back, but I swear I tried."

"It's not your fault, Meeka," the prince took a deep breath, "I gave him too much leeway. Not anymore. My uncle is a dead man."

"He fled once he got his magic back," I explained.

"I will find him, and I will kill him myself," Ajax ground out.

Demetri knelt beside us, fiddling with my chains. He was able to get the ties off from my ankles, but the chains around my wrists wouldn't budge.

"These chains won't be broken with magic. We will need to find a stronger tool," Demetri shook his head.

Ajax rubbed at my ankles where the bands had cut into my skin.

"Do you think you can walk?" he asked gently.

"I don't think so," I reluctantly left the comfort of his arms, but with my injuries and no magic, my body was exhausted.

"What's going on out there?" I tried to keep the defeat from my voice. Despite the searing pain in my arms, I would need to be strong.

"Demetri sent me a message he was on his way and so was the military. I went to meet him but when I came back, you had left. Tieman told me your plans, how you'd come here, and how we would ride at daybreak. When you failed to return, we led the men here to fight." The prince ran his hand through his hair.

"Trafi was with me, have you seen her?" I asked, trepidation growing in my stomach.

"We haven't seen her," he shook his head.

"We have to go. We have to stop this war, Ajax," I met his eyes. Understanding passed between us, "together Ajax, we can make this country better, together."

He stared at me, reaching deeply into my soul. He nodded once, and even though I knew our marriage was a farce, it felt real in that moment. We felt like a team.

My heart beat as though it were on fire.

I swayed, and he caught me.

"First, we need to bandage your arms. Then we need to get these chains off you," he clenched his jaw, nodding to his brother. Demetri tore two pieces of fabric off his tunic and used them to bandage my arms.

"Thanks," I murmured, feeling slightly better.

Ajax gathered me in his arms, "save your strength."

Normally I would have fought him, but not today. He was right, I was exhausted. I didn't have the energy to pretend I didn't want him to hold me.

Once I got these chains off, I would be strong. And then I would fight.

Ajax carried me out of the tent where two horses lay waiting.

"Demetri, find Trafi," I ordered. He nodded, jumping on the horse and taking off without question.

"That was easy," I murmured.

Ajax smiled down at me.

"He's been waiting for your commands since the day he met you," the prince's lip quirked to the side.

He gently placed me on top of the horse, jumping up behind. He pulled my body in close, cradling me with his strong thighs. He held me like I was the most precious thing in the world.

I felt his breath against my hair as he led the horse forward. We were on the outskirts of the encampment, along the forest border.

In the distance, the clearing gave way to a field. I took in a sight I dreaded to see. Battle.

"We should go around the fight, get you healed up properly," Ajax leaned down to speak in my ear.

I nodded reluctantly. I wouldn't be able to help much in this state, but still I winced thinking of riding away from my people.

"Be quick, then," I took a deep breath. I needed to stop this. I needed to end the fighting.

Ajax kicked the horse into full speed. We circled far from the battle, but I could see the men and women clashing with swords and magic. Fire sprouted up amongst the fight, and the acrid smell of rotting flesh suggested there had already been casualties.

I tried not to overthink the carnage that would ensue if we were not quick. We needed to get these chains off quickly, but the longer we rode, the fainter I felt.

In and out of a daze, thoughts of war were soon replaced by the steady motion of the horse's galloping and the comforting feel of Ajax' chest. Maybe I didn't hate riding horses after all. I took a deep breath breathing in the hypnotic smell of this man holding me tight.

My head swam the closer we came to the village. I felt almost drunk, like I was floating.

"Ajax," I whispered.

"Yes, Meeka," I could hear the smile in his voice.

"What if our marriage wasn't fake. What if it was real?" My head rolled from side to side against his chest as dizziness started to take hold.

Ajax' body went rigid against mine. I wanted to take back what I said. I didn't mean to say it out loud, but it was too late. I heard Ajax inhale deeply, but before he could respond I passed out.

# CHAPTER 51

"How long was I asleep," I panicked sitting up frantically. I was in a small hut. A fire raged to my side, and chains and metal tools hung from the ceiling. It was a blacksmith's forge.

"Less than an hour. How do you feel?" Ajax stood before me, sweating.

"I feel better," I looked down at my hands. The chains had been removed. I striped the bandages from my arms. Already the cuts had begun healing, it must be my magic.

*Hofsadora?*

*I'm here.*

*Did you see what happened?* I asked.

*No, I was blocked from this world. But I felt his presence. The fallen one has returned.*

*He wanted my blood.* I stated.

*Because his power is in your heart.*

I shivered against that thought. The curse of my stone heart. That darkness lived inside me, but could I banish it as I did the shadow?

I pulled power around me. Fire erupted in my palm. "Let's go."

"Are you sure you're ready?" Ajax looked me up and down. "I don't like this."

"As ready as I'll ever be," I stood. I felt strong. I had overcome so much in my life. I had survived against all odds. Now was not the time to cower. No, I had defeated the shadow – I would not allow him my soul. I would bring my people back together.

Ajax nodded and led me out of the forge, where the horse was being fed and watered.

"Then let's do this," he winked at me, grabbing my waist and lifting me onto the horse. Once again, he jumped behind me and pulled me in close, holding me protectively.

We rode swiftly, no time to spare. I hoped Demetri found Trafi. If only we could have prevented the war before it started. It would take something greater than words to end the fighting now.

"About what you asked me..." Ajax started once we were well on our way.

"Forget what I said. I know you only married me because you had to. I'm not mad anymore, I get it. There are things we must do as leaders for the good of our people despite our feelings."

It shouldn't bother me. I really did understand now that there were bigger things at stake. Nonetheless, my chest clenched.

"That's not true, Meeka." Ajax sighed, sounding frustrated.

"What's not true?" I asked.

"That I married you because I had to."

I felt his breath against my shoulder.

I stilled, my heart racing.

"Then why?" I questioned, ignoring the way my stomach fluttered.

"Since the day I met you, I've been drawn to you. I can't help it. You make me-"

"I make you what?" I breathed out.

"Well, irritated when you interrupt me," he murmured.

"Well, if you'd only speak plainly," I complained.

"Did you mean what you said? You want this to be a real marriage?" He asked holding his breath.

"Do you?" I bit my lip.

"Just answer the question, Meeka," he sighed.

"I want you to answer first." I was a coward.

"Gods, Meeka, see this is what I mean by irritating," he scoffed.

"But I'm your greatest weakness, aren't I?" I asked playfully.

"You really are." There was no humor in his voice now.

"I don't know Ajax. Maybe I've lost all sense, but I can't imagine doing this without you," I spoke softly, almost under my breath. Heat rose to my cheeks at the admission.

"I don't want to do anything without you, Meeka. I want to be by your side always, I want to laugh with you, I want to get irritated with you, I want to love you." He whispered it in my ear pulling me closer. My heart raced and my stomach tied itself in knots. His mouth was so close to my ear, I could feel the brush of his lips against my skin. I wanted to turn around and claim him, I wanted him to be mine and I wanted to be his.

But we were on the verge of a fight I wasn't sure we could win.

"Ajax, I-" I didn't know what to say. Did I tell him I wanted those things too? For the first time in my life it was the only thing in the world I truly wanted? We needed to focus on this battle. We needed to stop this war. How could we feel happy when our people were dying?

"I think we should talk about it once all this is over," I brought my hands to my face, rubbing my eyes.

"Fine," he ground out, pulling away slightly.

We rode the rest of the way in tense silence. When we finally made it to the battlefield there were only a couple hours of light remaining. My stomach dropped as I realized this fight would leave scars on all our hearts.

The lines between sides blurred. The fighting had turned into a bloody mess. There was no order. There was no one in charge to ask for a plan.

"Take this," Ajax shoved a blade into my hand, "fight, Meeka, don't die."

I grabbed the sword from him but I didn't want to kill these men.

A soldier on horseback came galloping toward us, sword drawn. Ajax met his sword, but the man simply jumped off his horse, rolling on the ground, using the leverage to slash our horse's knees. Ajax and I went flying.

I used my magic to shield against the fall, throwing air around to buffer my arm as I came crashing to the ground. I scrambled, finding my blade a few feet away, and quickly pounced for it as a soldier approached. He blasted me with fire, but I pushed it away. I still didn't have much practice using my magic, but I would need to think quick to survive.

*Hofsadora, are you with me?*

*I'm here.*

I grabbed the sword and slashed out at the soldier, but he brought his own sword down, parrying. I struggled to my feet as I defended myself blow for blow. I finally met my target, slicing my blade across the back of his leg, severing a tendon and causing the man to fall. He wasn't dead, but all the same, I felt sick at the thought of ripping his flesh.

I looked around frantically for Ajax, but he was lost in the throng. Another soldier came barreling at me, a woman dressed in military garb. She swung her blade, going straight for my neck, but I ducked. She brought the blade back around, but this time shifted her stance, turning into a fox.

The fox lunged at me, catching my arm in her teeth. The wound that had almost healed was ripped open, and blood began to flow. At the taste of my blood the fox choked, turning back into the woman, who spasmed on the ground. I ignored her, running deeper into the mob, trying to make my way to the center of the battle. I knew what I needed to do.

I spied Ajax several yards away, but I couldn't get his attention. He was occupied with a soldier whose magic swirled around them both, encasing them in a bubble as they fought.  I would have to hope Ajax was as strong as he claimed.

I ran further, ducking blows and avoiding magic. I spotted Tieman and rushed to him. He was on the ground, a soldier hovering above, ready to hack off his head. I threw out my arm, throwing fire at the soldier, sending him running and screaming, while patting the flames from his body. Hopefully it wouldn't kill him. The more people I could keep alive the better.

I heard a scream toward the forest edge. Even in the clamorous ring of battle, the shout reached my ears, and I knew it had been intended for me. Trafi.

Pulling Trafi by the hair was Captain Fintir. The scoundrel. He would pay. I needed to get to Trafi and fast.

A dagger came flying toward my chest. Before I could react, Captain Bellamoni leapt in front of me, taking the blow to his arm.

"Bellamoni," I gasped.

"Go. Get Trafi, I'm fine," he gestured to where Trafi had now disappeared into the woods. I hesitated to leave him injured, but he continued to fight on, creating a path for me through the fighting.

I ran.

# CHAPTER 52

I followed Captain Fintir and Trafi's steps, tracking broken branches and the impressions left by their struggle. The forest grew dimmer the farther I wandered, the tree cover growing so thick as to block the sun. I crept quietly, trying to dampen the sound of my footsteps, as I had been taught while trapping in the North.

After prowling through the woods until I could no longer hear the battle, I spied them. Captain Fintir still held Trafi by her hair, dragging her along as she kicked and lashed out. They approached a small cottage buried deep in the woods. Trafi was wearing metal cuffs, the same ones that had chained me earlier. She wouldn't be able to use her magic.

I clenched my jaw, fury begging to lash out. I warred against my usual instincts, not wanting to be rash. My life wasn't the only one at stake.

"You've brought her then, good boy." Lieutenant Neriai exited the cottage, greeting Captain Fintir with a clap on the back.

Captain Fintir threw Trafi to the ground. She moaned against the gag in her mouth. Not wanting to be spotted, I slowly and quietly climbed the nearest tree until I was safe in the upper branches.

"The little spy herself." Captain Fintir kicked Trafi in the side. She buckled in on herself, curling into a ball with a groan of pain.

"And the princess?" Lieutenant Neriai questioned.

"She saw us leave. I suspect she'll be here soon." Captain Fintir and Lieutenant Neriai looked around the clearing into the woods but didn't spy me.

So, this was meant to be a trap.

"Good. Chain her to the well like the dog she is." Lieutenant Neriai commanded Captain Fintir before heading back into the cottage. Captain Fintir pulled some rope out of his bag, using it to tie Trafi to the rundown well centered before the cottage.

I waited for Captain Fintir to go into the cottage before climbing down.

"Pst," I threw a pebble in Trafi's direction, trying to get her attention. It took a couple of tries before she finally looked up in my direction. Her eyes went wide and she shook her head manically, nodding for me to leave.

"It's ok, I know it's a trap," I whispered, not sure if she could hear me. I stayed behind a large tree trunk, shielding myself from the cottage's view.

"I will be right back. I have an idea. Just hold on a little longer." I tried to give her a reassuring smile, but her eyes were wide in fear.

I turned to run farther into the woods. I made it two steps before a man stepped out from behind a tree in front of me. I skidded to a stop, my heart dropping in my chest.

"Ajax, you nearly gave me a heart attack," I panted.

"So did you. What are you doing?"

"They've got Trafi."

"And where are you going now?"

"To get help."

"I'm coming with you."

I hesitated only briefly before nodding and grabbing his hand, pulling him farther into the woods along my side.

"How did you find me?" I asked when we were out of earshot of the cabin.

"I saw you leave. I fought my way through to you."

"You should have stayed to fight with our men."

"Tieman has it under control. We've retreated, but only to regroup. The fighting will continue soon. We should be quick about this."

"I know." I ran a little faster.

"What are you looking for?" He asked, glancing around at the dark and silent woods. Too silent.

"Shh," I gestured us both to a halt, "just wait."

We stood in silence, my eyes darting around the shadows.

"Wait," Ajax turned toward me, "I hope you're not thinking-"

"So, we meet again, princess," the blemmyes interrupted.

"Hells," Ajax murmured, rubbing his face and taking a deep breath. He turned toward the blemmyes, poised to fight.

Only this time there wasn't just one, but three.

"I come not to fight, but to follow up on my offer," I stood tall, mustering as much regal authority as I could imagine.

"And why would we support you, princess?" One of the other blemmyesi answered.

"So, he has told you what I said," I turned to Ajax, "that's a start at least."

Ajax shook his head but didn't take his eyes off the blemmyesi.

"You want to rule our people. You who have brought nothing but war to our forests?" the blemmyes spit out, taking a step closer. I resisted the urge to step backward.

"I don't want to rule you. I want to lead our people toward peace. With input from the blemmyesi," I explained.

The blemmyes laughed.

"And why would we trust you? A daughter of traitors and murderers. A liar."

"Like you, I've lived in the woods. I've been beaten and hated. I've struggled to survive. That isn't the life I want for my people. Including you."

"And what would you have us do?"

"My friend has been captured. Help me get her back."

"And what will you give us?" The blemmyes curled its taloned fingers.

"I will put a blemmyes on the council. No longer will your people fight in the pits. No longer will war come to this forest."

"And you'll do this if we save your friend?" The blemmyesi looked around at each other, tempted by my words.

"No," I narrowed my eyes making sure they were listening, "I will do this regardless. Whether you help me or not is your decision to make. I will not force you. But either way, your people will no longer live in fear of ours. That is if we win this war."

I turned and pulled Ajax with me. I didn't wait to hear what the blemmyesi would say. If they decided to help, they would find us.

# CHAPTER 53

Back in the clearing, Ajax and I waited, hiding in the brush. Trafi was still tied to the well. No one else was outside.

"How many are in the cottage?" Ajax asked.

"Not sure. Captain Fintir and Lieutenant Neriai. I wonder if the whole council is in there hiding from the real fight. Cowards."

"My uncle?"

"I haven't seen him since his magic returned."

"Do you have a plan?"

"Not particularly. This is meant to be a trap, that's all I know. Do you have any ideas?" I asked, turning toward Ajax. My stomach flipped when I realized how close we were. How badly I wanted to brush against him, to feel even the smallest amount of contact. But now was not the time.

"I think we will just need to wing it then." Ajax traced a finger across his lip in thought, as if he knew how much he was distracting me.

"We need to convince them to be on our side. And then we need to stop this fighting."

"You say it like it's simple." Ajax sighed.

"Maybe it is," I furrowed my brow.

The cottage door creaked open and Lieutenant Neriai and compatriot Lexim walked out.

"She still hasn't come. Maybe we overestimated her loyalty to you, spy." Lexim sneered at Trafi.

"Ajax don't come out until I give you a signal," I stood and entered the clearing.

Ajax tensed, irritation simmering in his eyes, but he didn't stop me. He trusted I knew what I was doing. I hoped he was right.

"Silly, Lieutenant Neriai, I've been right here all along." I strode confidently toward him, pushing down the fear that tingled down my spine.

"There you are, princess, we've been looking for you," Lieutenant Neriai drawled.

The remaining members of the council came out of the cottage then, spreading out around me. I eyed them each wearily. Lieutenant Barrow came through the door last, stopping in his tracks.

"I thought she was dead," he exclaimed, going pale.

"Nope, I'm very much alive," I shrugged my shoulders.

"What is the meaning of this, Lieutenant Neriai? I thought we were here to fight rebels." Lieutenant Barrow fussed.

"She is the face of the rebels, is she not?" Neriai countered.

"She is married to our prince." Barrow asserted, looking around nervously.

"Who the rebels killed." Lieutenant Neriai seethed back.

I snorted. Was that the lie they were telling to get people to rally to their cause?

"I'm not here to fight you. I'd like to come to an agreement with you." I crossed my arms against my chest.

"We don't negotiate with traitors," Lieutenant Neriai sneered

"I am not a traitor, I am your rightful Queen." I stood as tall as I could muster.

A few of the men looked around confused. It was clear the council had been lied to. Not all these men supported the military regime. I would use that to my advantage.

"There is no need for the fighting to continue. We can meet like adults, I will keep you all on my council."

"But you are only a child." Lieutenant Neriai smirked.

"A child? And did you care I was a child when you killed my family? Did you care I was a child when you banished me to the North to forget, to live amongst a cruel and harsh people. Did you care I was a child when I had to hunt for my meals so I wouldn't starve. As I watched my brothers and sisters, my mother, die? You stole my throne, killed my family, took everything from me. I am no child. I am your Queen."

"So, what is it you want? Revenge?" Lieutenant Neriai narrowed his eyes.

"No. I want peace. I want both sides to come together, to start anew."

A few men took steps back, no longer wanting to be a part of whatever they planned for me.

"Don't listen to her, she lies!" Captain Fintir shouted. He took several steps until he was in front of Trafi and grabbed her by the wrist.

"Stop," I yelled.

"Or what? It's about time you and your family stopped plaguing this country." He yanked Trafi off the ground, bringing his blade to her throat.

*Hofsadora, what do I do?*

*You fight back.*

*But I need them on my side.*

*Not all of them.*

I blasted my power out, knocking Captain Fintir to the ground. A few of the other council members rushed at me, but I dodged them, running to Trafi's side before Captain Fintir got his bearings.

I pulled a dagger from my boot, sawing through the rope that tied her to the well. Two of the men grabbed my shoulders, yanking me off, but I had already severed the ties. She was free but still chained, unable to use her magic.

I threw wind and pushed the men away, panting. Two more charged, swords out, one blasting fire in my direction. Trafi and I took cover behind the well. I used my dagger to rip the gag free.

"Thank the gods," she breathed.

"Can you fight?" I asked.

"Kind of, but these chains won't make it easy." A blast of fire surrounded us.

"Come out princess, the two of you cannot fight us all alone." Captain Fintir uttered.

"They are not alone." Ajax strode lazily into the clearing, sword drawn, looking like a god of war.

"Prince," Lieutenant Neriai breathed, shock in his voice. A few more of the men looked around confused.

Suddenly, several of the council members turned on their own, their conviction wavering the minute they saw the prince alive.

"Drop this charade. It's over." Prince Ajax strode toward Captain Fintir, death in his eyes.

"Your uncle said you were murdered by the rebels. By her." Lieutenant Neriai interrupted, shock still in his voice. I almost pitied him then, a fool. "My lord, I-" he began but didn't get a chance to finish.  General Alexi came striding out of the cottage, a wild smirk on his face, dagger in either hand.

"Oh, shut up, won't you, Neriai." The General flicked his wrist and the dagger went flying, hitting Lieutenant Neriai in the chest. He crumpled to the ground.

*Something is wrong. The shadow returns.*

"General Alexi," I whispered.

Ajax followed my gaze stiffening. Alexi held another blade in his hand, not just any blade, but one made from that strange metal that squashed magic.

"Uncle," Ajax tensed and I could see the panic on his face as he looked between his uncle and me. "Don't do anything stupid."

General Alexi only laughed, his head flying back maniacally. He straightened, glaring at me with a smile full of corruption and hate.

The dagger flew straight for my heart.

Ajax leapt.

I watched in horror as time slowed. No, this couldn't be happening. Not now. Not when he was almost mine.

Ajax crumpled to the floor.

The dagger, intended for me, speared straight into his heart.

I bent down where he lay, cradling his head, as his life bled out. I put my hands over his heart, desperately trying to stop the blood.

General Alexi approached.

"What have you done!" I screamed at him.

"It's this thing," he screeched, clawing at his face, "the shadow is eating me alive, you need to die, red devil!"

The words hit me with a raw force, my past falling into place. These were the same words Pa had used. Pa had been possessed by the shadow just as the General was now.

I didn't answer but froze as the General turned his rage on me, death in his eyes.

Ajax grunted, struggling even as his life bled out. He pulled the dagger from his chest. With his last remaining strength, he flung the dagger at his uncle, catching him between the eyes. General Alexi dropped instantly.

The shadow peeled away from his body, screeching. The men watching stumbled in fear, shock and panic rippling through them to see what their General truly was. Captain Fintir turned to run, but Lieutenant Barrow stopped him with his magic, paralyzing him.

I turned back to Ajax, kneeling over him, hugging his chest to mine.

"Once again you've saved me," my tears poured, dripping onto his forehead.

"No, Meeka, it is you who have saved me." His breathing hitched.

"Don't you dare die, Ajax. I'll kill you if you die." I cried.

He laughed then, even as his life slipped away, the sound filling me, touching me deep.

"I warned you before, that sound can turn a heart of stone to fire," I uttered through sobs. A surge of power flowed from my core. The stone inside my chest burned. "You don't need a heart, Ajax, when you have mine."

*You found a way to break the curse.*

*I what?* I asked, startled.

*Your heart was made for love, not hate. Your heart of stone has turned to fire. Light burns through you and the power will seep out at your will. Love and sacrifice break all curses. Two hearts can beat for one.*

My hair was fire waiting to be released. My heart was a stone of ice waiting to be thawed.

I watched in awe as the wound slowly began to heal, the stone in my heart melting as the power flowed into his chest.

"For so long, I could not cry, I could not grieve. But I grieve you, Johnny Pullver, my prince, Ajax, my husband. And your laugh has turned my heart into fire. You have thawed my heart of stone."

Fire roared in my heart – in my very soul, healing all wounds. I would give Ajax my heart. Two souls united, filled with the flame's light – and where there was light, there was no darkness.

I stroked Ajax' hair as life seeped back into his body.

"Meeka?" He rasped, as color returned to his lips.

"I'm here." I squeezed his shoulders, holding on desperately, hope filling my soul.

He smiled, green eyes sparkling as he pulled me in and kissed me.

# CHAPTER 54



I raced through the woods, desperate to get back to the battle. The people needed to know this war was over. Evil's hold over this land had met its demise. The time for healing had arrived. With General Alexi dead, and the shadow exposed, the remaining council members had relinquished their weapons, confusion and sorrow, and perhaps regret, overcoming their lust for war. Captain Fintir had been subdued and chained, to be dealt with by law in the capital.

Lieutenant Barrow was able to rid Trafi of her shackles, and I reluctantly left her in charge of Ajax. It was now up to me to end this, once and for all.

I ran down the hill into the valley. Movement caught my eye.

"You came," I gasped, spying a whole tribe of Blemmyesi marching toward the valley.

"We found you charming," the blemmyes grated out.

"We are here to stop this fight, not drag it on. I need you to make me a path to the center of the valley." I nodded at the blemmyes, whose vacant eyes scanned the valley as he nodded back.

I followed the tribe into the melee, who used their strength to barrel through the clashing of swords and magic. Soldiers and warriors stumbled back in terror to see the blemmyesi parading through the fray, their red-haired princess striding along in the middle.

Spying Tieman, I darted through the tumult, using my power to fight off anyone who came near, though the blemmyesi protected me fiercely.

"Tieman, we have to stop this fighting," I shouted over the noise.

"Meeka, you're alive," he gasped with relief.

"I had a bit of a hiccup but I'm ok. I'm going to stop this war. I need to get to the center of the field." He nodded and grabbed my arm, pulling me deeper into the battle.

The closer we got to the center, the more bodies we had to go around. I jolted at the sight, but I was no stranger to death. Death was a creature that had stalked me many times, but like the shadow I would not give it power over me.

"This is as close to the center as we come," Tieman nodded.

"Back away, Tieman," I gestured for him to move. He did so, the blemmyesi following suit, pushing others back with them.

I'd been told repeatedly that I was powerful. I would test that power now. The world was full of forces. I would make them obey my command.

I crouched in a ball, drawing the world in around me.

*Hofsadora, open my magic, give me all that you can.* I took a deep breath.

*But your heart cannot survive that much power.*

*I do not need to survive. I only need to stop this fighting.* I closed my eyes, willing my body to calm.

*You don't know what you ask.*

*You said you were a queen. Command the opeki now.*

I could feel Hosfsadora's hesitation, but then I heard her sigh.

Soldiers grabbed their heads, falling to their knees. Power snuffed out. Those with magic could no longer use it. The opeki had obeyed Hofsadora's command.

*Now it's your turn.*

I took breath after breath of air, gulping in the sky. Wind rushed from all directions, knocking those around me off their feet. The whole valley filled with a swirl of mist. I noticed men falling to the ground, reaching out to steady themselves. But some still fought regardless, lost in the rage of battle.

I spoke to the earth and the earth responded. The ground shook violently, throwing those who still stood to the forest floor. Trees fell on the hillsides, barreling down and crushing tents.

Still, there were those who fought.

I called to the very core of the world. To the energy of life itself. Fire erupted around my body, encircling me but not burning. Those around me cowered in fear. I told the fire to spread, and it listened. Trees went up in flames, fire hovered over the heads of those who fought, threatening but not burning.

But then I began to shake. I couldn't hold this much power for so long. My body was failing.

*Hofsadroa, help. My heart bleeds.*

*I cannot help much longer. There isn't enough of you or me.*

*But we are so close to ending this.*

*It cannot be done alone.*

My eyes rolled back in my head and I fell to my knees. I tried desperately to hold onto the source of power. If only I could muster a little bit more, it would be enough. But death lingered on the horizon. I was going to fail.

A hand landed on my shoulder in the chaos. It was gentle, even among the jumble of screaming and fighting. Somehow, Ajax found me.

I looked up into his eyes, putting my hand over his. I jolted awake with life. Though he had no power of his own, we were connected now, our hearts as one. With him, I was whole. With him, I could do anything.

I let his warmth strengthen me. Reaching out, I touched the mind of each and every person in the field. I let them understand me, showed them our dreams and hope for the future. It felt like an eternity passed. Ajax fell to his knees beside me, and we held each other as my magic and my opeki finished the job.

The world around us slowed. A hush fell across the clearing.

Finally, the fighting stopped.

Ages seemed to pass by dizzyingly. My heart pounded slowly, wanting to give out, wanting to give up on this life and continue to the next. I closed my eyes against the pain, Ajax's warm body next to mine keeping me steady.

*Your heart still beats.*

*You sound surprised.*

*So, it is true. Two hearts can beat for one.*

Hofsadora appeared before me. Dressed in flowy capes, the opeki's black hair flowed as though underwater. A crown sat upon its head.

*I can see you.* I gasped.

*Because I have willed it.*

*You are beautiful.* I smiled. I must be dying.

*You will not die today.*

Hofsadora leaned down and brushed the sweaty hair from my face. The opeki smiled down at me, radiantly, then blinked out of sight.

I stood slowly, regaining my composure. The men and women surrounding me stirred as though waking from a dream. Some looked at me in awe, others in horror.

"People of Skirsgard," I shouted, trying to amplify my voice with the wind, "the fighting has stopped. It is finished." My voice cracked with the strain of having used so much magic.

My people began to recognize me, pointing to my fiery hair whipping in the wind. Murmurs about who I was passed through rows of soldiers – the prince's wife, the lost heir, the one who had died and now was back.

"Listen," I shouted, "there will be no more fighting. I want to serve this country. I want to be your queen, if you'd have me." There was so much more I wanted to say but I was so tired.

"My queen," a man nearby knelt before me. He was dressed in soldier garb, fighting against me, and yet he knelt for me. I wanted to cry in relief.

Others followed. Both my kin, and the soldiers.

Deliberately, the whole valley began to kneel.

I teetered, but Ajax caught me before I could collapse.

"You, stupid, beautiful, thing," he cradled my head against his chest. I didn't have the strength to argue.

"I'm so tired, Ajax," I breathed into his embrace.

"Let's find you somewhere to rest." He picked me up, cradling my body across his.

"How are you even standing?" I mumbled.

"You healed me, Meeka. I'm ok now." He whispered. The relief I felt was all consuming.

"Can I trust the fighting won't continue?"

"Demetri's already shoved Lieutenant Barrow and Tieman together. If they can get along, anyone can. They will begin clearing the field. It's mostly soldiers here, and soldiers have a way of separating battle from life. But don't worry about that now." He brought his lips to my temple.

"But there will be those who need to mourn," I stated.

"And they will have time. But now we need to rest." Ajax would take no more arguing, and I didn't have the strength.

# CHAPTER 55

A week later, we recovered enough to return to the capital.

My kin and the remaining council members had already left to begin preparations for the coronation. Soon we would follow.

Ajax stood beside me as we looked out over the valley, preparing to leave.

"I was thinking about that fountain in the middle of the square in Tyev," I muttered, "it used to have a statue of my grandfather. I think we should put a monument to remember those who died here."

"I think that's a good idea," Ajax smiled.

"And we need to do something about the hungry," I turned toward him.

"We will," his eyes sparkled as he met mine.

"Also, I was thinking-"

"Meeka," Ajax interrupted me, "we are going to fix this country, we are going to do all these things, but first we need to get back to the capital." He placed his hand on my lower back, steering me toward the carriage that awaited us. We would return to Tyev tonight.

"Is it just us going in the carriage?" I asked, breath hitching.

"Are you nervous to be alone with me, wife?" He asked wickedly.

"No," I squeaked, though I very much was. We hadn't been alone since his confession. Since my own. And with the coronation happening as soon as we reached the capital, we had yet to discuss what would happen afterward.

"After you," Ajax gestured for me to enter the carriage. He came up behind me, taking the seat across.

We sat in silence for a time, but I could feel the weight of Ajax' stare on my face. I sat looking out the window, nerves getting the better of me.

"Meeka-"

"Ajax-"

We spoke at the same time. Ajax chuckled and I bit my lips, nodding for him to continue.

"I love you, Meeka-"

"Ajax-"

"No," the prince gestured for me to stop, "for once, Meeka, let me get this out." He rolled his eyes toward the carriage ceiling.

"Fine, continue," I bit back a smile as heat spread across my cheeks.

"I love you, Meeka," Ajax found my eyes and held them, "I think I loved you since we were kids. You didn't know me then, but my father was a general in the palace. I would follow you around, but you never gave me the time of day."

"Really?" I laughed, "I don't remember that."

"Well, it's true. The day I found you in the garden with a knife in your chest, the day I found out my father was a traitor, I vowed to help you and one day find you again. I've been searching for you my whole life." He reached out and grabbed my hands.

"Ajax, I should thank you -" I started before he interrupted me again.

"I don't want your thanks, Meeka," he shook his head, "when I found you again that day in the snow, I had never felt such relief. It was as though my whole world was finally coming together. I know I've betrayed you, and haven't always told you the full truth, but believe me Meeka, the whole time I just wanted to love you." He looked down at our interwoven fingers.

"Ajax, I -"

"Wait, let me finish," he interjected.

"For the sake of the gods, I can't even get a word in," I scoffed, but couldn't help the smile and tears threatening to let loose.

"I love you, Meeka. I've been through hell and back. I've been beaten. I've been tortured. I've fought in the pits. I've been stabbed in the heart. But none of that can compare to the agony of a life without you." He took a deep breath and let go of my hands, sitting back in his seat. His eyes met mine with a fierce intensity.

"I-" I stuttered. I took a deep breath, silence lingering between us.

"Oh, now you're silent." Ajax ran a hand through his hair. I couldn't help the grin that broke across my face. Of course, I loved him back.

*Why do you torture him?* Hofsdora interjected.

*It's a bit fun.* I admitted.

He scoffed, irritation written plainly across his face, as he scooted to the side and looked out the window, pouting.

I moved to the spot next to him, grabbing his face and turning it back toward mine. I gave him a sweet smile, and he rolled his eyes. I didn't want him to feel lonely ever again.

"Ajax, I love you, too," I grinned, pulling him close. Electric sparks radiated in the space between us.

He looked at me, eyebrows raised.

"Are you sure?" he asked and if I denied it now, I knew it would shatter him.

"I loved you ever since you were Johnny Pullver, and even though I tried to hate you as the prince I couldn't. My heart is yours. Forever, Ajax." I spoke sincerely.

"Does this mean you will stay my wife?" The sparkle in his eyes and the grin that broke across that beautiful face were enough to melt an iceberg.

"For eternity," I beamed.

"You can't take that back," he teased.

"I don't plan on it," I bit my lip and crawled onto his lap straddling him. I planted my hands on either side of his cheeks and looked him deep in the eyes. "If you think I was hard to find, I'm much harder to get rid of."

"Oh, I have my ways. I could torture you." His eyes twinkled as he placed his large warm hands around my waist, pulling me closer.

"Is that a threat?" I moved my hands to his chest.

"It can be," he sucked his lips in his teeth hiding a smile.

"Prove it," I scrunched my nose but couldn't contain my grin.

He brought his hands slowly up my back until the tips of his fingers rested along my neck. Pulling me close he kissed me softly against my collarbone, working his way up my neck and along my jaw.

"You definitely are my weakness, Meeka," he spoke into my mouth then kissed me softly, "and my strength."

He brought his mouth on mine then, the hunger from weeks of pent-up tension finally coming to an end.

I basked in the satisfaction of his kiss but wanted more. My hands searched his chest, moving to his hair, and he grunted against my mouth as my fingers laced within the silky locks. He brought his hands to my lower back, pushing me closer, until our bodies were intertwined.

"Meeka, I'm going to have to show you what it truly means to be husband and wife if you continue to do that," he stated, panting.

"How long until we get to the palace?" I asked, breathless but not wanting this to ever stop.

"We have a few more hours," he winked and pulled me closer.

"Then you better explain what you mean," I giggled as he grabbed my face and kissed me with his soul.

# EPILOGUE

———

"Does she have to pester me constantly?" I scoffed, leaning against a tree to catch my breath.

"Oh, quit complaining," Ajax grabbed my wrist and pulled me close. He wrapped a hand around my waist, the other behind my head as he brought his lips to mine.

My stomach still dropped at his touch, unable to contain the butterflies.

"I'm not complaining, I just need a moment of peace," I huffed but Ajax only chuckled and tucked a piece of crimson hair behind my ear. He brought his other hand to rest on my swollen belly.

"Only a couple more months. You've survived a lot over the last few years, I think you can handle being pregnant a little bit longer." He grabbed my hand, leading me away from the tree and down the forest road.

"I'd like to see you try," I narrowed my eyes and swatted him in the chest.

A horse barreled down the road, kicking up dirt.

"Demetri, what is it?" Ajax grabbed the reins as Demetri jumped from the horse's back.

"They've arrived," Demetri panted out.

"They're two days early," I squealed, grabbing the horse, trying to fling myself over its back.

"Not so fast, you," Ajax pulled me off.

"Ajax, I've been waiting years to see my family," I protested.

"Then what's ten more minutes? We walk." He glared. I wouldn't win this argument. I sighed but knew he was right.

I pestered Ajax with questions the whole walk back to the palace, giving him little room to answer. He only chuckled and shook his head.

"Do you think they will remember everything now that they are here? Will they have their opekis back and their magic? I wonder what kind of magic they have." I continued.

"We will see." Ajax put his arm around my shoulders, pulling me in tight.

"Do you think Timtim is tall now like Ceceil? I wonder how Yesi is doing with all those kids. I'm sure she'll give me some unwanted advice." I bit my thumb, lost in thought.

"I'm sure." Ajax smiled down at me.

"And Pa?" I asked, taking a deep breath.

"You know he went missing last year." Ajax squeezed my hand.

"Should I tell them the truth?" I had been warring over this for some time now. After the country finally settled and bridges amended between sides, I debated going back North and confronting him. But he wouldn't remember what he had done. What good would it be to kill an old man with no memories.

"It's up to you." Ajax kissed my temple. I loved the feel of his weight around me. I took a deep breath luxuriating in our closeness.

"He is probably dead now. I don't see much point in bringing it up," I whispered as the baby kicked. "Oh, there she goes again!"

Ajax brought his hand down on my stomach and grinned.

"She will be born into a better world." Ajax paused on the road as the castle came in to sight. He met my eyes and I looked up, still dazzled by the sparkling green depths. "I love you, Meeka."

"I love you, Johnny Pullver," I teased, tilting my head, allowing his lips to meet mine in a soft kiss full of love and promise.

About the Author

Harper A. Burge graduated from UC Berkeley with a degree in Earth and Planetary Science. She lives in Texas with her family and enjoys reading, writing, game nights, and traveling. You can follow her writing journey on social media @authorharperaburge.